To Tame the
Sentry Being

To Tame the Sentry Being

Michael Georgiou

The Book Guild Ltd

First published in Great Britain in 2018 by
The Book Guild Ltd
9 Priory Business Park
Wistow Road, Kibworth
Leicestershire, LE8 0RX
Freephone: 0800 999 2982
www.bookguild.co.uk
Email: info@bookguild.co.uk
Twitter: @bookguild

Typeset in Adobe Garamond Pro

Printed and bound in Great Britain by CPI Group (UK) Ltd, Croydon, CR0 4YY

ISBN 978 1912362 752

British Library Cataloguing in Publication Data.
A catalogue record for this book is available from the British Library.

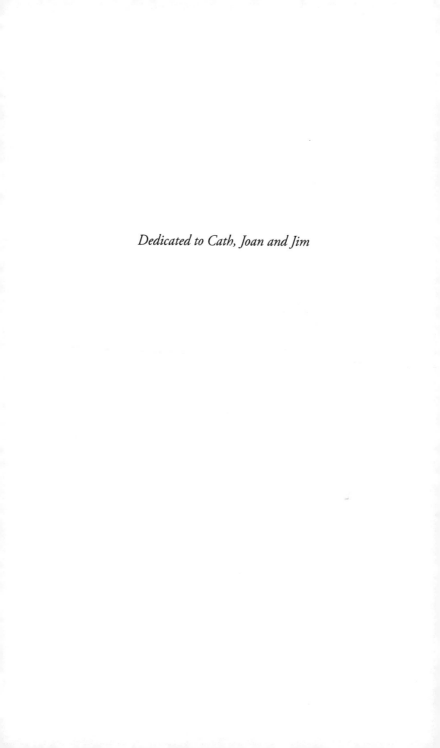

Dedicated to Cath, Joan and Jim

Prologue

Encounter

New Year's Eve

The fiery firmament above them bled flush crimson, the wind howled while rain surged through the stone-cobbled streets; it was the time of the Holy Star of Sechen. *The red eclipse is truly upon us – has it already been a year since the last one?* Bowenn ruminated as he picked up his eternally loyal blade.

"Time flies when death looms, the days grow shorter and the whole universe moves in a plot against you." He recalled his father telling him these words many years ago. Bowenn chuckled to himself; the old man had been in so many battles he must have thought every day was going to be his last. It was not the battlefield that took his father in the end but a small infection he got in his finger, while carving the chair where he would later be found, cold and stiff. *Sad way to go,* Bowenn reminisced, not proper for such a renowned warrior; he should have died on the battlefield, sword in hand, cutting down as many Alpelite savages as humanly possible.

In many ways, he had already overshadowed the accomplishments of his ancestor; his own valour had seen him rise through the ranks to become General of the Southwestern Border. He had not seen as many full-scale battles, and none as legendary as the defence of Verkins River, but had fought in more skirmishes than he would dare count. However, these were mostly just Alpelite raiding parties crossing the border, hacking down all human life having the misfortune to encounter them. He scoffed. *They're like bacteria... and bacteria must be wiped out before they fester.*

Placing on his helmet from the side of his bed, Bowenn eyed his reflection; this armour gave him a sense of pride, while wearing it he was more than just a wrinkled old man from the deprived town of Lowton. He was a sword, a human weapon defending his species against all its would-be predators. After giving his bushy moustache a final groom, he placed his steel into its sheath and walked downstairs.

"I'm leaving," he called to his wife.

"Why?" she responded, appearing to him from the dining room. "It's almost midnight."

"Sorry, Verena, but duty calls." He could see the faces of his children peering around the side of the door. They had his blue eyes, the colour of stormy waves, like his mother's before him.

"On the night of the eclipse? What kind of duty is it?"

"Intel's come in; a raiding party apparently, shouldn't be more than ten or so. I'm going to headquarters to gather a repelling force."

Drip. Drip. The harsh downpour from the increasingly ferocious storm could be heard slamming against his house like the sound of distant drums.

They always find ways of making it past the border, but for what reason? Why cross the border just to meet an opposing force and be killed? Moreover, why tonight of all nights? He quickly snapped out of this line of thought. *Useless pondering it, we will never understand their way of thinking – they're not even human.*

She smiled at him, but he could not muster one back. He wanted to tell her how much he loved her, but he could not do that either. Simply turning his back on her and his children, he exited the building into the deluge and beheld the inflamed sky. The rain spewed and thunder roared as a sinking, uneasy feeling ran up his spine. *Is this finally the night?* Walking around to the stable, he stared at the house he had lived in for over twenty years. The house where he had first made love and later raised his children, but which had never felt like home. At least, never as much as the battlefield. Mounting his horse, Bowenn rode towards the only subject he ever truly understood.

As he rode through the stony streets of Lowton, he heard laughter and music coming from the taverns he passed. Lowton, like most other towns subsidiary to the capital, was rundown and riddled with poverty. Bowenn and his family had to deal with myriad homeless while travelling through the marketplaces. This night, be that as it may, was a time of celebration for the coming of New Year, the time when the golden Star of Sechen passes the blue moon Vurtus to illuminate a red glow throughout the sky for one full angelic night. Bowenn remembered his own childhood and how his mother always used to cry on this night over how his father, away on military campaigns in Alpelite lands, was never there to celebrate with them.

He continued pressing forward through the streets. "Drink with us, General!" a woman shouted, opening one of the tavern windows. He ignored her and carried on; he did not trust the young. The times were changing, a new age of pacifism was seeping through the youth of his country; many were becoming sympathetic to the Alpelite cause. There had long been claims that the human ancestors had done the Alpelites wrong by unlawfully taking their land. Myths and legends had always told the tale of how human life had not even originated from this planet; how, many years ago, human beings appeared seeking refuge, travelling from a dying star in a distant part of the cosmos.

Ridiculous, Bowenn thought, *ridiculous stories orchestrated to brainwash and gain support for the enemy cause. Old tales of space travel.* He laughed aloud to himself. *There is nothing out there in the stars – nothing.*

Still, the times were changing. In the days his father's squadron rode to war, the whole town of Lowton would gather to wave, cheer and declare how they were all in thoughts and prayers – and when they returned, they were treated as heroes. Yes, the times were indeed changing, there was no such adoration for the modern-day soldier.

"An old man from the wrong generation, too stuck in the traditions of the past." The words his wife uttered whenever these frustrations rang through his head. *Maybe you are right*, he thought, *but it is too late to change*. His sword, the badges he had earned for his valour on the battlefield, they were what was important, not the adoration of the townsfolk who were too cowardly to fight for themselves. *See what their pacifism brings them if a bloodthirsty Alpelite horde breaks through the border*. He would continue to fight, kill and even die for them, despite their lack of gratitude.

Headquarters consisted of one room with different sections for weapons, training, eating and nursing beds for the injured; it even had an inside stable for the horses. On this night the hall was almost completely empty, except for a group of men together on wooden tables to one end. After he dismounted from his horse, one of the men noticed him, quickly whispered to his friends and in unison they stood up to face him. "General!"

Bowenn moved purposefully forwards, undeterred by the fact he was interrupting their feast. "What can you tell me of the Alpelites' movements?"

"A mere raiding band, Sir. Southwestern Watch identified a boat moving in our direction. Chances are they mean to bypass our location and make it across Caledon Meadows."

"What is your name, Private?"

"Rengard, Sir," he replied, wiping his mouth before he

answered; he was a young man, black-skinned and of stocky build. Bowenn speculated he could not be any older than seventeen.

He looked at the other faces; there were eleven in total. "And where, Private Rengard, is everyone? Where is Captain Oakghart or Captain Simms?"

"Captain Oakghart is on compassionate leave, Sir, while Captain Simms was ordered to take many of the privates to Asterleigh to await further orders from the Supreme Leader."

This shocked Bowenn; how could he, as leading general of the Southwestern Border Blockade, not have been informed of this beforehand?

Rengard continued, "The word only came in an hour or so ago, Sir."

Bowenn narrowed his brows. "But that cannot explain the lack of ready arms here, Private? Surely they haven't all accompanied Captain Simms to the capital?"

"No, Sir, many are out celebrating the New Year." Rengard coughed into his hand. "You see, we don't normally get called into combat on the night of the eclipse."

How could the capital have left us so short-handed? Even though he outranked Captain Simms, he could not call him back if it were a direct order from the Supreme Leader. *What was happening in Asterleigh to leave the Southern border so undermanned?* Well, he had a mission to carry out regardless. He studied each of the young men's faces; none really resembled warriors, but if intel were correct, then they still outmanned the enemy. Plus, he was aching for combat. He could not lie; this was what he lived for. What he craved above all else. The sweet single rush of humanity. Spirit raised, he shouted to his men, "Gentlemen, gather your arms! We have Alpelites to kill!"

Conditions had worsened as the group travelled north into the vast empty fields of Caledon Meadows. His feet felt as if they were about ready to drop off from the damn cold as they journeyed through the open plains. There was no life out there, only grassy hills stretching for hundreds of miles; however, Bowenn had an intimation of where the raiders should be heading. The closest village on the outskirts was Hampshed to the northwest. Alpelite tracks were never too hard to spot, not for a seasoned professional such as himself. The Alpelites would also be on foot, as they must have used a small boat to bypass the border. The only difficulty was the cursed weather. The rain had become a complete storm, the wind had worsened, and the daylight had all but vanished. *Lucky,* he thought, *to happen tonight of all nights.* The eclipse was giving a dark red-tinted light to help them weave their way through the meadows. *Beautiful really*, he concluded, gazing towards the sky as the faint astral light of a shooting star pierced the black and red veil. It was indeed beautiful, despite the weather. He would normally be spending this night at home with Verena and their two children, staring through the window at the sky, telling them spine-tingling stories of warfare. He now could not wait for next year, so he may tell them the story of this night.

He struck up a conversation with what appeared to be the youngest of the group. "How old are you, boy?"

"Thirteen, Sir," said the baby-faced lad.

"I saw my first combat at thirteen," he boasted loudly, trying to be heard over the raging gust. "That sword," Bowenn pointed towards the sheath strapped to the lad's belt. "You know how to use it?"

"I think so, Sir."

"What's your name, son?"

"Adnan, Sir."

"Well, Adnan, were you born in Lowton?"

"Yes, Sir."

"This is your first mission?"

"Yes, Sir."

"And… how do you feel?"

Adnan did not reply; Bowenn was starting to speculate he would be having a better conversation if he were talking to a dead mule. After a moment, however, the lad did eventually perk up. "I feel scared, Sir."

Bowenn stopped in his tracks. Something about the tone in which the boy had answered made him forget all previous warlike mannerisms; he was thirteen after all, only a few years older than his son. He mulled over this thought until a shout from one of the privates riding ahead interrupted him.

"Sir, we've found a body!"

What could only be described as a monster was lying face down in the muddy plain. Bowenn had encountered many Alpelites out on the field, but it never failed to shock him just how ugly the beasts were. Its three horizontal eyes and pig-like snout had an expression of stiffness and an almost-smile was upon its motionless face. Many of the younger members of the troop were looking upon the corpse with awe, as they gazed for the very first time upon the beasts the townsfolk used to sing songs of horror about. 'The scourge of humanity' they called them when Bowenn was a child. *Well, that may be the case, but luckily for us this one's dead.* Bowenn dismounted and fell to his hands and knees to scan the body in more detail. There's no wound left from either sword or arrow, *so what killed it?*

"It's not unheard of for the Alpelites to kill each other while on these raids. Perhaps they had an argument, Sir?" said Rengard, observing the situation from horseback.

"If that were the case there would be an entry point of some kind, but there doesn't appear to be any sign of a struggle."

"Perhaps a sickness killed it, Sir?"

Perhaps, Bowenn thought, *but this was not the way the Alpelites treated their dead. They followed a strict religious ritual for commemoration, even when they butchered one another. They would not just leave it out here in the open.* He was still surveying the body when a different voice caught his attention.

"Sir, there's another one…"

Two? This was beginning to make the uneasy feeling in the pit of Bowenn's stomach grow. *Had someone already come to intercept the raiders?* Bowenn and the remaining troops made their way to the private crouching over the second body. *It's the same,* Bowenn deliberated after another inspection. No sign of an entry point, with the same facial stiffness and an almost-smile across the face.

Bowenn lifted his sword to them all. "Continue

forwards. With any luck, this trail will lead us to the remaining Alpelites and they can join their brothers in the next world!"

The crimson sky was darkening as it fell later into the night. In a couple of hours, the twin suns of the east would rise and the first day of the New Year would officially begin. He was starting to wish he had stayed at home, as the gale once again picked up strength. After a hundred yards, they came upon a third body, and a fourth fifty yards after that, then a fifth. Eventually, they reached a chasm at the bottom of an enormous slope – the horses became visibly nervous, neighing loudly and refusing to exert themselves beyond the hilltop.

"Leave them here!" Bowenn roared as the sound of thunder cracked the sky, his curiosity at an all-time high, his usually ever-rational mind leaving him. The only course left was to follow the trail of bodies and find its source. He lost one of his boots in the mud and perhaps his mind along with it. It had become so dark he could not have seen another body on the ground even if that were where his mind was focussed; his eyes were fixed up towards the top of the hill and the last remnants of the once bright light of the eclipse. He did not feel anything at this time, no fear nor excitement; it was as if some external force was drawing him onwards. Drip. Drip. His mind was coming in and out of consciousness, like awakening from a deep sleep, one that had lasted his entire life. His ears had all but burst and yet he persevered on, as though it was his intrinsic need to do so. He made out a faint voice whispering, soft and soothingly, like a lullaby sung from some place and time long forgotten in his past. The sweet sounds filled his mind, compelling his body to grow numb. *What is this feeling that has overcome me? Am I dreaming?* Drip. *I must be dreaming, yes of course that's it. Oh, Verena, I know I'm there lying beside you. Shake me. Pull me out from this nightmare. Before I become forever lost in it. Mother... I can hear you singing... like you did all those years ago... I can see the light... I can't stop myself...*

A white light was illuminating the darkness in the open plains an extra eighty or so yards before them. So astral and captivating as if it were emitting from the stars themselves. Drawn to it like moths to the flame, Bowenn and company maintained their death march. Moving upon the white luminous source he could distinguish a figure surrounded by the celestial glow. He could not make out any facial appearance; all he could see was white and blinding.

"To pass between the black void. To reconfigure the fragments and matter. To separate the spirit from its transient shell. To tame the sentry being..." The rumbling storm was deafening but Bowenn and the others could hear these words spoken as clear as day. As they approached, the figure sensed their presence; it turned and Bowenn could determine the outlines of its face. It appeared human enough, with a bald head and face covered in strange markings. The one aspect, however, which did not seem human were the eyes – two black sunken eyes that appeared to have no light within them. Its skin was a shade of colour Bowenn had never seen before, a type of light grey azure tone with red veins visible on the outside, curling, twisting and forming patterns. The Entity's whole body, to Bowenn's absolute astonishment, was illuminating, pulsing through different stages of brightness.

"Life form, what planet is this?" the strange Entity asked, in a way that cut through Bowenn entirely.

"V-v-vena!" Bowenn managed in a startled response. *Could it be true, could it actually be from another world?* "What happened to the Alpelites? Was that you?"

The Entity inspected its two illuminating hands as if it were the first time it had ever seen them.

"Energy…" it said, "the energy of the universe… in these fingertips…" Reaching down to a lifeless Alpelite corpse by its feet, the being withdrew the sword from its sheath, studied it, and continued its stare into Bowenn.

Silence engulfed the plains, and it was as if for a moment calmness and serenity might linger – before the sudden crack of thunder abruptly pulled Bowenn back to his senses. Recognising the danger, the whole troop withdrew their swords. His heart and mind were racing; for the first time in years, he felt himself tremble. Like a lone reed caught in the tempest, he stood and stared for what felt like eternity, before the glowing Entity lunged forwards and it was over in a second.

Bowenn was on his back staring up towards the crimson night sky; the bodies of his comrades lay motionless beside him, covered in blood. As the rain from above fell onto his face, his last remaining thoughts were with his wife, children, and all he would miss. His mind also went to his parents and how proud his father would have been at the way he had died, with a sword in hand. This brought small comfort. But also how sad his mother would have been, and this filled him with nothing but sorrow. A thought too went to young Adnan, whose lifeless eyes he could feel staring his way. The darkness closed around him and, as Bowenn's ending arrived, he did not feel the fear that he had once pictured. He heard the roar of loud thunder, and then... Bowenn finally awoke from the nightmare.

1

Sy and Ed

296 Days until the New Year

He was dreaming this night, as he did most nights, of the stars. He dreamt of distant planets and galaxies; of cosmic dust and supernovas; black holes and white. Standing alone upon the shores of the vast Asterleigh Lake, he stared up towards the silk-white clouds holding the statue of the great god Medzu. He knew this dream as he had dreamt it many times over. Therefore, it came as no surprise when the statue of Medzu moved; first its hand rose towards the sky, then its head turned towards him. He had learnt the skill of lucid dreaming many years ago from a book in the Grand Library of Asterleigh, so this time he was determined not to look away; he was going to hold the gaze of the transcendental being for as long as he possibly could. The light was beyond blinding, yet brought him no discomfort; his one desire was to continue this lucid state to see where the light brought him. However, like the many nights before this one, he could not hold its gaze. And, once again, he awoke just as the lucent reached its celestial brightest.

He sprang up with a curse. *Why? Why can't I travel any further into the dream?* He reached out for a match to illuminate the darkness, only to notice with surprise that he was no longer in his room. He did not appear to be anywhere; there was no light nor colour, no physical material of any kind. The bed he slept on, the chairs and dressers, all the books and toys in his room were gone; no walls nor ceiling, no outside, there was only nothing… he looked down towards his hands, but they too had vanished. *Am I still dreaming?* As this line of thought concluded, he experienced the sensation of falling. He was descending in a spiral, like a stone plummeting into the depths of the ocean, he collapsed into the vast blackness of space and time. He was shooting past planets and stars now, moving so fast they were in his eyeline for only a fraction of a moment. He was moving closer and closer. In the distance he saw a white hole spinning, before it gradually disintegrated, transforming into a great eye of many different colours and shapes – colours he had never seen before, and shapes in dimensions he never knew existed. The lids opened and blinding light was once again all he could see. He heard the word "Ed" as if from memories of long ago.

"Ed," the voice repeated, echoing around his empty consciousness. *Ed? Is that my name?* The light was growing but so too was the voice. "Ed!" The voice was a deafening yell. *No,* he found himself pleading, *not now, not yet, please just a few more seconds.* He opened his eyes to find his brother's hand upon his shoulder. Ednon glanced up towards him, his face covered in sweat.

"Are you okay, little brother?"

Ednon looked at his hands to see whether they were visible to his eye; reassured they were, he clenched to see if he could feel them. Once he finally determined he was no longer within a dream state, he responded with a panted "Yeah."

His brother, though four years older, shared many appearance traits – both were dark-skinned, with long curly hair and deep brown eyes.

"What were you dreaming of?" Syros asked.

"Same as every night."

Syros did not need to question further. He had lived in the same house and slept in the same room as his little brother ever since the day Ednon was born; the two of them used to go into a great deal of discussion trying to interpret the dreams. Syros had once theorised it was a sign from the god itself that Ednon would grow into a famous warrior who would one day win the war against the Alpelites in Medzu's name. Although, to Syros's disappointment, Ednon never took any interest in the military and instead chose a life of pacifism. Ednon had much grief from the other children of Jovian village, who teased him as a coward whenever he did not join in their fights and games of wrestling. However, Syros was always there to come to his defence when their words of taunt and insult became acts of physicality. Ednon remembered when his brother once hit one of the tormentors across the head with a rock the size of his hand. He could not lie and say he did not appreciate the action. Their grandfather, on the other hand, did not approve whatsoever; his brother was not allowed to leave their room for a whole fortnight in punishment. As a sign of solidarity Ednon also stayed in their room, opting to read old history books while his brother played with a wooden sword.

Those days were long behind them; his brother was no longer a child playing with toy weapons. He was a man with facial hair starting to break out across his face and the wood had now turned to steel inserted into a sheath across his midriff. On the night of Syros's announcement, Ira had told him if he were to leave he was never to come back. He remembered thinking his brother was going to retract his plan, as the threat of never seeing each other again would be too great for him to go – but he left anyway. Now the only time Ednon saw him was these occasional visits during the night when Syros would break back into their old room to tell him of his new life in the Asterleigh training camps.

"How was your New Year?"

"Fine," Ednon lied.

The night had been a disaster. Instead of going to a celebration of the New Year with the other villagers of Jovian, where the adults would drink and laugh while Ednon felt out of place with the other children, his grandfather had come down with a sickness and Ednon had spent the night caring for his needs. He did, however, manage to spare enough time to cast his gaze towards the crimson night sky.

The passing of Sechen did only happen once a year; he dare not miss the sight of it.

"I will be leaving tomorrow," Syros announced in a proud voice. "My first military campaign. You won't be seeing me for a while. Time for me to write my pages within the history books, little brother."

These words, as well as the way his brother spoke them, aggravated Ednon. "Why do you have to go? The war will continue with or without your involvement. The state doesn't care whether you die, they're using you!" He found himself almost yelling, only refraining so as not to wake their grandfather asleep in the next room.

Syros laughed. "Little brother, whenever you speak I seem to hear the words of our grandfather. Perhaps you and the old man should take your pacifism to the forest and join the Venians."

Ednon had only seen a Venian once. He had been an infant, travelling with Ira and Syros through Molosis Forest to their new farm in Jovian village on the outskirts of the capital, Asterleigh, when he had noticed something peering at him, hidden within the trees. He could still picture the large emerald eyes staring into him, sparkling within the darkness, as if they were surveying his very life essence.

"There is no destiny, Sy, no universal plan. The universe is entirely impersonal. There is only chance; that is all life is made up of, chance after chance. There is no valour in death, there is only death. The Supreme Leader and the military will not care if you die, but I will..." he paused for a moment before completing, "and so will Ira... "

The smiling face Syros had previously shown was gone.

He had always known his younger brother was smart – it must have been the benefit of all his constant reading while he himself was out training his body for battle.

"You speak as if you see the whole universe, Ed, but you can't possibly know everything. I was born to do this. If I die in battle then fine, but it will be for something greater than I am. There are still wonders left in this world, little brother, you do not know what happens after death, your books couldn't possibly have taught you that. Perhaps we awake in a world a little less war-torn than this one; or perhaps we are reborn as fish or plants, free from the knowledge of how dark conscious thought can become. Death is a certainty, little brother; the path afterwards isn't."

With tears beginning to pour from his eyes, Ed sat up in his bed as if to give himself greater dominance in the argument. "You speak as if you want to die!" he shouted at the top of his lungs, not caring whom he woke up. "I am sad all the time. Are you really going to add to my sorrow?"

"We all feel sorrow, little brother, every creature, man, woman and child. None of us asked to be born into this hell, but we must find our own happiness, a purpose to guide us through existence." A look appeared in Syros's eyes, an expression Ednon had seen only rarely. "I am going to kill them all, little brother... Mark my words."

He stood up and withdrew his sword from its sheath, and pointed it upwards while eyeing the tip. The blade was long and polished – Ednon could see his own face reflecting back at him. "I found my purpose, Ed, perhaps you should find yours."

"Put down the blade, Syros."

Both brothers turned to see their grandfather standing by the open door to Ednon's bedroom. An extremely old man, his skin the same dark tone as the brothers, with a long white beard and bald head with hair only to the sides, Ira was holding himself up on two wooden crutches. His face was pale and his eyes were almost completely glazed over.

"Grandfather!"

"Come to give me another lecture on hatred, old man?" Syros smirked.

Ira let out a deep sigh. "No, Syros, no lectures on hate. I fear they have always been lost when you and I talk. I still see only the boy whose trembling hand I held while leading him away from that burning hell. Not the man you have become." He coughed violently into his hand, which stopped him in his tracks.

"Let me get you some medicine."

"No, Ednon, sit down. I want you to hear this as well," he said, turning his attention back to Syros. "Sy, I do not blame you, we live in a system that builds young men to hate. You, like many others, have fallen prey to the way things are, how they have always been. More bloodshed won't heal the hatred within yourself, nor will it solve the conflict between us and the Alpelites…" He coughed again, this time almost falling to the ground. After a moment, he managed to recover his bearings enough to continue.

Pain crossed Ira's wrinkled face. "Perhaps I am the one to blame. When the two of you came to live with me, I knew you would be filled with this hatred. Ednon was too young

7

to recall what happened that night, but I knew you, Syros, would be old enough to remember everything. Perhaps I should have done things differently. Maybe I should have shown you more love, but I knew from me alone it would never be enough. But, Syros…" he pointed a wrinkled finger towards Ednon. "Look at Ed, despite this cruel world he has a golden heart, look at how much he cares for you, don't become another nameless soldier to die for senselessness, don't do it for me… do it for him."

Syros was focusing on the floor. Ednon was surprised to see how long his brother had held his tongue; usually whenever his grandfather went into his long speeches, Syros would interrupt with a witty remark or retort. It had, of course, to Ednon's knowledge, been almost two years since the pair had last seen each other. Syros broke the elongated silence by uttering the words "I am only my steel." Placing his sword back into its sheath, he lifted his head to look into his grandfather's eyes.

Ira gave his straggly grey beard a stroke. "You certainly have your steel, but lack humanity."

"What would you have me do? Stay here and do what? Live and die here as you will? You're a coward."

"Yes, I am. But sometimes a little cowardice within yourself can do wonders."

"I hate you."

"That is a shame. But I fear I will not be the one who ends up saving your halo that now seems so lost within the darkness."

A long pause followed. Ednon could feel the tension within the room. He was thinking of what to say, what

8

combination of words would prevent his brother from leaving and persuade him to stay here with him and their grandfather, but he could think of none.

"I'm going," his brother said after a while. "Nothing you say will change my mind."

"I know," Ira conceded.

Syros kissed Ednon on the forehead. "Stay golden, little brother," he said, before making his way to the bedroom door. As he passed Ira, his grandfather uttered softly, "Keep safe, Syros." Syros stopped for a moment, seemingly thinking of an appropriate response, but he did not say anything and merely continued to walk out the door. He did not even glance at his grandfather and brother, who were both standing in the middle of Ednon's darkened room, watching him briskly leaving their lives.

2

A Monster's Hate

295 Days until the New Year

He awoke to the sound of wailing and the stench of ash. He felt unsettled. *What could possibly be happening in the village to cause such a noise?* He sat there petrified, wishing the horrid noises would cease. Next to him, his baby brother awoke in his crib and began to cry. Syros covered his ears trying to deafen out all sound, but the scent of burning cinder grew underneath his nostrils as black smoke entered his bedroom. Where were his father and mother? Could they not hear Ednon? They usually came in whenever his brother was crying – so why were they not here? He was becoming so scared he shut his eyes and pressed his hands harder against his ears. His mind was racing out of control; he needed to calm his rampant thought process.

He repeated a mantra in his mind. Something Ira had once taught him during a family visit to his farm in Jovian. His grandfather told him it was a technique he should use whenever he felt anxious or scared. He sat cross-legged, stiffened his neck and back and repeated the phrase *aaaiieoor…* until his mind blanked completely. The noise of screams faded along with all previous anxiety. His mind was focused. He knew what he as an elder brother had to do. Getting up from his stance, he moved stealthily over to his brother's crib, picked him up in his arms and found a hiding place in his wardrobe. He sat there for hours, waiting for the grisly cries to end, whispering "It's going to be okay, Ed, it's going to be okay…" as if it were once again a mantra. His brother had stopped crying and was now staring with his large amber eyes back into his own.

It felt like an age since the howling had ended, but he was too terrified to move. When Syros finally left his hiding place, clutching his brother, pale morning sunlight had crept in through the window. It was all but silent. The smell of ash was still discernible as he stretched out a shaking hand to open the bedroom door.

His house was empty. He shouted to his parents but received no response. He searched their rooms, but found nothing. Smoke was entering the house from beyond the front door. Heart pounding and body trembling, he decided to go outside and find its source. He left his house to a sight that must have been concocted in the darkest of nightmares. The street was covered in bodies, neighbouring houses were ablaze, blood spilled across every corner of the village, pouring down the cracks in the road as the rain did on a stormy winter night. He felt completely separated from his self, as if this was not something he was witnessing, as though it was all a bad dream and at any second he would awake from it.

The distant suns had barely risen. It was still an early horizon as he walked around the village surveying the motionless faces of his fellow villagers. He had lost all contact with his senses. He knew what he was searching for but dared not think it to himself. Ednon had once again started to cry as Syros came across two bodies he recognised above all others in the centre of the village, one male and one female, lying face down in the cobbled street. Still with his brother cradled in his arms, he reached down to turn over the body of the woman and looked into the lifeless eyes of his mother.

He awoke with a roar and, without skipping a heartbeat, landed a heavy punch to the granite wall on his right side. He hardly felt the pain as his hand swelled. He had dreamt of that night many times but never had it been so gut-wrenchingly vivid. He was gasping rapidly and was beginning to feel the pain surge through his hand.

"And a good morning to you as well…"

Two comrades from Zelta Squadron were in the beds to the left of his own; Saniya, the woman who had spoken, and next to her a male, Torjan. Saniya was of an olive skin tone, with light brown hair curled up into dreads. She possessed a scar stretching vertically across the left side of her face from the forehead down into her thin lips. Torjan was an exceedingly large man. *Still a boy in fact*, Syros had to often remind himself. Torjan was actually younger than Syros, but his sheer size fooled many into thinking him older than he was. He stood at six feet seven inches tall, of black skin, a completely shaven head and an enormous midriff with arms each the size of large ale barrels. Many presumed Torjan fat, but Syros had arm-wrestled his stocky friend numerous times on drunken nights out in the Asterleigh taverns, as well as engaging him in swordplay in the training camps; he was nothing but pure muscle. Both had concern etched across their faces.

Syros wanted to lie and say he was fine, but he knew panic and shock was what he was still unwillingly portraying. He tried to hide the tears as they formed in his eyes. He felt so much anger with himself. He was supposed to be all steel, but steel doesn't cry. That was something only life forms did. Saniya sat down on the side of his bed and placed a gentle hand on him; her touch was smooth and comforting, much like a mother's.

"It's okay, Sy, we all have messed-up dreams sometimes," she said as she stroked his shoulder back and forth. He considered her bright blue eyes. *Without the scar she would be very pretty,* he found himself thinking. Within this moment he got an inexplicable urge to kiss her. Saniya was two years older than him at seventeen and had never before shown him any sign of tenderness. In fact, she acted like she outright hated him most the time.

He slapped her hand away, unnerved by the sign of affection.

"Oww!" she yelped. "Sorry I even tried. It's nice to see you show some emotion for once."

"What do you care about my emotions?"

"Sometimes you make me so angry."

"Good."

"You're a dick." She punched him on the shoulder. Despite Saniya's slim build, the power she used in her punches never failed to amaze Syros. He no longer worried about his fist because now there was a much greater pain. Syros considered whether he was going to hit her back, but before he could decide she stood up from the bed and violently pushed past Torjan, leaving him alone with his heavyset comrade.

They sat together on their beds quietly before Torjan broke the elongated silence with the question, "Want to get some fresh air?"

"Yeah," Syros grimaced while rubbing his shoulder, attempting to quell the aching.

The two of them strolled out onto the stone-paved streets of East Asterleigh, dressed in the gold-braided purple military uniforms of Zelta Squadron. Syros studied the sky; surprisingly, it was only two nights since one of the worst storms he could remember. He queried it now the suns were out, central in the almost cloudless blue veil. Asterleigh seemed so different on a sunny day, tranquil and peaceful; plants looked to have more life and people walked around with happier expressions. It even appeared as if the great Medzu statue was smiling. Syros had always questioned divine intervention. To him, the idea of enormous cosmic gods dictating all life within the universe was completely ridiculous. However, that was until he moved to Asterleigh and saw the Medzu statue with his own two eyes. As tall as a mountain and resting upon never-moving wool-like clouds, the statue was beyond most people's comprehension. It had no eyes, indeed no eye features of any kind, but what seemed like an endlessly spinning spiral filling the entirety of its rounded head. It had hands and feet like a human, only much bigger. Its thin body was made up of strange textures and patterns. *They're like diamonds of a deep shade of indigo*, Syros thought to himself whenever he saw it, *and they're always shining, no matter what.* Throughout the darkest of nights the light of the statue was always emanating, leading even the most stumbling drunkard back home. He often had a small chuckle watching the faces of tourists as they saw the inconceivable statue in the sky for the very first time.

Maybe it wasn't a statue, many questioned, but Medzu itself sitting perfectly still in the heavens. The statue was too grand to have been made by sentient life – human or other; the body did not seem to be either wood, stone or mineral of any kind. Moreover, why do the clouds never move, no matter if in wind or storm? The clouds around the one on which it sits dissipate, so why not those ones? *It must be divine intervention, but if Medzu does exist, where is it?* And if it exists does that mean the other gods of legend also exist? A question from Torjan brought Syros's thoughts free-falling back down to the ground of Vena.

"You off to see your cute florist girlfriend?"

"Her name's Dashera."

"Of course. If only you would hold your tongue when talking about her, I could get some rest during the nights."

"Whatever…"

"I was joking! You know, Sy…" Torjan paused for a moment, considering whether he should continue. "You're not very easy to be friends with."

"Then why are you?"

"Because I like you."

"That's good to know."

"Did you go to your grandfather's farm last night to see Ednon?"

Syros nodded. He was still filled with guilt over how the situation had played out. He knew he must have upset both Ednon and his grandfather with the way he had acted. He was beginning to suspect the horrid dream he had was retribution from the universe for how coldly he had behaved towards the old man. He did not hate Ira by any means and didn't understand why he said that he did. They just held different ideals. He was wrong to call him a coward as well. If there was one thing Ira wasn't, that was a coward. His grandfather had been one of the first to voice opposition to the military campaigns and to call for a peace between the humans and the Alpelites. And for doing so, Ira was often scorned and mocked. He stayed true to his convictions no matter how unpopular they were and that was its own type of bravery.

Torjan slapped him on the back. If it had been anyone else Syros wouldn't have minded, but his friend had hands the size of small boulders and enough strength in them to carry one twice the weight of him. So, try as he might, Syros couldn't prevent himself from giving a small yelp.

"Cheer up, Sy!" Torjan roared from his belly. "Suns are out, you're off to see your cute florist girlfriend, and in a month or two we'll probably both be dead, killed by some pissed-off Alpelite. Life's not that bad, eh?"

Syros thought this over and gave a rare smile. "That's if Saniya doesn't kill me first." And they laughed. Other Asterlieghians looked over towards them, wondering what the commotion was.

"I hope I didn't upset her too much."

"Well… " Torjan beamed from ear to ear. "I think she becomes sensitive with things concerning you."

Syros understood what his friend was getting at; the thought disturbed him, not because he found Saniya unattractive, quite the opposite. He had always considered Saniya to be a close friend, for joking, drinking, war fantasies and wrestling – most of the time, he completely forgot she was a girl at all.

"What about you? She's single and you're single."

"She's not my type."

"Why? Even with the scar she's still very pretty."

"Yeah, I know… she's just not my type." Nervousness had appeared in Torjan's voice. "I've got to go, Sy. I'm spending the day with my Ma and her husband. Say hello to Dasyian for me." He ran off down the street, the ground practically shaking underneath his sheer weight.

"It's Dashera!" Syros shouted after him.

Left alone to his own devices, and without the distraction of his loud, ever positive friend beside him, Syros sunk deeper into anger. The thought of that night many years ago, still playing through his head, allowed darkness to enter him. He now could not wait for his first battlefield, to swing his sword and take an Alpelite life. The thought of doing so almost made him salivate. He pictured piercing his blade through the heart of a cowering Alpelite begging for forgiveness, then soaking himself in its blood. He snickered gleefully as he walked through the marketplace. Soon, after all these years, his fantasies were going to become a reality.

He became so excited he kicked viciously at a fruit stand, causing it to collapse and all the produce to flow into the streets. The owner, an elderly woman, made a motion to shout before quickly stopping herself after noticing Syros's military uniform. All the other civilians glanced away nervously. There was a growing voice of discontent at the heavy toll of death and the taxes needed to fund the state's expansionist policies. Views led by men like Syros's grandfather, longing for change in the make-up of the military state led by a single person – the Supreme Leader.

Syros had never seen the Supreme Leader; he didn't know if they were male or female or what skin colour they had, and he did not even know their age. All he knew was the last name – *Gibbon.* Syros often made enquiries about them to his superior and captain, Lars Raynmaher, who shook his head each time Syros brought it up, saying, "I don't know anything. And even if I did, I wouldn't tell you." He did get the information about the last name on the night of Sechen's passing the previous year when he, Torjan and Saniya had found the General of the Eastern Border blacked out drunk in Mundie's Tavern. After promising to buy more pints of ale, the three of them together managed to prise the information out of him.

Dashera was in the midst of opening her flower stand. There were many different flower stalls within the marketplace. Syros had often suggested she should try a change of product to gain more of an income; the best suggestions he could usually muster ranged from an open-air tavern to an arm-wrestling stand, where people would be able to see if they could best Torjan. Dashera normally shot him down with an angry glance, telling him to "Shut up." Tall and slim, she was five years older than Syros at the age of twenty, with long blonde hair, pale white skin and bright green eyes. He reached out and groped her backside, but was unnerved to see her recoil away.

"What's wrong?" he asked, sensing what was going to come.

"Why did you kick over that old woman's stall?" she said angrily. "Why would you do something so heartless?"

"Not sure," he said, with a devilish grin. "I guess I must be excited."

"That's psychotic," she said, while organising the sunflowers, zinnias and orchids into their respective pots. She sighed to herself. "Tonight's the night... the night you leave on military duty?"

"Yes, does that make you feel pride?"

"No" she responded sharply. "No, it doesn't... why do you have to go, Sy?"

He felt his blood boil once more. *Why did they all ask him that?*

He considered her bright green eyes. "You know why…"

Dashera had a pained demeanour as she returned his deep stare. "I felt so much sorrow for you, you know, when you first told me what happened to your village and your parents. I cried so much for you… I thought I could help your hatred, I really did, but it's only grown over time. Truth is, you scare me, Sy. You've always scared me…" She finished apprehensively, picking up a handful of red tubers before placing them in their designated area.

Scare her? "You will be thankful for my hatred one day. Hatred isn't a curse, it's a gift. The only thing stopping the Alpelites from destroying our way of life is the hatred we have for them, giving us the strength to fight back."

"So, hate once again fights hate. For how long have we tried that?"

"Okay, let's say we give the Alpelites what they want." He motioned with his arms. "Their land. What do you think will happen? They will let us move to some other distant part of this world? No, they will slaughter each one of us, because they hate us, and that's only natural." He pointed to her flowers, which she had sorted into bunches. "We remain in packs always – it's the way of all life and nature. The Venians are together in the forests, the Willtors in the underwater kingdoms and the Alpelites occupy the mountains. It's the way of life to stick with one's kind. There is no natural home for us on this planet so we must fight for one."

Unlike many of the staunch members of the military, Syros was of the belief human beings had not originated from this planet. With that, he held one thing in common with the pacifists. He had read enough evidence in books to see humans were not a part of Vena's past. However, although he acknowledged that humans may have done the Alpelites wrong by unlawfully taking their land, this did not make Syros feel any sympathy towards them. You must take what is necessary for a species to survive. Survival is the only thing that matters in life whatever the cost – that does not make you evil or unique, it merely signifies the fact that you are living.

"The Alpelites are not the enemy…"

This infuriated Syros, who was looking at her with nothing but hatred. *They weren't the enemy?* He had never heard anything so ridiculous.

"What do you know? The Alpelites are nothing but savages. I've witnessed it with my own two eyes. All you've ever known is the safety of the capital and your fucking flowers!"

A crowd was circling around them. *Wrong time to do this,* he thought to himself. It was surprisingly warm and sunny, plus the first day of the New Year was always the busiest in Asterleigh. There must have been hundreds of people walking throughout the marketplace.

"I feel for you, Sy, I really do. I hope you don't always remain so full of hate…"

Her condescending pacifistic nature was the last straw for Syros. He struck her across the face as hard as he could, causing her to fall back into her stand.

The crowd that had been drawn by the noisy bickering let out a collection of gasps and shouts. An enormous stallholder from a neighbouring stand, almost the size of

Torjan but twice his age, came running over and laid a heavy punch across Syros's head, making him stumble backwards in a daze.

"You military dogs," the man snarled. "Thinking you can always act as you please. Come on, punk, why don't you test yourself against someone who will fight back!"

He was sizing up for a fight, which Syros normally would have accepted as he was always up for a good scrap, but the powerful blow had caught him off guard. He felt as if he were about to lose consciousness.

Stumbling back and forth, Syros went to his sheath and withdrew his sword. The crowd that had circulated around them quickly dispersed, with startled yells of "Mad man" and "Monster." He had completely lost control. He was going to do it; he was going to cut the man's head off and show it to the crowd.

"Stop!" Dashera had risen to her feet, the right side of her face beginning to visibly swell. "Go home, Sy, and not to the military camps, but back to your grandfather and brother." She sounded genuine in her care.

Syros stopped himself, cursed at her, before placing his sword back into its sheath, and then stumbled his way through the crowd who were separating to make a path. He felt all eyes staring at him, passing their judgement, but he did not care, because deep down he knew he was better than each and every one of them. He knew they also felt this – *So keep on fearing.*

"You're a real killer," hissed a cold voice.

The words came from Mercivous, one of Syros's comrades of Zelta Squadron. He had chalky white skin and sunken eyes with constant black bags; his chin and nose were pointed and sharp, and his long hair silver, despite his young age. Usually ever silent, Mercivous appeared to have lost all humanity many years ago. The only time Syros ever saw his ghoulish brother-in-arms express any emotion at all was when he witnessed violence or was administering it himself. He was leaning on the wall of a nearby alleyway, soaking in the entirety of the whole crazed pantomime.

"I could tell when I studied your eyes, the first time I saw you." Mercivous gave an unnerving smile. "You're just like me."

Syros kept silent, unsure of how to respond. He had lost all previous indignation; it was now the sensation of fear that overtook him, coursing through his very being.

"I look forward to sharing this upcoming campaign with you. I believe it will be most interesting…"

I'm nothing like you, Syros thought to himself, watching the icy cold figure of Mercivous as he slowly immersed himself into the shadows of the alleyway. *I'm not a monster.* He questioned this again, with the events that had just transpired, and Dashera's warm, beautiful face that he had only moments ago bruised.

"I'm not a monster…" he whispered, experiencing a feeling as frosty as winter form inside his stomach.

3

Phantom in the Library

"What are you doing?" A high-pitched voice pulled Ednon out of his trance. He opened his eyes to see his next-door neighbour Amelia peering at him inquisitively.

"Meditating."

"Why?"

"Ira tells me to do it every morning," he paused and smiled at her. "He told me it improves my attention span while helping me forge a deeper connection with the universe."

The suns were beaming down upon them. Ednon was sitting in the middle of the open fields surrounding his farm. He came out here every day, once in the morning and once again at night. Ever since he could remember, Ira had always taught him the benefits of taking time out of the day to create a mental state of nothingness. His grandfather had also tried to teach Syros the same lesson, but his brother grew weary of such incorporeal exercise and stopped. He once stated to both Ednon and their grandfather that he no longer wanted to waste his life with "nothing" and would be putting his time to better use, which usually involved finding a makeshift punching bag or sharpening whatever objects he found lying around.

"How do you do it?" Amelia asked.

"It's easy. See this stance I'm in?"

She nodded.

"Just copy what I'm doing."

She sat down beside him. Ednon felt his face redden.

"Like this, Ed?" she asked, trying to copy his position.

"Yep."

"Now what?"

"Close your eyes."

"Oww!" she yelped. "Why do we have to do this in the field, there's so many bugs and prickly leaves. Can't we go inside?"

"It's sunny."

Once again she shut her eyes. Ednon opened his slightly to make sure they were, in fact, closed, plus it was a chance to look at her. He did not know what intoxicated him more – how beautiful she was or her pure unconditional kindness. Almost the same age, she had lived in Jovian ever since Ira brought Ednon and his brother up here from their old village down south. He continued to stare mindlessly, as if he were once again under a trance, until she opened her eyes, confused at the lack of instruction. He looked away, embarrassed she had caught his gaze.

"So…"

She reached out and grabbed his hand. "What do we do next, Ed?"

Ednon literally could not think, which was ironic when trying to teach someone the method of meditation. He cleared his throat and regained his stance.

"All you need to do is try to wipe everything from your mind."

"Everything?"

"Yep… try and clear your head of every thought."

"Well, that's going to be impossible."

Ednon wondered what she meant; he would have liked to have thought it was because they were now sitting so close that their faces were only inches away from each other's.

After almost a minute of them sitting with their eyes shut, Amelia broke the nothingness. "I told you this was going to be impossible."

"It will be if you keep talking…"

They tried again, this time lasting slightly longer. Ednon could feel the tall grass underneath him, stroking his skin as Amelia had earlier. He could feel small insects moving slowly over him; he could smell the sunlight mixed with Amelia's sweet aroma as it drifted into the ether. She was so close he could almost feel her life-essence.

"I think a bug went up my nose…" she announced, once again breaking the silence.

A while later, Ednon entered the back door of his farmhouse and was surprised to find Ira standing by the kitchen window.

"Grandfather! You should still be in bed."

"Don't worry, Ednon; I was just talking to Abacus."

Amelia's father was sitting on one of the wooden chairs. In contrast to Ira's smile, Abacus had a deeply worried expression upon his face.

"Ednon," Abacus announced, getting up from his chair to greet him.

"Hello, Abacus."

The man was large and muscled, in his late thirties and shared many similar appearance traits with his daughter. He had the same freckles and strawberry blond hair, only much shorter.

"Is Ami still playing outside?" He tried not to show it, but Ednon could sense pain emanating from his look.

"No, she went home a while ago."

"Then I best go home too." Abacus looked to Ira, who was continuing to idly stare outwards upon the fields. "Goodbye, Ira…" Ednon could swear he heard a slight waver in the man's voice.

"Goodbye, old friend."

Abacus gave Ednon a pat on the shoulder before proceeding to make his way to the door.

"What was that about?" Ednon asked, after he was sure Abacus had left.

"What do you mean?"

"Mr Abacus sounded worried. What were the two of you talking about?"

Ira turned, and in this moment showed him the same pained expression that Abacus had displayed. "You will find out in due course…" and with that, he coughed so violently he fell onto the hard floor. Ednon rushed over, helping him to his feet and onto a chair. He stared into his grandfather's eyes; they seemed so distant and far away, as if they were no longer a part of him. Ira continued to hack into his hand. "Ednon…"

"What is it?"

"I need you to do something for me."

"What?"

"Travel to Asterleigh." Another coughing fit broke his flow. "Go to the Grand Library and bring back *Poems from Worlds Long Gone.*"

"*Poems from Worlds Long Gone,*" Ednon repeated. "Okay. Let me bring you to your bed. It won't take me long to get to the capital and back."

"No!" Ira demanded assertively. "I wish to have a moment of reflection underneath the sunlight. And Ednon…"

"Yes?"

Ira smiled again, but this time it was a genuine one. "Take Amelia with you and heed some advice. Once you take her hand, do not ever let it go."

Ednon, with Amelia beside him, made his way through the grassy meadows towards the capital, Asterleigh. It was a mere fifteen-minute walk from their homes in Jovian. Instead of joining the busy roads of men, carts and horses travelling back and forth from the capital, the two decided to take the path through the meadows, to walk through the long winding grass.

"Okay… I've got one," Ednon said, after passing a herd of cows. "Why do cows like being told jokes?"

"Why?"

"Because they like being amooooosed!"

"That was awful…"

"Let's hear your joke then!"

She thought it over for a while as the two moved closer towards the gates of the city walls.

"What do you get when you cross an angry sheep with a moody cow?"

Ednon shook his head, anticipating the answer.

"An animal that's in a baaaaaaaad mooooood!"

Ednon continued to shake his head, as they laughingly walked past the sentry garrison and through the open gates of South Asterleigh. The streets were swarming with people. *Always so different on a sunny day*, Ednon reflected; everyone seemed happier. Ednon watched a family with two sons playfully fighting with each other and his mind drifted to Syros. It had been well over a month since he had last seen his brother on the night after the eclipse. He must have already set off on his military campaign. Nerves swirled around his stomach; he hoped Syros was okay and he wondered whether he would write. He never used to; when he had moved away to the military hostel in Asterleigh, he'd normally sneak back to their home on odd nights to engage him in discussion. However, with Syros travelling so far away, he assumed there would be no chance whatsoever of his brother keeping in contact. He felt his eyes fill up, but quickly wiped them before Amelia noticed. Ednon made a conscious decision at that moment that, if there was a way to bring his brother back, he would do all he could to make that happen.

After travelling through the congested streets, Ednon and Amelia found themselves in front of the gilded doors of the

Grand Library. It was more of a temple than a library, as large as a palace, its marble walls patterned in gold. The Grand Library of Asterleigh had apparently stood for thousands of years, many centuries before humans had even inhabited the area. Statues of all five gods of mythology flanked the pathway leading to the entrance. He looked at Medzu. This statue was infinitely smaller than the one looming over the city from the clouds. It did not have the colour pattern, nor was it emitting a heavenly glow.

"Here we are," Amelia said, interrupting Ednon's thoughts. "I've walked past this building many times with my parents, but this will be the first time I've ever gone in."

Ednon was a regular visitor to the Library, borrowing books for either himself or the sickly Ira. It was the only reason for him to ever visit the capital. Ira used to take him before his sickness, saying it was not for the books or the knowledge they held, but because he found the atmosphere calm and cerebral. He told Ednon this was where, as a young man, he would meet with other local pacifists, to discuss ways of trying to change the military state into a democracy. He would say it was the perfect place to hold these kinds of treasonous meetings because "it was almost always completely empty".

They both entered through the jewel-encrusted golden doors, where they were instantly greeted by the old caretaker of the Library, with book in hand and sitting by her desk only yards away from the entrance – the elderly Ageth.

"Ednon!" she beamed. "It's good to see you... and who is this young thing you have brought?" She tilted her glasses to get a better look at Amelia's face. Ageth was short and skinny and black of skin, with wrinkles covering every inch of her visible body. She had worked in the Library for most of her long life, using a wooden walking stick for assistance to move around its dimly lit halls. She was even older than Ira and almost as wise, Ednon found himself thinking, whenever the two were in discussion.

"This is Amelia," he explained to her in an elevated half-shout. He had to remember to speak loudly as she was almost completely deaf. "She's my next-door neighbour from Jovian."

"Oh, you've got yourself a girlfriend, Ednon, well isn't that the sweet—"

"She's not my girlfriend!" Ednon interrupted, his face enflamed. He glanced over to Amelia, who was looking just as awkward.

"What have you come searching for today, my little burning star?"

"Ira sent me. Do you remember where the book *Poems from Worlds Long Gone* is stored?"

The old woman thought to herself for a moment. "Row Q, right next to the fountain, third book on the left, middle row."

"Wow," Amelia gasped. "How did you… "

"Years of walking these hallways. When you spend as much time here as I do, you start to dream of books and where they are located. So, how is dear Ira?"

"Ira's not been well lately but he's been doing…" He queried whether he was going to tell her the truth. "Better."

"Oh dear. Please tell him to come and visit when he's feeling well."

"I will."

"Ednon, I'll wait outside. I saw someone selling ice cream. I will get some for when you're done."

The two of them thanked the old woman and Ednon, now by himself, continued to explore the Grand Library attempting to find the area Ageth had told them to search for. The library was extensive and seemed to stretch on for miles. The halls were completely desolate except for the shadowy figure of a man lurking in the corner of his eyes each time he passed a new row of vacated aisles. Ednon assumed it was a man. In fact, he could not determine any physical appearance whatsoever. He could only see a face partially bandaged with white cloth and two bloodshot eyes that matched Ednon's stare each time he glanced over. Just as the time before, they were in a long black cloak that ran far down past their arms, hands and feet. He had seen this figure the last time he had visited the Grand Library and, much like this occasion, the two of them were the only people present. The shadowy figure was watching his every movement, as if it was surveying an animal that was about to be hunted.

Ednon had asked Ageth about the figure the last time he had visited. She had just smiled and answered with, "Must be another keen reader."

Ednon was deep in the darkened depths of the library, surrounded by rows upon rows of books. This side of the building had no windows, so he did not have the benefit of any natural light for assistance. He picked up a lit lantern hanging upon the white marble walls and was searching for either the fountain Ageth had mentioned or an indication of the start of row Q, when a distant, far-off voice caught his attention.

"This world will end…" It was so faint Ednon questioned whether he had truly heard it. However, he could feel a presence behind him. Lantern in hand and nerves jangling in his stomach, he turned to see the bandaged figure only a couple of feet away, looming over him like a shadow being cast from an early sun.

"W-what did you say?" Ednon asked, fear etched into every syllable.

The shadow was large, twice the size of Ednon. The cloak surrounding it was the darkest shade of black he had ever seen; its eyes were red, fierce and terrifying. They were open wide and not wavering from Ednon's own. He could sense only emptiness and a dark fluorescence emanating from his shadow-like stalker.

"This world will end…" This time, there was more clarity in its emotionless voice.

The figure started to move towards him. Ednon stumbled backwards onto the floor, trying desperately to get away. The figure was only an arm's reach from him; its red eyes grew fiercer, gleaming like rubies in the dark. With each step, it moved forwards, with hand extended to within touching distance of Ednon's face. Ednon had never thrown a punch before, but this seemed as good a time as any. He curled his hand into a fist, let out a sort of feeble war cry, and attempted to strike the figure. However, just as he was about to make contact, to his astonishment, his hand moved through it, as if it was not truly there at all.

"What happened!" Ednon gasped, heart and mind rattling. "Why did it go through you?"

"Stand upon your feet, my shining lodestar." The bandaged being's eyes locked onto Ednon's own, refusing to flicker for an instant.

What did it call me? Ednon questioned. However, he felt something change inside him after he heard these words. He no longer felt afraid. In fact, he had never felt this confident.

He stood with purpose, looked intently at the shadowy figure, right into those sharp bloodshot eyes that for some unknown reason felt so familiar, and asked in a clear, calm voice, "Who are you?"

"A shadow," the figure told him. "Lost molecules and matter. Dispersed within space and time, searching long and tirelessly for you, my young starry wayfarer."

"What do you want with me?" Ednon asked. *Is this thing for real? Is it, truly, even here with me? Is this really happening or am I merely dreaming once more?*

"Your essence glows like the brightest of lights engulfed within the darkest of nightmares." It was as if it were not truly present there in front of him. "Yes... I am sure that it shines within you. When the time comes, child, you must leave this world behind. The gods' hands are in motion; plans from long ago have begun. The end has come riding upon the Star of Sechen, travelling across the cosmos. This world will soon cease to be..."

"There must be a way to stop this from happening?" Ednon shouted.

The figure appeared to be shaking its head. It was hard

for Ednon to see, only a few dim lanterns were illuminating his field of vision.

"This world has had its chance; it no longer deserves its place in the universe. There is only misery and death here."

"It's not all misery and death. Many of us are trying to change it."

"Whether you do or you don't no longer makes any difference. As I said before, this is a plan from the gods. We are merely pawns in their games, helpless and subservient. The only course left is to escape, and hope the darkness left lingering from this world doesn't follow you when you go."

Ednon had so many questions racing through his mind that he did not know where to begin. "How will I know when the end comes?" was the question he found himself asking. "What will I have to do when it's time?"

"Stay close to your friends. The old and the new. When the time does come, you will know it. We shall next meet upon the shores of Xerus."

The lanterns upon the walls witnessing them flickered violently. *Did it say Xerus?* Ednon asked himself. Xerus was one of the five worlds sharing its planetary rotation around the twin suns along with Vena. His grandfather once told him if there was life on another planet within this solar system, it would most likely be Xerus; but how could he ever possibly get there, through the black void of space?

The figure's dark cloak swayed from its movement. "Sleep tight, my divine prince. Follow where your dreams lead you... " it finished quietly, before slowly dematerialising, much like smoke fading within air, into the shadows of the Library.

4

The Placid Forest

They had been riding east for many weeks, under still azure darkness and radiant sunlit days. Syros and his fellow comrades of Zelta had finally crossed beyond the borders of the human territories and had entered into the realms of the unknown. It had taken its time, but Syros could sense his first bloodshed. The moment for which he had been craving almost his entire life was soon approaching. He had found all the travelling tedious at best. Saniya had not spoken to him once since he had upset her back in Asterleigh, which left the downtime dull and uneventful. Torjan had tried to broker a peace between them many times, either while on horseback or by the fireside while they camped. However, she had refused each time. *I don't care*, Syros thought to himself when he saw her being so painfully unsubtle whenever she passed him. *Makes her more in the mood for battle if she remains angry with me.* They were not out here on vacation, as some of the other members of Zelta Squadron seemed to believe with their joking and games. *We are here to kill the enemy not frolic on the fields.* Most of his cohort had already begun to shun him; even Torjan was growing weary of his cynicism and moody behaviour. *I don't care anymore*, he once again told himself.

He felt the anger grow inside him each day. Whenever he slept he dreamt of Dashera's face and when he awoke, he felt a little more coldness engraving itself inside him. The feelings of enmity and angst held onto him so tightly, he couldn't any longer remember a time without them. He pictured his grandfather going off on one of his tangents on hatred and he felt like punching something; and Ed, he was always the faultless one. No matter the circumstance, Ed would always find a way of reminding the world of how perfect he was. But he must admit deep down that he did miss them both, especially Ednon. They at least did not scare him, not as Mercivous did. He had not appeared to have taken his eyes off Syros ever since they had first set out upon their campaign. Not for one moment had his cold dead stare stopped fixating on Syros, with those baleful eyes that penetrated through the flickering flames of the campfire, while displaying a haunting and menacing smile. Syros was no longer in doubt that the devil rode here beside him, wearing false human skin.

"Maybe he's got a crush on you!" Torjan laughed, after Syros mentioned this while the two of them were sequestered away from the rest of the squadron. Syros gave a small shudder when his broad-muscled friend uttered this, as if cold ice was suddenly poured down his back. "Perhaps he's under the same spell as our dear Saniya. You always have been extraordinarily pretty, Sy. Who can blame them?"

Syros had winced when he heard this. However, his friend was not wrong. Syros had never found it a difficulty attracting members of the opposite sex. With his big brown eyes and chiselled features, he often found women staring his way. Nevertheless, for some reason, and as with most other things, this also brought him anger. *Why do I feel like this?* he found himself thinking. *Will these feelings always be burrowing away inside me? Does it ever stop?* He felt like hitting something, but restrained himself from attacking Torjan, as he was now, truly, the only friend he had left in this world.

"Can you and San please make up already?" Torjan asked while picking up a bundle of logs. "I'm tired of acting like an ambassador charged with getting two rival species to stop warring."

"No one asked you to do that, Torj."

"True, but damn do I miss the old trio. You're off by yourself, looking all miserable as per usual. While she's with the other female members of the company, pretending to be interested in the same crap they're into. The whole situation's damn depressing."

The two of them walked back to camp. The evening was dark and restless as they moved through the remote yet serene woodlands. They had journeyed deep into the woods to find a suitable tree to cut, so deep in fact that Syros genuinely did not know where they were.

He gazed around anxiously. "Torjan? You do remember which way we came?"

Torjan surveyed every direction. "Umm… no… not really."

"Brilliant," Syros sighed. Dusk was fast becoming night; all natural light would soon vanish, plus they had never been this far east. For all they knew this forest could stretch on for an eternity.

"It's alright, we could go… oh, who knows, let's continue walking the way we were going."

"If it's the wrong direction, then we'll just be walking further away from camp."

"Damn it! Why didn't we mark locations to remind us of the way?"

"You were distracting us with all your relentlessly dull talk of Saniya and her precious feelings."

Torjan glared at him. "Fuck off! All I ever do is help you, but lately you've become unbearable."

"You really think I care?"

"Yes."

"Why?"

"Because I'm your friend!"

Syros made a dispassionate motion before spitting on the ground.

"If that's the way it's going to be…"

Syros watched Torjan, believing he was about to walk away. However, Torjan instead dropped the logs he was holding, faced him and, without a hint of a warning, struck him hard across the face, knocking him to the ground. Syros arose quickly and tried to land a punch, but Torjan dodged it and returned a blow of his own into Syros's stomach. Syros had been punched many times throughout his short lifespan, but none were as hard or held as much strength as the ones from the gigantic Torjan. He felt the wind go out of his lungs. The pain was unbearable, but Syros managed to rise with the help of the adrenaline flowing through his body and lunged again for Torjan, who quickly manoeuvred him into a headlock. The blood rushing to his head, Syros landed some jabs into Torjan's ribs, but it was like hitting a sturdy rock with a broken feather and did not seem to have any effect. After a minute or two of Syros's head being crushed between Torjan's enormous arms, he decided to call out for a truce. Exhausted, the two of them fell to the floor panting heavily.

"You always were the better fighter," Syros conceded.

"Well, I am twice your size."

"That you are… How ever did you get so big?"

"Not sure… I just woke up one morning to find all my clothes were ten sizes too small for me."

The two of them laughed. And it was as if everything that had been said previously was forgotten. After a moment, however, Torjan repeated, "We are your friends, Sy, no matter how much you may deny it. We both are, me and San."

Syros placed his head into his hands, utterly drained, both physically and mentally.

"Sy, I realise you have a lot of anger; that's one of the reasons I was drawn to you. However, to go through life with so much is a waste. Chances are, we will probably both die out here past the border, so don't spend your last moments neglecting the people who actually like you, mate." Syros did not respond immediately, so Torjan proceeded. "I don't mind it when you release your angst with me, but Saniya doesn't deserve it. She's more sensitive than she lets on, as are most of us. Hell, I bet even that creep Mercivous has a sensitive side to him, as miniscule as it may be."

Syros once again did not answer. He continued to sit upon the broken branches and displaced logs, his head remaining firmly in his hands.

Apparently unnerved by Syros's silence, Torjan pressed forwards. "So how did it go with Dashera before we left? You never did tell me."

"I hit her…"

"What?"

"I hit her," he repeated with greater clarity.

Syros's eyes were covered by his hands, so he could not gauge the reaction from his stocky friend. The mood surrounding the secluded area had changed, however, and the wind had just turned a little colder.

"Torjan?" Syros asked tentatively, beginning to feel a strange, unfamiliar feeling creep up inside him. "Do you think I'm a monster?"

A lengthy pause followed, as Torjan thought over his response. The heavyset lad eventually responded with the single word, "No."

Syros's eyes started to fill. He could feel his lips tremble; he was about to do something he had not done in many years. "I don't want to feel like this anymore…" Tears rolled down his face. No matter how hard he fought he could not keep them from streaming. Torjan came over and silently placed

41

an arm around his shoulder. It was the first time Syros had openly cried in front of someone since the day he had found his parents on the street of his old village. On that occasion, he was in front of his brother who was only a baby and would not remember him doing so. Sensations swept over him as the tears continued to fall. It was strangely calm and salutary. He sat there in the windswept leaves underneath a lone oak, lit only by the blue moon Vurtus, which had come out from its hiding place behind the clouds. Small wild animals and insects scurried past him and Torjan, who sat there silently for close to an hour.

"What are humans doing so deep within our forest?"

Startled, the two of them jumped to their feet, withdrew their swords and turned towards the speaker. A face was sticking out from the tree behind them, almost as if it was carved into it. It had large glistening emerald eyes, light-green clear skin and an extraordinarily small nose and lips. The blue moonlight from Vurtus reflected off its skin, causing it to twinkle softly. It had an extremely kind face, which was all Syros and Torjan could see of the being; the body still appeared to be within the tree itself.

"Are you a Venian?" Syros asked, already knowing the answer. He had seen the species once before when he was a child travelling through Molosis Forest with Ira and his infant brother, straight after the massacre that had killed their parents. Even though the Venians were a renowned passive species, Ira had quickly gripped him by the hand, telling him not to go any closer. Though at the time all he saw were their green eyes gleaming in the darkness, there was no chance this wasn't the same life form that he had seen on that day many years ago.

"If, human, that is the term you want to use, then yes, I am what you call a Venian. Although that name has only been used since the ancestral human beings first arrived here." It spoke softly and quietly, much like Mercivous did. However, unlike Mercivous, whose every syllable caused a chill to run down the spine, this creature's voice was nothing but soothing.

The tree separated from the bottom of its trunk to as high as Syros's eyes would lead him. The two of them retreated backwards, uncertain of how to deal with this new situation. The Venian emerged from the tree and now its full body was on display. Its legs, arms and body were thin, quite like the stem of a plant, with small light-brown patterns running horizontally up its legs and arms. It appeared very much like a flower with its large ovate-shaped head and beyond thin body structure; but flowers did not twinkle delicately in the pale moonlight, nor did they walk upon feet that slowly approached with each step they took.

"Now, humans…" the Venian said, its glimmering eyes dancing with their own. "Won't you tell me what you are doing so far from your border and so deep within our placid forest?"

Syros had to think quickly. Perhaps he should not tell the creature they were travelling as part of a large-scale military campaign east on a mass invasion of Alpelite land. Nor would it be wise to say they had got lost cutting down trees to be burned upon a campfire.

"We are mere travellers." Torjan quickly came to the

rescue. "Travelling the world to gain the knowledge to write a novel so profound it will one day solve the conflict between ourselves and the Alpelites. See, we are both pacifists, much like yourself."

The Venian stared at them blankly and then opened its mouth to release a sound utterly unlike anything Syros had ever heard before, but if he could find a similarity, he would have said it reminded him of laughter.

"Such pacifists," it howled, continuing to make the strange vibrations. "Only moments ago, I witnessed the both of you attacking one another. I know very well what you humans are doing. I am not so very short-sighted; I have eyes in all trees, plants and blades of grass. I have seen you humans riding other saddled mammals in high numbers heading east. But lying has always been a very mammalian characteristic, as has war. I was merely trying to determine whether the two of you broke this never-changing mould."

They gave a nervous smile, unsure of how to act. Syros could not tell whether the creature was upset or not. He read no emotion on its face, but the words it uttered and the way it spoke to them gave Syros the impression the plant-like life form was amused by them.

"You're the first Venian I've ever seen," Torjan said.

"I feel that is more your human doing than it is our own. I remember the ancestral human refugees used to come visit us within the forest almost nightly. However, as the war deepened, the less frequent those visits became. Shame, you always were a most intriguing species."

"You said you remembered," Syros began, having

completely forgotten his tears from earlier. "How old are you?"

"I am almost as old as Vena itself, our race is many but we are also one, sharing all thoughts, experiences and memories. I have witnessed much in my long life, but this is the first time a human being has ever caused me to laugh." The wind around them was blistering; leaves flew in all directions, as the Venian took further steps forward.

"Usually, you humans are so un-humorous. Both you and the Alpelites have begun to lose appreciation of this world and all it has provided; you spill each other's blood upon its dirt, causing it to sink within our roots. Vena is feeling the cost of your savagery."

"The Alpelites are the ones who are the savages!" Syros spoke in a voice loud with anger, as he did most times he talked about the Alpelites. "They break through our borders, raid our villages and kill our people."

"Yes, but I've seen you humans do the same. And if I recall correctly, those wondrous temples and homes within Asterleigh, that you all inhabit, were built by the Alpelites... not done so easily by a race of savages. There is more to a being than your predetermined hatred, human. How many Alpelites have you met? How many have you talked to, much in the same way I am talking to you now?"

"None," Syros admitted. "And I don't intend to. If I ever meet an Alpelite, I will kill it – and without any remorse." He finished coldly as Torjan shot him a worried glance.

The sentient plant moved upon him quickly, standing only inches away from his face. "Now... you are a most interesting life form," it whispered, beginning to search his eyes. "I can feel only sadness coming from inside you. Perhaps before your time does come, you can find a little peace within the variable chaos."

"If you wouldn't mind," Syros began, not troubled with how close the creature was, or indeed its vague words, "could you show us the way back to our comrades?"

"I could…" the Venian murmured. "However, your lives lingering will only bring more bloodshed to this already blood-soaked world. Perhaps I should just leave you here and a young Alpelite child may still have a father when Sechen comes by once more. Although…" its tone quietened as though it was speaking only for itself, "I guess it doesn't really matter now anyway…" It paused for a moment in a deep reflective silence, before lifting its voice in an excited, almost child-like way. "Yes. I think I will help you humans, for making me laugh so much earlier."

"Thank you," they both replied sincerely.

The shimmering life form swiftly moved past them, its whole body becoming even more phosphorescent from the light of the moon Vurtus, which was now central in the cloudless night sky. "This way, humans." Its thin lips stretched out to something that could almost resemble a smile. "We must all find our own salvation. You mammals will find yours on the battlefield doing what your kind does best; while our salvation… has finally come falling from the stars in the sky."

5

Ira

For how long have I been enticed by you? When did your gaze first draw me in, governing over my stream of consciousness – my kaleidoscopic eye? And, once again, you have me falling, deeper and deeper into the void of nothingness, and for what? Where are you leading me?

He felt the sensation of plummeting and, in what felt like no time at all, identified the muddy ground beneath him. He sensed the rain and the wind rustling against his skin. *Where am I? Who am I?* He had forgotten himself. Had he even existed before this moment? He opened his eyes to find himself upon the top of a high grassy ridge, surrounded by hills and meadows that seemed to stretch open for an eternity; the sky was a dark shade of red, the star and the moon were passing. He continued to survey his surroundings; emerald-eyed beings were standing over him, staring gawkily. Meeting his gaze, they fell into a bow, uttering "You have arrived…" before they steadily receded into the bespattered terrain below them. He checked his own being. Why were his hands illuminating like this? He could feel something within them, a feeling that covered every inch of his being, circulating underneath his cold grey skin; it was life itself. *For how long has this been my shell?* As the wind and rain picked up to a fierce pace, he found himself quietly whispering, "To pass between the black void. To reconfigure the fragments and matter. To separate the spirit from its transient shell. To tame the sentry being…"

Ednon opened his eyes. He was back in his own body in the grassy fields around his farmhouse. Strange visions had begun to fester within his personal nothingness ever since he had spoken to the shadowy figure in the darkened depths of the Grand Library. He had not told Ageth, Amelia or even Ira of his conversation with the shadows – would they believe him? Ednon was not known for lying, but some stories were just too fantastical to believe. The figure had spoken of the world ending. Well, many claimed of the world's imminent destruction. He passed them all the time in the streets of Asterleigh, smelling of booze and shouting in almost unintelligible voices. However, it felt different this time, as it wasn't a man who had told him this. It didn't appear to be a life form of any kind. He was scared; life was spiralling, beginning to overwhelm his mind. He placed his head within his hands. He could no longer travel into his nothing. Too many thoughts were within him, clouding his judgment. Along with worries about his grandfather's rapid decline in health and his loss of communication with his brother, he also heard the ghostly words of this shadowy figure playing continuously through his head.

He got up from his stance and glanced skywards just as a shooting star pierced the black veil. The night was warm and still, without a single cloud. The moon was on full magisterial display. Taking a long breath inwards, he decided to go for a short walk around his farm before he went bed-ways. Mournful howls echoed in the distance. *Wolves*, he thought to himself. Good thing all the animals are already locked within the barns; perhaps it would be wise for him not to stay out too late. As he walked, he tried to make sense of his latest vision. *That figure told me the end came riding upon the Star of Sechen,* he deduced to himself, *and in that vision I was looking up towards the crimson eclipse.*

Pieces were coming together within his mind. The shadow had told him that the only option left was for escape onto the shores of Xerus, but he still had no idea how he would be getting there, or indeed how many people would be able to accompany him. He would like to think he could take everyone, all humans, Alpelites, Willtors and sentient plants. No one should be left on this planet if it truly was the end. He changed his mind; no, he had never believed in destiny. It went against every conception of the universe that he had. There must be a way to change this planet's fate. "There is a way to change this planet's fate," he said out loud, newly filled with optimism. He thought of his brother, Ira, Amelia and Abacus, and even Ageth. He had too much to lose to let it all go willingly. He would fight for them, even without the physical strength.

How many different worlds were there? How many different races of species? Were all worlds like this one? Was Xerus much like Vena? He felt something brush up against his leg and lowered his gaze to see a strange blue-skinned creature with large white eyes shaped like diamonds. The life form was small, only two feet or so high. Two antennae hung to the ground, much like long hair on a person. Its body was transparent with what looked to Ednon like bright orange organs gently floating round its insides. Its arms were bright blue flippers. Its lips and nose were both barely visible, the nose in particular was almost completely non-existent. A spiral marking appeared to be engraved on the strange animal's forehead. It was sparkling slightly, illuminating the almost complete darkness. *Such a beautiful creature,* Ednon thought, kneeling down to get a better look at its face.

"Hello. What is your name?" Ednon was half expecting the creature to respond. It didn't. However, appearing to return his smile, it uttered a small joyous squeaking noise. "Are you hungry?" he asked, confused at what had attracted it towards him. Reaching inside his pocket, Ednon retrieved some grain that he had previously used to feed his farm animals and placed it in front of the creature's face. It clapped its flippers together approvingly and gave a squeak before proceeding to eat the grain out of Ednon's hand.

"Where did you come from?" Ednon queried, not expecting the creature to answer, especially now since it was using its mouth to nibble furiously on the grain. The organism was emitting a strange presence; it felt calm and loving. *It can't be from this planet.* Ednon had never seen anything that even slightly resembled the small transparent creature. The loud howling of wolves once again broke his deep contemplation. He glanced back to the life form. He could not leave it out in the wild to fend for itself; much like himself, it didn't look like a fighter.

"Come with me," Ednon told it. The small life form, however, was hesitant, unsure whether to comply with the demand. Ednon gave a sigh and outstretched his hand containing the grain. It clapped its flippers together gleefully and trudged alongside him, following the open palm.

Ednon entered the back door to his farmhouse. He had left the creature locked within his barn. It seemed happy enough, instantly going over to the herds of pigs, sheep and chickens as if it was striking up lively conversations. Something about the organism lured him in. Maybe it was the eyes or the beautiful transparency of its skin, but something inexplicable made him feel warmth, much like Amelia did. He would go see it in the morning, and if Ira was up for it, he would take him as well. He would also very much like to show it to Amelia. He felt overwhelmingly positive; yes, tomorrow was going to be a good day. He was certainly in need of one, considering the chaos and conflict his mind had been under since his visit to the Grand Library earlier that morning.

His home was dark and only dimly lit by lanterns upon each of the walls. The stones were old and battered, paintings of stars and grassy landscapes decorated the bland

51

lack of colour. He took off his muddy boots by the back door quietly, trying not to wake the sleeping Ira. It was way past midnight but, for whatever reason, he had found this the perfect time to go into the fields to meditate under the ever star-filled night skies. *Why did that vision come to me?* He often dreamt of strange scenarios where he was inside someone else's body, experiencing their thoughts and emotions, but never had they come while he was trying to achieve his state of nothingness. Sometimes he even dreamt of great battles on worlds trillions of light-years away from this one. Thousands of strange creatures and life forms being led by gigantic gods into war; he even saw himself among them sometimes, leading the armies from out ahead as if he were a general.

He opened his bedroom door; the room had been stripped of anything relating to Syros, almost as if he had never been there. Ednon remembered when his brother used to play with a wooden sword, and how he'd hit it against the battered walls of their bedroom whenever he got angry; usually due to a fight he had had with their grandfather. "One day, Ednon, you will write the books of my exploits," Syros used to tell him, giving him a wide grin. "Humanity will win, little brother, and I will play my part to defeat the monsters."

Ednon got into his bed; he had not heard any coughing from Ira since re-entering the house. *It's good he's sleeping*, Ednon thought. *At this stage, it really is the best thing for him.*

"Ednon." The gravelly voice of his grandfather startled him. The old man was standing by his door. He was wide-awake and dressed as if it were midday and he was about to do something of importance either with the village elders or in the city. The messy hair that remained on the side of his head was brushed and he was even wearing a tie.

"Yes?" Ednon said, unsure of what to make of the situation.

"If you wouldn't mind, would you please accompany me outside? There is something I wish to discuss." Ira started to make his way down the hall and out into the fields. Confused, Ednon got up from his bed and assisted his grandfather who was swaying slightly, struggling to get to his sanctum of the cool open-air underneath the majesty of the tranquil night stars.

He helped his grandfather onto one of the wooden chairs in the yard that were positioned to survey the vast acres of grassy fields which were, and had been, his farm for most of his life. Ira gazed skywards. "Not a cloud in sight... It's as perfect a night as any for this."

Confused, Ednon sat down on the chair beside him. "A perfect night for what?"

Ira's glazed eyes filled with frailty. "My sweet child, I am going to be forthright with you. I have not feared death for a long time – in many ways, I have longed for it dearly. All my life I have prided myself on my knowledge and my own inward lucidity. As I feel them fade away due to sickness and old age I see less and less reason for lingering. I am afraid Syros was right. I am a coward and yes, I have always been, but not for death, but for what life may become for me in the future if I should continue this dawdling. My boy, this pains me greatly to say."

"What are you trying to tell me?"

"My burning star…" Ira breathed heavily. "I no longer wish to live under the density of this fog. My life has only become a burden upon you and I fear I am not a burden anyone should bear, especially one as young as you." He closed his eyes and tilted his head backwards upon his chair. "Do you remember when you asked me what I was talking to Abacus about?" His voice was almost completely quiet. "When my consciousness departs to wherever lost consciousness goes, you will stay with your friend Amelia and her family. Ednon, remember what I told you? About when you take her hand, not ever letting it go…" he wheezed violently, and his speech became even weaker and more sluggish. "Please don't forget."

"I won't," Ednon said, wiping his eyes.

"Good," Ira said, the weakened grin still across his face. "Your smiles are what dreams are made of; genuine pure smiles from your loved ones are what makes life worth the struggle." Saliva spat from his crusty mouth as he coughed violently. "Ed, go to them now. I have already ingested the poison. My light will soon fade… go quickly." Powerlessly, he outstretched his hand to find him.

Ednon caught his grandfather's hand. It was cold, colder than ice. He glanced around the fields and thought of what his grandfather had instructed. He could quickly run next door to inform Abacus and maybe try and find an antidote, but it looked like his grandfather had only a few minutes left. He could not leave; the thought of not being there at the moment of Ira's death he was sure would haunt him for the rest of his life.

"I'm going to stay," he uttered in a shaking voice.

"My dearest Ednon, you will one day become the awe-inspiring visionary who will change the fate of our species. Of that I hold no doubt. You don't hate – sometimes I question whether you are human at all. When I heard the news of what happened to my daughter, I was filled with so much hate." He began shaking his head as his face tightened, with pain etched into every syllable of his voice. "I wanted so badly to kill the ones that had done them that injustice. It was all I could think about, and it's all I dreamt about. And for that, I have always been a hypocrite; what we show and who we truly are is usually so different. When I told Syros that it was the State that conditions man's hatred, I was wrong." He shook his head violently as tears fell from his tightly sealed eyes. "It's this whole damn planet!" his voice erupted in bitterness. "I fear, Ednon, you may never truly know what's lying within the hearts of strangers. These ghouls masquerading as thinking and feeling life forms won't deserve you. They won't even come close."

A long silence followed, only the trees and the grass gently rustling in the gentle breeze could be heard, along with the deep unsteady breaths of Ira's life dissipating. Ednon sat there with him for what seemed like hours, savouring each passing moment. After a while he managed to look upon the face of the almost completely vacant shell that was once his grandfather. "You taught me so much. No matter how much inner turmoil you were in, you did what was right for this world to end the hatred. That does not make you a hypocrite; all it does is make you human."

"My boy, I'm far more of a hypocrite than you know.

55

Life is merely a dream that quickly fades, but it is a glorious dream we must all work in unison to savour, for the generations still to come. So they may live in a better world."

These last words hit Ednon hard inside his stomach as he remembered the warning of the shadowy figure, and how he had spoken of the world's imminent ending. He had previously planned to discuss the shadow's words with Ira, but had got home late from Asterleigh with Amelia, and Ira had been asleep throughout the entirety of the evening since he had been back.

In his last moments, his grandfather gave a slight smile and spoke in a voice quieter than a whisper. "If you see Syros, Ed, if you see him…" his voice grew fainter. "Please tell him these words …" But his voice finally faded and the light in his eyes along with it. His consciousness also left to go wherever separated consciousness goes when no longer bounded. His grandfather's cold hand still holding his own, Ednon no longer cried. He solely searched the night stars and imagined a world where he would be able to meet him once more.

6

Vows of Moonlight

Syros and Torjan walked across the verdant fields, back to the encampment of Zelta Squadron. With a smile and a wave, the Venian left them at the edge of the forest before slowly receding into the ground – as if Vena itself was demanding a reunification. The creature was happy, almost too happy. Something about it made Syros feel perturbed. It even appeared to be whistling to itself as it illuminated their way through the empty woods. *Maybe I'm overreacting*, Syros thought. It was, of course, his first ever interaction with the life form – perhaps they were always so cheerful. However, he and Torjan had both initially entered the forest to cut down wood. If the creature spoke the truth about having eyes in all trees and plants, it surely knew what Syros and company were planning on their campaign. A species so renowned as being pacifists should not have behaved so harmoniously towards them. He also could not get out of his mind what it had said; "Our salvation has finally come falling from the stars in the sky." He repeated this aloud to Torjan after a few minutes of walking. "What do you think it meant?"

Torjan just gave a disinterested motion as the two finally reached their destination.

"You took long enough!" shouted Steph, a lanky blond-haired lad and a comrade from Zelta.

"The lovers have returned. Enjoy your nice romantic walk, lads?" laughed Hurus, another of his brothers-in-arms. They were both sitting around a high-burning fire in the dead centre of camp.

"Where is everyone?" Torjan asked as he and Syros sat down to join them.

"Most are in bed," Hurus explained. "Raynmaher is in his quarters writing his reports to be sent back to the capital. Oh, and before I forget, he said you both were to take over night duty for making us wait. So why did you take so long getting back? And you didn't even bring the wood!"

"Where is Saniya?" Syros interrupted.

Hurus grew visibly annoyed. "Not sure, most likely in her tent with the other girls. Are you going to answer my question or are we going to pretend you haven't been gone all evening?"

"Got lost," Torjan explained. "A Venian had to show us the way back."

"A Venian!" Steph's eyes sprang wide open. "I saw a Venian once when I was a kid... Went to take a shit behind a tree when I saw a head sticking out from it. Almost scared me to death."

Syros stood up from the campfire. "I'm going to find Saniya."

Torjan gave him a knowing look. The two had been discussing her as they made their way through the forest, following the sparkling back of the life form.

"Did Torjan not give you a good enough time?"

Syros knew he was joking, but the words still caused his blood to boil. No matter how slight the affront might be, he was never one to let his ego get bruised. He clenched his fist in anger. Sensing this, Torjan firmly grabbed him by the wrist.

"He was only joking…" Torjan whispered, glancing up towards him.

"Blimey, Sy, will you chill out for once?" Hurus grimaced. "Torj, how do you put up with this?"

Torjan released his arm. "Sy is alright. As long as you can handle a few unprovoked attacks and a constant moody attitude, it's actually quite the rewarding friendship."

Syros swallowed his pride, took a deep breath in and uttered the single word "Sorry" before moving past them in search of Saniya.

"Did he really just apologise for something?" Hurus laughed. "Perhaps we should all lose ourselves within the forest; it may end up stopping the war!"

There were twenty of Syros's comrades in camp, with each tent holding three people. Only three females had left on the campaign east and they shared the same quarters, so all

Syros had to do was walk round the camp until he heard a woman's voice and that would be Saniya's location. The night was late but almost all tents still had lights emitting from them. Many of Zelta Squadron stayed up until the early hours of the morning, telling stories or playing games, and, if they were crafty like himself, they drank alcohol they had managed to conceal before making it across the border. As he moved round the camp, with ears and mind focused, he eventually heard hushed female voices. He moved closer and determined this was the tent belonging to Saniya and co. He felt nervous; he could not just barge in, that would be ungentlemanly, plus who knew what state of undress they might be in? He was visualising this scenario when he heard one of the voices mention his name.

"So where do you think Syros and Torjan went?" said a voice he recognised as another of his comrades, Narcisi.

"Not sure. If you ask me, the further away Syros is from us the better," said a different voice he identified as the third girl of the group, Petula. Syros knelt beside the tent, just far enough to still hear their voices distinctly. He was never one for eavesdropping, but learning someone's true thoughts and feelings about you was an opportunity too rare to squander. He picked up a nearby flower and moved it round his fingers as he focused his full attention on the voices.

"Something about him really is unnerving," Petula continued. "Unlike the rest of us who signed up because we have nowhere else to go, people like him and Mercivous signed up because they love killing… "

"Sy is not so bad." His heart lifted a little to hear Saniya stick up for him.

"Come on, Sandy…" This almost made Syros laugh out loud. *Sandy?* When Syros first met the fierce warrior in the East Asterleigh training camps, he had made the mistake of calling her 'Sandy'. After that day, each time she saw him for months afterwards, she gave him a heavy punch to say 'Hello.' But Petula clearly did not bring out the same reaction in her that he once had.

"You only like him because he's handsome. If he was more like Mercivous, I doubt you would be able to tell the two apart."

"Syros is lost, but deep down I know he's a good person. There's a kind-hearted boy there, it's just buried underneath all the anger and sorrow he carries from what happened to his parents."

He did not know how he felt about what she had said, but the flower he had picked was now violently crushed within his hand, leaving it bleeding from the thorns. He flexed his hand in and out of tension, watching the blood slowly drip onto the grass. He wished he had never told her that story, but on one drunken night out in Asterleigh, and after one too many drinks with constant calls for him to 'Open up', he had eventually caved in and told her about the day he had found his parents lying in the street of his old village. After that moment, the way she reacted to him changed; she no longer punched him a 'Hello' and her eyes filled with sympathy whenever she saw him – eyes he began to despise. Syros didn't want her sympathy, or anyone else's. *We all go through experiences that change us*, he told himself. Some experiences just change us more than others. He often imagined what life would have been like if they were still alive, but constantly stopped himself whenever these thoughts went on too long. For his own sake, he should not dwell on them.

He didn't want to eavesdrop any more. In fact, he no longer wanted to see her or anybody else. He wanted to retreat. To leave to where he would no longer be seen by anyone. Getting up from his position he started his withdrawal, until he heard one of the voices. "I think I will go see if they've come back."

He turned around to see Saniya emerging from the tent's opening.

"O-oh!" she stammered. "Where have you been? I was getting worried," she said, seeming to forget she was supposed to be mad at him.

Syros stared at her in shock. She had let her light brown hair down from its usual curled-up dreads, allowing it to flow naturally in the wind. In all the time they were roommates in Asterleigh, Syros had never seen her with her hair any way other than how she normally kept it. It may have been his imagination but something about her eyes also seemed different, more full and radiant. He had always considered her beautiful but the way she stood in front of him, in her nightwear, lit only by the moonlight, melted something inside of him.

"Your hair…" he murmured after a moment of marvel.

"Do you like it?" she asked. If Syros was not mistaken, he almost would have said she was blushing.

"Yes." He moved towards her and gazed into her eyes. They seemed so alluring and esoteric, meant only for him. She even appeared to be glowing like a faraway star, coming in and out of brightness. There was a famous saying that many love-astray drunkards, or beggars masquerading as poets, uttered about absence causing the heart to grow fonder. He had never cared for pretentious love-sickly drunks, but, within this moment, he was inclined to agree with them. *Why am I having these thoughts? It must be the moon that is getting to me...* He wanted to go over and undress her, to see what her naked skin looked like in the moonlight. To caress her gently, and then use his mouth to explore every inch of her illuminated being. He imagined the groans she would make and the cries of pleasure she'd howl as Vurtus towered above them both. Embracing the glow fully until it vanquished the surrounding dark, and then becoming one with her while announcing his love, before they transformed into nothing more than dispersed particles. He was staring for too long, he knew it. So, chances were she also knew this.

"I—" he began. This was hard, harder than anything he had previously done. He coughed in nervousness. "I came to say that I was sorry... if I hurt your feelings, I didn't... sometimes I don't..." He could not find the right combination of words. Failing completely, he continued his stare, waiting for a response that did not return immediately. The clouds in the sky parted and, much like within the forest with the Venian only moments earlier, zaffre-blue moonlight covered his location, filling everything between them with calm tranquil light. They stood there for a moment as shadows of clouds passing the moon caused the light to flicker, as if there was divine intervention for their moment of re-coalescence.

"Sy?"

"Yes?"

"Do you hate me?"

"No."

"I'm glad." Her lips began to tremble.

He wanted to run and hug her while telling her everything was going to be alright, but something within prevented him from doing so. If Syros could have one hope come to fruition, it would be for him to lose this unwelcome part of himself and forget it was ever once there.

He was standing still, filled with ambivalence, unsure of how to react to his inner confliction, when Saniya broke through his inertia by moving upon him suddenly, entwining him within a deep embrace. Momentary feelings of warmth swept over him and for an instant he forgot himself and all his misgivings. He forgot his life of blood and death, anger and hate, all that had happened previously and all that was undoubtedly still to occur – in this moment, he felt newly defined.

She recoiled away from him in embarrassment. "I'm sorry…" she said apprehensively, glancing upwards to match his eyes. "I know you don't like hugs."

Underneath the at-rest night sky, filled with ever-burning golden stars, he gave a rare smile, grasped her gently and swiftly brought her back within a warm embrace. Silently holding her for as long as he dared.

They walked back to the raging campfire. Now alone, Torjan raised his head to see the two of them coming towards him.

"What?" Syros asked, probing the reason for his friend's beaming grin.

"Nothing…"

The night had grown dark, the clouds had concealed the moon, so the only source of light was the campfire. It must have been the early hours of the morning as the other members of Zelta Squadron were sleeping soundly within their tents. The three of them sat there in a moment of silence before Torjan laid back onto the ground and started a loud bellowing laugh. Syros and Saniya looked at each other in bewilderment.

"What?" Syros chuckled, bemused by his friend's strange behaviour.

"It's just…" Torjan lay on his back, facing the stars. "Tonight is a good night. That… and my legs have become completely numb."

"Are you drunk?" Saniya asked between her laughs.

Torjan gave a shake of the head, and weakly raised his right hand upwards before letting it fall clumsily back down onto his chest. "Steph and Hurus went picking during the daytime, through the meadows seeking herbs." He made a noise that sounded more like a girly giggle. "Those guys are fun…"

"You've been taking herbs?" Syros asked, his interest significantly raised. "Did they leave any?" Struggling, Torjan sat upright, with a smile that now dwarfed the width of the moon.

Deeper into the night, the three of them lay on their backs, senses reduced, with both mind and body stimulated. Movement had become a chore that was not worth the expense. Reminiscing old memories and first encounters, plagued with laughter, was all the three in their newly found state were capable of. The grass beneath them was so long it rose above them; the moon had once again come out from its hiding place and the stars were back on display.

"Man… this should last forever," Torjan said, as the three laid on their backs, scanning the cosmos.

Syros gazed upwards and thought of his little brother back in Jovian. Ednon and Ira always had a fascination with the stars above, for as long as they had grown up on their farm together – and now he understood why. They were beautiful, peering down upon this planet in all their benevolence, far away from all war and death, heartache and sorrow. Truly anything was possible in the night sky and on the planets that stayed so isolated away from their own.

"What do you think happens after you die?" he asked the two of them, his mind shifting away from the stars.

"I heard from old shamans that our consciousness travels to a distant part of the universe where we are judged by the five great Gods of legend," Torjan explained. "Dependent on the lives we have lived, they decide what we shall be reborn as – then we start again with new families and bodies, as well as new destinies to fulfil."

"But how could anyone possibly know that? Especially some senile old shaman to whom you have to pay coins to hear his knowledge." He thought it over within his mind. "I don't think I want to die."

"That's a step in the right direction! We probably shouldn't have joined the military then."

"Yeah," he agreed, disheartened. "Too late now, though.

Once you sign up, only death relieves you from your duty. That's something they don't tell you when you're a kid, between the stories of glory and valour." He turned his head to Saniya who had been unusually quiet. She gave a small smile as he faced her and their eyes locked.

"Why did you join the military, San?" Syros wasn't sure if he had ever asked her. Saniya became visibly nervous. Sensing this, he instantly felt horrible.

"I'm sorry…"

"Don't," she said, quickly interrupting him. "Don't feel bad, I…" She stayed silent for a moment, choosing her next words carefully. "I've never really felt as if I had a home. The one home I did have did this to me." She indicated the scar running down her face. "Nor did I feel I had much of a family. I have always considered the two of you to be my true family, making the military my true home." She blushed again, much like she had when he was alone with her earlier outside her tent. He had never heard her speak so openly before – more than ever, he felt terrible for all the times he had been insensitive towards her.

"Well," Torjan began quietly, sitting upright. Proceeding to retrieve a knife from the belt around his waist, he slowly started to cut into the palm of his hand.

"What are you doing?" Saniya shouted.

"If we are indeed a true family," Torjan said, opening his palm and showing them the wound, "then we need to share the same blood."

"You're going to regret that when you become sober, mate."

"Come on… how about we do a vow… a blood vow."

"A vow that states what?"

"How about…" he stopped in a moment of thought. "How about we swear that we will all die on the same day."

"But what happens if one of us dies first?"

Torjan gave a shrug. "Chances are it will be in the same battle. If that is the case, I guess we should go out fighting."

Syros, while not totally certain if he completely meant it, said, "Sure, why not?" He turned to Saniya, whose eyes were already fixed on his own. After a moment, she too agreed. His hand was already bloodied from earlier, so cutting into his palm this time around didn't appear to make much of a difference. The three put their hands together, collectively held them upwards to the moon and spoke their everlasting vow.

After a while of lying on the grass next to the campfire, flicking in and out of consciousness due to fatigue, Syros heard footsteps moving towards them. It was Mercivous and two others, Deckard and Koman, two extremely stocky lads who were only slightly smaller than Torjan in both height and width – and just about sharing a brain cell between them. They had been drawn to Mercivous ever since the beginning of the campaign. *Could I have been among them – if I did not have Torjan and Saniya with me?* he questioned as the three of them walked over, with the two heavyset youths eclipsing Mercivous by a good foot.

"We've come to relieve you of your night duty," Deckard told them. He was carrying a bag round his waist. Syros thought to ask what was in it, but stopped himself like he did most times Mercivous was in his presence.

"Don't you three ever sleep?" Torjan asked nervously.

"We've been on quite an adventure," Koman snickered. Within an instant, Deckard opened his bag and threw a severed head to the ground. It rolled a short way and then stopped, revealing three eyes all facing vertically and dark brownish skin stained with blood.

"We found this primitive savage wandering the meadows alone," Mercivous uttered coldly. "It struggled… but not for very long."

Torjan, Syros and Saniya, leaving the three to their ghoulish cackling, walked back to their pavilions. Having said goodnight to Saniya, the two lads re-entered their tent quietly so as not to wake their sleeping comrade.

"Freckon," Torjan whispered, as the two entered through the flap. "Are you awake?" The boy lifted his head slightly.

"Yeah…" he said, before placing his head back onto his pillow.

"Still having problems sleeping?"

He did not answer, opting to avert his eyes while remaining silent. Freckon was a short timid lad, who stood at just over five foot and was extremely skinny. He was only thirteen years of age but his appearance made him look even younger – short brown hair with a freckled face and wide-open eyes, which gave the impression he was in a permanent state of terror. Syros had the feeling that Freckon feared him, as he rarely talked whenever he was present. He had, however, found his young comrade in deep discussions with Torjan whenever he faked sleep.

"More nightmares?" Torjan asked, as he and Syros

positioned themselves in their respective beds. The young lad did not answer, once again choosing silence.

Syros could relate to the freckle-faced youth more than he knew. As he laid his head down upon his pillow, he too felt anxiety run through him. It had been close to a perfect night, one of the best nights he had known in quite a while. However, once again, he found himself silently begging to whatever divine powers were at play. He prayed that this night, he too would not have his deep sleep infested with any form of nightmare.

Dreams

In the silent still void of nothingness, all matter congealed into one large burst that spread waves throughout the entire fabric of space and time; creating the limitless cosmos. Through the ocean of chaos and uncertainty, independent consciousness began to rise from small microorganisms fighting for the slight chance of momentary existence within the once great void; and, rising through the possibility, the human race, though new and ungainly, began to make its mark within the universe. Striding through fear and uncertainty, the zealous life form began to create its own civilisations. However, fearing the unknown of death and the subsequent path it leads to, the species too late discovered that the one true conflict was within. Eco destruction and endless warfare threatened the still unfamiliar species with complete annihilation; sensing the end, they then decided they should instead be turning within themselves to find the answers, to the dark matter and to the spirit molecule that cycles within all life during the universal course. Whether genuine or metaphorical, the human race found through extraction and inner conflict that death was not the end and nothingness was solely that; it was always merely nothingness – nothing more nor was it anything less. The human race began to spread throughout the universe wielding the silent secrets of the cosmos. The world they left behind and the civilisations that had taken thousands upon thousands of years to forge soon returned to nothingness. And humanity was born once again amongst the stars, but mistakes were always bound to reoccur. Having lost all previous knowledge of worlds and the silent secrets of the cosmos, eyes were once again fixed only upon the ground; fear and prejudice once again began to fester in minds; love soon became hate; exploration became stagnation and alluring dreams became turbid nightmares. Now the once sanguine life form travels the vast silent skies searching for what it once believed was home, now, once again fearing the eventual finality of death. Without the knowledge of the one simple law to all life within the universe, all things, no matter how bright, eventually fade. No matter how much one individual may transcend, they will eventually, without exception, all return into the great empty void. However, the cosmos is nothing other than incalculable; perhaps what once was isn't any longer. Perhaps what we witness is not actually what is truly there; and perhaps the true answers are all lying sequestered within forgotten dreams.

7

Suns of a New Age

It was the day of Ira's funeral; he was dressed in black. Ednon had met so many new faces this day it was hard to keep track of them all and was surprised at just how many had known his grandfather well enough to come and offer their sympathy at the secluded cemetery on the outskirts of Jovian. There must have been close to two hundred people who had arrived to pay their respects to the at-peace visionary. They all came up to Ednon, shaking his hand while offering their utmost reverent condolences. Even old Ageth had come out from her sanctuary of the library, crying uncontrollably and holding him for so long it made him feel uncomfortable. The suns were central within the sky and sunlight was beating down. It did not feel much like a day for mourning. In fact, it had been continuously sunny ever since the passing of Sechen and the bringing of the New Year. Ednon wished he could return to Abacus's farm and retreat into the room they had given him following Ira's death. He was growing tired of these new faces and their fake sincerity; it was beginning to cause unwanted pains to form in his stomach. Sensing his discomfort, Abacus sent him a glance.

"Do not worry, Ednon. You will only need to greet a few more."

"Why do I have to greet them at all?"

"It's because your grandfather was a much beloved man. And you, being Ira's genetic relation, well, there are many who are curious to see just what kind of boy you are."

"Will Syros return from military duty?" he asked in hope.

"We have sent word to your brother. I wouldn't hold out too much hope though, Ednon. The military isn't known for showing this kind of compassion, especially towards new recruits."

Ednon wondered if Syros had been in any battles yet. He had dreamt the previous night of being dressed in golden armour, wielding a sword and killing strange beasts with over a dozen eyes. Perhaps Syros was right when they were both children and his theories, of Ednon's dreams being a sign of him growing into a great warrior, were true. He was starting to speculate he was on the wrong path and his purpose in life was war, and had never been peace.

Feeling even worse than he had previously, Ednon looked to the large congregation behind him. "How did he know so many people?"

"Your grandfather was a very popular man within Asterleigh and the surrounding villages. He used to preach in the streets when he was young; I couldn't tell you the number of times he was beaten or jailed for the unpopular ideals he spouted. Still, he held true to his convictions and before too long he no longer needed to, as the number of followers grew, and our Order was finally born."

Ednon looked at Abacus, intrigued. *Order? What Order is he speaking of?* Before Ednon could utter a response, Abacus announced loudly, "He has finally arrived. Ednon, this is the man I have most wanted you to meet." Three distinguished figures had made their way up the grassy pathway.

"Ednon, this is Luther," Abacus gestured to the man in the middle. He was fat, pear-shaped and standing only an inch or so taller than Ednon, using a short walking stick to assist his movement. Dark-tinted shades made it difficult for Ednon to get a proper look at his eyes, while a bald head placed his wrinkles on full display. The two men surrounding him were both tall, almost double the height of the exceptionally small Luther.

"Abacus, my dear chap. How are you?" he said in a deep voice as he shook Abacus's outstretched hand. "And this must be…" Luther turned his attention to Ednon. "Ira's grandson… the deepest of condolences, my young maverick. Ira was a great man in his prime, however, I fear years do horrors to the consciousness. But suicide…" he shook his head. "I'm afraid none of us knew how unsound of spirit he had truly become." He stopped and let out a long sigh, which sounded to Ednon as nothing but fake. "Suicide has always been an act of cowardice, especially when he had someone so young as yourself to shepherd."

"I don't think suicide is an act of cowardice nor do I feel it is selfish. To choose when one exits this world is one of the only genuine freedoms we have."

Luther let out a gruff laugh. "Ha! I'm impressed, child, you truly must be of Ira's genetic heritage. You should come to some of our meetings. I feel they are the perfect place for a young progressive such as yourself. Memphis!" he shouted abruptly to the enormous man on his right-hand side. "Give the lad a treat."

The man reached inside his pocket, then handed a single wrapped sweet to Ednon. He wanted to tell the man to take his offering and shove it, but managed to stop himself. "Thank you," he said, through gritted teeth.

Luther placed a hand upon his shoulder; despite the warm weather, it was surprisingly cold to the touch. "Do not fret, lad, for one day soon the suns shall both rise, illuminating the darkness – and the new age shall be ushered in; as our dissonance reaches its most violent and bloody it shall come, and then a glorious light shall engulf these lands, curing all of our collective sorrow." Luther gestured to the two men beside him and together they silently walked past. Ednon watched as they moved further away. Still with gritted teeth, he tossed the sweet to the ground.

"What's wrong?" Abacus asked.

"I don't like what he said about Ira. My grandfather was not a coward."

"Luther has always had a forward way of speaking, I am sure he did not mean it like that. He is a very important man within Asterleigh. When the time comes, we will need men such as him to be on our side."

"Side? A side in what?"

Abacus studied him thoughtfully. "Perhaps I should take you to one of our next meetings. There will be plenty of chances after we move to our new home in Asterleigh."

"You don't have to go through all that trouble just for my benefit, Abacus…"

"Don't worry about it, Ednon. It would not be right for you to remain living so close to your old home, considering what has happened. Plus, I feel it is time my wife, daughter and I left our small cottage and traded it in for a larger home."

Ednon did not know how he felt about moving to the capital. He had always enjoyed the grassy meadows and rural areas, but if Abacus's heart was set on the move, he had no right to try and change it. He nostalgically scanned the vast sunlit meadows, cottages and farms. He liked it here, he did not want to leave, not in the slightest.

"When do you think we will go?" he asked, fearing the answer.

"As soon as the funeral is over, my wife and I will begin house-hunting…" Abacus stopped himself. "That is, of course, if it's okay with you?"

Ednon did not answer. Standing on the high hilltop next to the cemetery, he merely continued to look out over the seemingly never-ending meadows to the south, west and east, and then to the outskirts of Asterleigh and its stone walls of resistance keeping it ever inviolable. From where he stood, he could also see the Medzu statue upon its clouds over the mountains to the north, like an ever-present sentry being on constant guard over the city. Even from this distance, it was a sight to behold. For so long now he had felt as if he were in a trance, as if his life was no longer his. The dreams and visions were starting to feel more palpable than life itself; he often found himself questioning what was real and what was only fantasy, but he no longer cared, because it did not matter – because nothing mattered.

Feelings and scattered thoughts that did not seem a part of him were now the only things that felt real. *Is it all a dream – all of it?* If it were a dream, he would very much like to wake up soon. He missed so much. He ached so much and now he hurt so much. When he placed his head down to sleep each night, he could swear he saw the shadows taking shape. Then, when he slept, he dreamt of nothing but stars – just endless stars over and over, bright and alluring, sad and profound and all utterly meaningless. He did not want to be here anymore – upon the ground, with his anguish. Will the dream end soon, Ira? Much like yours did, if of course you were ever truly real to begin with. Or will it last for eternity? Will sadness and death always be stalking behind, or will they finally leave when I bask within the cavern of the far-off cosmos, *isolated and shining like the brightest of stars?*

"Ed?" Abacus gently touched his shoulder. It felt real. The breeze caressed him gently; it too felt real. He heard hummingbirds chirping and the trees lightly rustling – but he was still not convinced.

"It's not real," Ednon said mindlessly, as if something extraordinary had caught his eye in the far-off distance.

"What isn't?"

"Everything…" he murmured, before walking his way through the cemetery gates.

The ceremony had begun; he felt all eyes upon him as he sat in the front row with Abacus and his wife Jernett. She was a kind and loving woman who had tried to make Ednon feel as welcome as possible ever since he had moved into their home and intruded into her family. She was always offering food and carried with her a constant smile, much as Amelia did, but he did not feel as if he belonged, because they weren't his real family. The only family he had left was his older brother, who was too preoccupied with feeding the anger inside himself to ever truly care for him. He felt very much alone in this world. Even with Amelia's warmth which, despite what his true self may have desired deep down, he could not return. Her face in particular stood out in the sea of mournful expressions; the bright-green eyes of her mother before her and the freckled face of her father. She stared at him with sadness. Right then, within that moment, he thought about what the shadow had told him of the world ending and a different feeling strangely swept over him. It was one of excitement. He wanted it all to end; nothing would bring him greater joy. There were so many mistakes that kept on repeating. The human race was nothing but a virus to the universe. Perhaps it was truly time for it all to end. He wanted to snap out of this line of thinking, but whatever had overcome him drew him back in. He placed his head in his hands and imagined; he imagined himself running as fast as he could, in which direction he did not care. He could run anywhere, the verdant fields were wide, perhaps he could travel all the way south to Lowton or even out to the border. He could, as he had been told so many times, 'go to the forest and live with the Venians.' He was sure they would accept him, from what he had heard about the species they at least sounded reasonable. Much more tolerable than humans had ever seemed. He was envisaging his new life, when he felt another hand on his shoulder. Having lost count of the number of different people who had done this today, Ednon turned disinterestedly to see who the owner of the hand was.

"Ed…" It was an old black man around the same age Ira had been, with a grey goatee running down far past his chin, and who was sitting directly behind him.

"Ed, my name is Fergus," the man said in a soothing voice. "I know nothing I say will quell the inner turmoil you must be feeling, but I wanted to tell you that your grandfather was a great man and an even better friend."

"Thank you, Fergus." The man sounded sincere, which was more than he could say for most who had spoken to him already. The way the man talked and the expression within his eyes gave Ednon the impression he too was in a great deal of inner turmoil. "Had you known my grandfather for very long?"

"Oh my, yes," Fergus nodded his head sadly. "For over fifty years. We grew up on the same street in Madale together. His mind was always one that was before its time."

"You had known him for that long? I don't mean to

cause offence, Fergus, but I don't believe I ever heard my grandfather mention your name."

"No, he wouldn't have... you see, we had a falling-out a long time ago."

"What over?"

"What else?" The old man gave a sad sigh. "Women." Sensing the personal situation, Ednon decided not to press the matter further. "It has always been a deepest regret that I was never able to reconcile myself with my once dear friend. And now it will be a regret that I carry with me until the day I follow him into the great beyond... but Ednon," he moved closer and whispered in a voice that could only be heard by them both, "I am here to warn you... You see the fat short man furthest to your right on my row?"

He peered down the row of people to see that the man Fergus was talking about was none other than the black-shaded Luther. Ednon nodded to Fergus silently.

"That man uses the name 'pacifist' only for his own selfish gain. In actuality, he is as much one as a starved wolf circling its sleeping prey. Be wary of him and the others who call themselves 'pacifists'. Your grandfather always stayed true to his convictions – I beg that you do the same." And with that, Fergus stood up, quickly making his way out of the cemetery. Ednon watched the man, contemplating what he had been told. His eyes then subconsciously fell back down to Luther, who was already staring back, matching his gaze.

8

Traditions of the Young

"Do you think Alpelites shit?" Syros questioned, shovelling up a pile of faeces.

"If they eat," Torjan wiped sweat from his forehead. "Then yes, they most likely shit."

Syros and Torjan, along with the young Freckon, had learnt from morning assignment that they had the unfortunate duty of cleaning out the latrines. Usually Syros would not have minded, but the weather was unbearably hot and the frustration growing inside him was not being helped by the suns' rays making the already rancid smell even fouler.

"Why is there so much of it?" Syros asked despairingly.

"Must have been the mushrooms we had for supper yesterday," added Saniya, watching the three of them while sitting on a nearby supply crate. "You two were out, so luckily you managed to miss the runs."

"Brilliant..." He was beginning to feel anger again. He had dreamt of his mother's face once more; that, mixed with the news that he was on latrine duty, caused unwanted emotions and thoughts to flow through him. He had forgotten what his mother's face had truly looked like, but he remembered light brown hair, full lips and a glowing smile. But now he questioned whether these memories of her were genuine or if he had merely fabricated them. The only time he could any longer see his mother's face was in his dreams, always lying motionless, the natural colour of her eyes gone, now complete black. *Perhaps it would be easier for me to forget her,* Syros questioned. But was that even possible? To forget someone in their entirety? Truth be told he could not remember what type of woman she had been, whether she was a kind and loving mother or a fierce and strict one. His grandfather always told him to try to hold on to the good memories of his parents, to help handle the grief he carried while growing up. But now, over twelve years later, he had forgotten most of his life before he and his brother began living with Ira. His father he could not completely picture; the only thing he remembered was bristly unshaven facial hair as he caressed it with his toddler-sized hand, and how it had felt rough and prickly. He did not want these memories any longer. They had become meaningless; they made him feel only emptiness.

"You going to help?" he turned to ask Saniya, annoyed.

She shook her head playfully. "Nope. Already done my duty for the morning. Narcisi, Petula and I cleaned all the cutlery and plates."

Lucky for some, he thought as he attacked the pile of faeces with his shovel. The heat and smell were getting to him. He needed to attack something living. He took off his military top and threw it aside. From the corner of his eye, he could see Saniya dart her eyes to him whenever she thought he would not notice.

"Wasn't Hurus put on latrine duty? Where is he?"

Torjan shrugged. "He's probably resting underneath the suns somewhere."

"And that's fair is it?" Syros demanded. He turned to young Freckon beside him. "What do you think, Freck? Is it fair that we have to dig through shit, some of his shit by the way, while he sunbathes… probably laughing at us." As expected, the small, timid lad did not answer and solely continued to avoid eye contact. Syros scoffed. "You've echoed my thoughts exactly, brother…" He did not understand why Freckon was so afraid of him. Was he really so much scarier than Torjan, whose arms were almost the size of the young lad's torso? He wondered what he was doing here. The freckle-faced boy had next to no physical prowess; he could not wield a sword and generally seemed terrified by the whole situation he was in. It would be very much what Ednon would be like if he was put in this situation, Syros speculated. *He is far too timid.* What could he possibly do in battle? Just stand there and stay quiet. Could the small unsure lad truly kill an Alpelite? He wondered what Freckon's story was, how he had ended up here in the military beside him, now digging up shit. Was it from loneliness or sadness that he had sought refuge here? Syros began to question whether he truly cared. He searched inside himself for a moment and found nothing, so perhaps he didn't.

"Where's Raynmaher?" he asked anyone who was listening. "What kind of military squadron is he running if a private refuses his order?"

If he were Captain, he would have Hurus severely beaten; he fantasied doing so, as he once again attacked the faeces with his shovel. He did not like Hurus. The way he made a joke of everything, his snide comments and he especially did not appreciate his laziness. He had thought he would find people like himself in the military. But he hadn't. Most treated this much like a holiday and seemed oblivious to the fact that any day death could find them – a three-eyed savage death. Perhaps, like nearly everywhere else, he did not belong here. He reflected over this sombrely as he threw his shovel aside, refusing to do any more work.

Saniya watched him sit down aggressively beside her. "You know Captain Raynmaher... he's probably in his tent writing reports or whatever the hell it is he does."

Syros picked up a nearby bucket and poured water over himself. It was the hottest day of the year so far. It had become so humid it was a struggle to stand up for too long, never mind doing acts of labour.

"I know what I'm going to do..." he announced, having been struck with an idea. "I'm going to find Hurus and then I am going to beat him until his eyes roll into the back of his head."

"Please don't."

"Why not?"

"Because it won't end well..."

"What would you do, if you were in my position?"

"I would probably beat him until he cries for his mother," she said, giving him a grin.

"Then why can't I?" he said, not returning one back to her.

"Because I know you and I know it will probably end up being more than a punch." She shifted closer towards him. "Just calm down for a moment and stay here... with me?"

Syros recoiled quickly, before she could touch him. He still did not like human contact, even after the time they had shared the previous night. That moment had felt more like a dream than it had real life. As though some imposter was in control of his body for one brief flash underneath the moonlight, forcing him to have thoughts and emotions he would normally never hold. Although the occasion itself had felt the most real thing he had ever experienced, it still did not seem like him, as if he had observed it from some place that was not his own darkened mind. But with the sunrise came a different mindset, and he felt the all too familiar gloom consume him; but mostly it was indifference that clutched onto him, much like a toddler refusing to let go of its favourite toy. Despite this, he felt a deep sadness to see the dejected expression in her eyes as he selfishly jilted away from her act of affection, and for that he was truly sorry.

"I've got something important to do..." he said, standing up, having remembered the new quest he had undertaken.

"Don't do anything stupid!" Torjan shouted after him, as Syros walked away, the foul smell of faeces following his every movement.

He made his way through camp. Most were already up doing their own odd jobs. They quickly turned away after they saw the expression of rage across his face. If he were to find Hurus he knew exactly where he would be. He proceeded to the outskirts of the camp and onto the blossoming meadows where, as expected, Hurus was lying on the grass chatting with the lanky Steph and Petula. They both glanced up at him nervously and muttered something quietly. Hurus stared upwards.

"Why is your top off? And why do you smell like shit?"

"Oh, you know…" Syros stood over him, trying to sound and act as intimidating as possible. "I was doing the job that you were supposed to be doing as well."

"Rolling around in faeces?" Hurus guffawed, seeking backing from the others, who did not return his laugh.

"Shovelling it actually. Didn't you hear Raynmaher read out the duties this morning?"

Hurus sent an absent look back. "I don't really pay much attention to whatever Raynmaher says, to be honest with you." Noticing the expression of rage across Syros's face, he continued, "But if you want me to help, then yeah, why not?"

"Good… We going then?"

"Hold your horses. I was in the middle of a conversation. Didn't your mother ever teach you patience?"

These words made something snap within Syros. All the aggression that had built up for over a month had reached boiling point; he could not contain it any longer. "Stand up," he demanded. He was proud it came across like a threat, because that was exactly how he had intended it.

Hurus's face paled. "Oh, what, you going to hit me, Sy?"

"I'm not going to hit you," he promised. "Stand up."

"You don't have to do as he says," said the red-haired

Petula. "He doesn't outrank you; you don't have to submit to what he says, Hurus."

Finding no other outcome and without wanting to seem weak, Hurus stood up and stared down at Syros. He was large and stocky, not weak in the slightest. However, Syros had fought many stronger. He gave a slight grin before smacking him as hard as he could with his right fist, and then continued to rain punches down on him until a loud booming voice caught his attention.

"Syros!"

Captain Raynmaher was standing by the entrance of the campsite, his eyes wide and fierce. "In my tent... now!"

Breathing heavily, Syros cursed the fact that he could not continue his exorcism of built-up anger. He arose from Hurus, who sat up, nose bleeding. "Mental case," he heard one of them murmur as he sauntered away. *Good* – he was glad that's what they thought of him. He didn't even know what a 'mental case' was but he kind of liked the sound of it. He did not care if they did not like him; that was never something he longed for. To be honest, he had no idea what he did long for. He thought back to the night before, lying with Torjan and Saniya as they had searched the night stars together, and how at peace he had felt in that moment. Perhaps there was something more...

Syros walked into the open pavilion of Captain Lars Raynmaher. The tent's interior was lit by a single lantern aflame upon a desk in the far corner. Maps and written reports lay messily; it appeared whatever his squadron leader did within his tent, he did in a most disorganised way. Captain Raynmaher, a middle-aged man with a thin, brown moustache, short brown hair and bright blue eyes, sat behind his desk at the end of the tent. After a moment of silently studying his papers, Raynmaher looked up towards him in a tired, almost lethargic, manner.

"Are you a woman, Syros?"

"Excuse me, Sir?"

"A woman…" Raynmaher once again asked, in a way that came across as being deadly serious. "Are you a woman?"

"No?"

"It's just that you are showing mood swings that are not too dissimilar to those of my wife. I am not going to punish you for hitting Hurus because truth be told the boy needed a good smack. However, these attacks must stop. My word, lad, no one knows what kind of mood you are in, when it is safe to approach you and when it is not. This quality you very much share with my wife."

"You're really not going to punish me, Sir?"

Raynmaher gave a shake of the head. "No, boy, I'm not going to punish you. As I said, there are many here who need a severe beating. Do you know how hard it is to lead a gang of unruly teenagers, then guide them to fight with all the vigour they can muster against an enemy that outnumbers them almost ten to one? Many here will die. I feel that out of everyone here only you and Mercivous have what it takes to rise through the ranks and become useful cogs for the human race. You both have the right amount of hatred, mixed in with the right amount of intelligence."

Syros felt a little unclean. He did not like being compared to Mercivous, even when it was meant as a compliment.

"These are sad days indeed, when women are allowed to join the military," Raynmaher continued, not sensing Syros's discomfort. "But our numbers being few, and the enemy numbers being many, we must take what we can."

"Saniya is the greatest fighter I know, Sir. She's much stronger than me and all the other males here, and by quite a distance, I might add."

Raynmaher nodded his head. "Aye, Saniya is a great warrior. But she too has her weaknesses. Don't think I do not notice the way that she looks at you."

Syros knew what his captain was alluding to and it made him fearful. He prayed Saniya did not love him; from that most unpleasant misfortune, he hoped he could spare her.

"A word of advice," Raynmaher said, noticing his silence. "Stay as far away as possible. Do not love, Syros; it will only hurt more when the time comes."

"Do you not love?" he asked daringly of the battle-hardened veteran. "Do you not hold love for your wife and children back home, Sir?"

Raynmaher studied his eyes while contemplating the words he was about to utter. "Do you want to know the sad truth?" he said after a moment of silence. "No. I don't. We are not individuals here, Syros. Individuality is the death of duty, and one day individuality will be the death of us all – on that you can trust me. We live and we die as something greater than ourselves – in that way, death is utterly meaningless. Never forget what you are, Syros, you are human as am I. We do what we must for humanity's sake. For both survival and for growth. The pacifists may scoff at us, but we are more human than they shall ever be." He finished, lifting his personalised gold patterned goblet and taking a sip from it. He groaned joyously, slamming the cup back onto his desk. "Nothing like wine on a sunlit morning," he grunted.

Syros thought over the words his Captain had told him. He knew this already. He had always known it. But still he thought of his little brother and how much he missed him. He thought of a calm serene life on a farm surrounded by the meadows underneath clouds and night stars, of his future wife and children, and then he thought of his friends.

"Sir..." Syros began. Raynmaher stared back at him, and in this moment, Syros saw his eyes too seemed to be lifeless and uncaring. "This campaign..." he tried to find the right combination of words. "After this campaign, is there a chance of me becoming unbound to the military?" He gulped as he felt sweat manifesting on his forehead.

Raynmaher stared coldly back, his eyebrows slightly raised. "That is your individuality seeping through..." he said in a voice that was almost a whisper. "To state it bluntly, no, Syros. You can never leave. Defection in these times when we have enemies even within our own lands is to be considered desertion, and desertion is a crime punishable by death." He stood up from his chair and made his way round to Syros, before placing a hand on his shoulder. "Do not fret, lad, after your first few kills it will soon be something that you can't live without. On that you can trust me. The travel is always a bore, but the bloodshed is far more rewarding. I feel it will not be too far away...." He walked towards the tent's opening. "We break camp at midday!" His voice erupted in a vibration that could be heard across the entire campsite.

"And Syros…"

"Yes, Sir?"

"Have a wash before we go."

Midday had come and the heat grew with it. As planned, Zelta Squadron had broken camp and rode horseback further and further east. The grassy meadows they had been travelling over for what felt like months were now rocky terrain. Mountains covered the distance ahead, rising high above even the clouds as they rode through an enormous canyon. There was no water, grass or greenery of any kind here, Syros reflected as he scanned every direction. No wonder the Alpelites yearned for their homes back within Asterleigh, as there appeared to be no life out here whatsoever. He still had not even seen an Alpelite, not a living one anyway. The fantasy had become a reality for most other members of Zelta. Many faces had paled completely as they too scanned the new, dead landscape. All except for Mercivous, who, unsurprisingly, had started to smirk. Syros watched him nervously while riding silently behind. *I am not like him* – he felt relief as the nerves grew inside his stomach. *I am like everyone else.* He sighed to himself quietly. "I'm just like everybody else…"

From the front of the squadron, Raynmaher called back for them to dismount. There was a group of figures heading their way from the far side of the canyon. After Syros dismounted, he squinted his eyes to see who the figures were and tightened the grip on his blade. He felt his heart pounding. *Is this finally it?* He could feel the sweat running down from his hand onto his blade's grip. He began to panic. *What if the sweat makes me drop my sword in the middle of a fight?* He would be as good as dead then. His mind was racing out of control and sweat was continuing to pour.

"Captain Simms, this way," Raynmaher signalled with his hands over his head.

As the figures moved closer, he could distinguish they were, in fact, human. Syros thought he counted ten or so as their faces became determinable. Much like his own squadron, they wore military uniforms. However, unlike the purple laced with gold braids, theirs were red and gold. They were all teenagers except for the one in front leading, whom he assumed was Captain Simms, as he was the only one old enough to grow facial hair. Not as old as Raynmaher, Captain Simms still appeared to be in his late twenties. However, his bushy beard and scarred face gave the young man a fierce look.

"Captain Raynmaher," Captain Simms said with his arms outstretched. "Thank the divine, intel was correct. We could use your assistance here in the land of the shit-smelling savages."

"Captains Simms," Raynmaher shook the younger captain's hand. "I am sorry to hear what happened to General Bowenn – most shocking, most shocking indeed."

"Ah yes. A damn shame. The old bastard was quite a bore, but he will be missed. It was a complete bloodbath apparently. I heard there were over thirty bodies of both Alpelite and human found upon Celadon Meadows on the night of Sechen's passing. They say a young private only the age of thirteen died in the conflict."

"He was only doing his duty."

"Yes, he was only doing his duty."

"What is your situation here?" Raynmaher studied the rest of the young squadron.

Syros noticed how shaken-up the privates were in comparison to their bushy-bearded Captain. Most were panting heavily, with eyes so wide it seemed at any moment they would fall out from their heads.

"We were inspecting one of the savages' villages, when we were attacked by a group of warriors." Simms uttered this last word with sarcasm. "We managed to fend them off pretty easily, but they were still able to take one of our own hostage before retreating back up into the mountains."

"Were there no closer squadrons nearby to receive your calls?"

"You were the nearest ones, I'm afraid. I don't know why the Supreme Leader has all the squadrons this far east, but whatever it is, it is on a scale which I have never seen before." Captains Simms appeared excited. "We could do with some assistance tracking down the savages who took one of our own, while that village up ahead still needs to be detained."

Raynmaher stood still, contemplating his next move. He faced Zelta Squadron, who had stayed in complete silence for his entire conversation with the ally captain. "Listen up!" he shouted his orders to them. "We shall split into two groups. Koman. Syros. Deckard. Freckon. Steph. Narcisi. Keenan. Jamison and Mercivous. You shall detain the village up ahead." He pointed a finger at each of them as he said their names. "Do not do anything rash until we rendezvous. Mercivous shall be in command until I'm back. The rest of us shall assist Captain Simms' squadron in tracking down the renegade Alpelites. Does everybody understand their tasks?"

Zelta Squadron shouted in unison to indicate they did. Torjan and Saniya had both made their way over to him, concern upon their faces. For the first time during the entirety of this campaign, he was going to be away from them both.

"Be safe, Sy," said Saniya. He could tell she wanted to hug him, and truth be told he wanted to hug her back. However, there were too many people around, so a small, sad smile was all they could give each other.

"Yes, be safe, Syros." Torjan placed a hand upon his shoulder.

"You both be safe as well," he pleaded. He had a wretched, ominous feeling; Mercivous was to be his leader. *This was not going to end well*, he thought to himself, as he looked over towards Mercivous, whose baleful grin had widened, now stretching from ear to ear.

9

Spectre of God

Ednon stood over the grave containing the collection of remains that were once his grandfather. It had been close to three months since they had laid Ira to rest, but, in his mind, it felt much shorter. The wind swirled as he placed the red roses upon the headstone. Ednon had finally made the transition to East Asterleigh. The house was large, much larger than the farmhouse he had shared with his grandfather and brother. He liked his new home, but missed Jovian – Asterleigh was always much too frantic. Abacus and his family had moved in not too far from a tavern, so even at night he was disturbed from his reading by laughing, drunken military personnel stumbling back and forth through the streets.

Thinking of both his brother and grandfather, Ednon's mind went to the last words that Ira had spoken. *What did you want me to tell Syros? Was it something deep and profound or was it simply that you loved him?* He looked down at the flower-strewn grave. In Asterleigh, tensions between the pacifists and military were brewing like an impending storm; he sensed it each day, growing increasingly sullen. Attacks were now becoming relentlessly usual. He heard stories of the Southern Military Barracks being destroyed in an explosion, leaving many innocent people dead. Military men were being stabbed in pubs and taverns; he had also caught wind of a tale about the General of the Western Border being completely decapitated, and his head then getting displayed in the streets. If Ira were here, what would he do, if he were able and in his prime?

"Excuse me…" A gentle voice caught his attention. The words came from a tall, blonde-haired woman with blue eyes, standing a couple of feet from him.

"Yes?"

"Are you Ednon, the grandson of Ira?"

"I am."

"Your grandfather was a quite brilliant man; I remember when I was little, he used to tell all the children stories on the night of Sechen's passing. He always made time for the young and the sickly. Of his kind, I fear there are too few left." Ednon studied her face; she couldn't be much older than Syros.

"Thank you." He had heard so many of these stories over the past couple of days that he felt as if they were all merging into one. "When did you leave Jovian?" he asked, confused as to why he had never seen her in the village before.

"I moved to Asterleigh when I was young, only thirteen.

97

My father taught me that whenever an opportunity presents itself, you must grab it firmly with both hands."

At this moment, he noticed that she too had brought flowers and, without wanting to cause offence, cautiously asked, "Who did you come to visit?"

"My father."

"I'm sorry…"

"Don't apologise. The man died doing what he thought was of the greatest importance."

"How did he die?"

"He was stabbed by a renegade Alpelite while returning home from military duty."

Ednon was surprised by the lack of emotion with which she recited her story. Even he was feeling choked up at the thought of waiting for a father to return from duty, only to find out he had been killed on his way home.

"I'm sorry…" he repeated, unable to find anything new to say. "My brother is in the military also."

The woman's eyebrows quickly rose. "A grandson of Ira, joining the military? How ever did that happen? Is that… Syron?"

"Syros."

"Oh yes…" The way she spoke seemed to signify the fact she had known this all along. "So, was he one of the ones who joined the mass campaign east?"

Ednon gave a slight nod. He had still not received word on his brother. Abacus usually gave a sad shake of the head whenever he asked if he had heard any news. Ednon wasn't even sure if Syros had been informed of their grandfather's passing and he wondered how he would react when he heard the news. The two had not been on the best of terms over the past few years, but Ednon still held happy memories of the three of them together. It saddened him to think of Syros not caring about their grandfather's death. But he had also seen how dark and violent his brother's mind had become. Even Ira, who was so well-known throughout the land for his inspiring words of peace and acceptance, could not change his brother from his own self-destructive path – and they had all lived together for over ten years. So perhaps even Ira knew that Syros was truly beyond the grasp of salvation.

The woman broke into his introspection. "I wish your brother good health. I am sure you will see him again before too long."

Feeling a little lifted, Ednon gave her a smile, as a man with a grey bushy moustache joined them at the graveside.

"Oh, Robles, are you finished?"

"Yes, Ma'am, I have left the flowers on her grave. Do you wish to return to Asterleigh?"

"Yes, Robles, after I lay these roses, we shall go." She remembered Ednon and seemed embarrassed that she had not introduced him. "Robles, this young man is Ednon, the grandson of none other than the great Ira."

"Ira…" Robles uttered, in a slightly surprised manner, fixing his stare upon him. "It is a pleasure, Sir." Ednon had never been called 'Sir' before and wasn't sure if he liked it. Something about the way the old man carried himself struck Ednon as being subservient, as if he were some type of butler or bodyguard. The grizzled man's waist had a sheathed sword strapped across the belt underneath his jacket, confirming his suspicions that it was most probably the latter.

"We must be going, Ednon. Do come and visit us sometime in Asterleigh."

"I will," he promised. Only in this moment, he remembered that he did not know her identity. "I don't think you ever told me your name."

"Ethna," she replied. "Ethna Gibbon."

"Well, Ethna, where in Asterleigh do you live?"

"The Temple of Yashin," the woman now known as Ethna told him. "Do you know of this building, Ednon?"

"Of course I do!" Ednon said in shock. "It is one of the largest buildings in Asterleigh. Are you telling me that's where you live?" He now questioned to whom he had been talking all this time.

Ethna gave a nod. "Do you remember what I told you about my father telling me to grab opportunities firmly? I very much took his words to heart. Please do come and visit us sometime soon, Ed." She gestured to the old Robles and together they walked out of the cemetery, leaving Ednon, now feeling a little perplexed, standing alone in front of his grandfather's grave.

After he had finished in the cemetery, he decided to walk through the meadows to Eos Lake. He made this journey a part of his weekly routine whenever he travelled to Ira's burial place. Usually he would take a book to read or, when the weather was especially hot, much like it was today, he would go for a short swim within the lake's still waters. The weather, to everybody's surprise, had still not cooled down. In fact, it had only become hotter as the days passed by. No one could explain this dramatic change within the ecosystem, apart from the drunks he passed throughout Asterleigh who, like with most things, claimed it was a sign of the world's imminent destruction. Usually, he would make his way past them without a second thought. However, with the words of the phantom he had met in the Grand Library constantly in his mind, he now gave their claims more attention. And the verdict at which he arrived caused terror to run through him. It was a type of fear he could only compare with the kind he had felt as a young child after realising that one day he would die, without any way of changing that inevitable outcome. He had locked himself in his room and cried for an entire week, after coming to the inner conclusion that nothing lasts forever.

Walking on the shores of Eos, he sat down beside the slow-moving tide. The sunlight reflected from the surface and into his eyes. He sat off the cuff of the water that pressed against his feet as it moved back and forth. He had been to the lake many times while growing up, with Ira and his brother; it had always given him a sense of calm and serenity. Not too far to his right a family played together. Two young children – a boy and a girl – and the parents sitting on the shore, basking underneath the suns. The children appeared so happy as they splashed one another, without a single other worriment. He craved longingly to return to that state, to once again feel like his old self, but that seemed like the most distant of hopes. Things could never go back to normal, of that he was certain. Small one-eyed fish only an inch-wide circled by his feet. They cast his mind back to the creature he had met on the night of Ira's death. It had not been there when he had gone back to the farm days later.

He wondered where it was. A creature that beautiful should not be on this planet. It shouldn't be anywhere near here. He picked up a stone and skimmed it across the lake, which caused ripples that disturbed the water's stillness. Ednon had travelled down to Eos not long after Ira's funeral, his mind feeling confused and chaotic; that was where Amelia had come to find him.

They had sat in silence observing the lake's tranquil surface, until she placed her head upon his shoulder. "You miss him, don't you?"

"Yes."

She grasped his arm gently. "I am here for you... we are all here for you."

He turned and considered her bright-green eyes. "I feel as if I am in a dream," he said, as the small, transparent, single-eyed fish nibbled between the toes of his naked foot. "That I am not really here beside you, as if this is not my real life, and that someday I shall wake up away from all of this."

He remembered her face brightening. "My dearest Ednon... if it is true that you are merely sleeping, and if you are only here beside me because of a dream, then I hope you do not ever wake up."

"Daddy..." he heard the young girl speak. "What is that creature there?"

He looked over at the family. The young girl was pointing towards a fierce light from underneath the water. From where he was sitting he could not see what creature she was talking about, but the light seemed familiar, as a strange yet esoteric feeling gripped him. Drawn to it, as if something unworldly was in control of his actions, he walked across the shore and closer to the source of the bright underwater illumination.

Her father scanned the water's surface. "I have no idea, sweetheart."

Ednon was at a better angle and could indeed see something within the waters. Whatever it was, it was shining in and out of brightness, and he could see the outline moving underneath the tides. Then, as quick as a flash, the creature's head appeared. It had large diamond-shaped eyes, an almost non-existent nose and mouth, and a strange spiral marking across its forehead. It was undoubtedly the same strange life form that he had found underneath the stars before the moment of Ira's death. It swam towards them using its two small flippers for thrusting, causing ripples to run throughout the lake.

"Mummy!" The young girl jumped up and down. "It's coming towards us…"

The child wasn't wrong. The little animal was indeed heading towards them, and at some pace. It reached the shore and made its way onto solid ground. Now that its full body was in view, it was without question the same creature. The family's faces were filled with shock as it moved upon Ednon. It trudged its way to his ankles, lifted its head and gave a small cheerful squeak before beginning to rub against him gently.

"Whatever it is… it holds some affection towards you," the man said, watching them both with astonishment. Ednon knelt and petted the shining organism's oval-shaped head.

"Where in all the stars did that come from?" the father continued, as his small children also felt confident enough to edge closer. Ednon wondered this himself – in fact, he had wondered about it continuously ever since his first encounter on that fateful night. Without warning, the spiral upon the creature's forehead started to glow and all traces of it disappeared, as if it had never truly been there to begin with.

"What on…" the man marvelled. Collectively, the five of them looked at each other, the same level of bewilderment spread across each of their faces.

Ednon walked back through the streets of East Asterleigh, his mind on the latest encounter with the small transparent life form. How did it disappear, in the way that it had? All logic dictated that what he had witnessed was utterly impossible. But he had seen it, and unless his eyes and mind were lying to him, it was real. Why did the life form appear to him, much like the shadow in the library? Why had they chosen him; was he so special? He did not feel special. He felt very much ordinary and insignificant. He could not change the path down which the fellow members of his race seemed to be heading – how could he, when he couldn't even change the path of his own sibling? His and all his race's destinies were out of his hands. He could only act the spectre and watch the movements of time play out. *Is this what you must feel, Medzu?* he thought, as he approached the great statue stationary within the sky. Do the gods weep at the actions of the lowly life forms? *No*, he thought cynically. *Medzu does not care about us, or any of the other gods for that matter. If they did, then why do they also only act like ghosts?*

If Medzu is watching, then why does it not appear, like it did within my dreams, to save us all from our own intrinsic slaughter? He hoped gods were not real, because if they were then he hated them for their insouciance. No god, no matter how powerful, deserves your unconditional love when it is so plainly not returned. We are nothing but specks of dust twirling within infinite chaos, abandoned and alone – of this, he was now utterly convinced.

Approaching his new home, he was surprised to see a crowd had gathered outside Mundie's Tavern. The mob was so thick that he could not make his way past or even get a sight of the military-frequented inn. But he did see black smoke rising fiercely up into the sky, and the smell of ash too was beginning to manifest underneath his nose. He moved closer, trying to gain some insight into what had caused the commotion. He was making his way through the muttering crowd when a hand grabbed him, stopping his advance.

"Do not come any closer, child," said the elderly man, whose arm had stopped him. "This sight should not be for your eyes."

"What happened?" Ednon asked, confused by the emotions many were displaying.

The elderly man did not answer and instead gazed sorrowfully towards the ground. The others who had gathered held haunted expressions while many had tears in their eyes. Not getting his answer, he pushed past and saw what the commotion was about. Mundie's Tavern lay before him, in a pile of smoking ruins. Not only was the building destroyed beyond recognition, but body parts too lay scattered across the streets, much like red paint spilt across an enormous canvas. He now recognised the emotion; it was terror that gripped them all. Surveying the area soaked with the blood of the once joyous crowd, whose lives had been viciously cut short, his eyes fell on a young girl, who could not have been older than five, lying motionless on the unhallowed soil. *An explosion?* It must have been another attack. *That could have been Am...* he thought, feeling his heart plummet to the bottom of his chest. Rage consumed him, while disgust suddenly burst his spirit wide-open. He remembered what he had thought at Ira's funeral, and how the human race was nothing but a virus. Clenching his fists, the shadow's words of the world's destruction played through his mind. *Perhaps it is truly time*, he pondered, staring into the eyes of the dead child, *and perhaps the sooner the better.*

Tales from the Past
The First Kill

"What are you doing?"

He lifted his eyes to see three boys from his village of Jovian peering at him speculatively.

"Reading…" Ednon responded cautiously.

"My dad says your grandfather is a coward and a friend to the savages," said Thumnas, the largest of the three. "He says he is a traitor to the human race."

Ednon kept silent; he knew where this situation was leading. The chubby lad had always hated Ednon ever since he could remember. He was four years older at the age of ten and was much bigger and stronger. Nor did he appear to place much stock on intellect. Thumnas often made threats to Ednon whenever he saw him, though when Syros was around the lad would not dare persist with the taunts.

"Where's your brother, traitor?" Thumnas violently kicked him. "My father says he is a wild animal that needs to be put down."

"I'm not sure," Ednon answered. "He's probably at home."

Thumnas kicked him once again, which caused the other two boys to laugh. "At home with your traitor grandfather? Not so brave without your brother to protect you, are we, coward?"

Ednon quickly checked his surroundings. It was only the four of them in one of the many fields that connected Jovian village. He had come out here to do some studying as Ira had instructed him to, as it was a sunny day and he should not spend it all indoors. It appeared that no one else was around, so for the time being he would have to deal with this situation himself. The three lads were much bigger and all older than Ednon, plus he had never been in a brawl before; chances are he would have no idea what to do.

"Fight me, coward," the lad demanded.

"My grandfather tells me not to…"

"Coward!" Thumnas kicked him again, more viciously than he had previously. The two cronies laughed and kicked Ednon as well. Ednon tried to stand but one of the boys pushed him back to the ground, where they instantly booted him once more. "This is what cowards get! This is what cowards get!" The boys screamed in excited delirium.

Then, from out of nowhere, like a lion jumping on its prey, Syros leapt onto Thumnas and rained down heavy punches upon the lad. The other two screamed in terror and pelted off through the meadows. At first, Ednon assumed the plethora of blood was something common in all fights. It was only afterwards, and following the subsequent reaction of his grandfather and all the other parents, that he realised Syros had a sharpened rock within his hand. Thumnas was now vigorously shaking as Syros continued to pound his face into the dirt. Thud. Thud. Blood was gushing out of the young lad's eyes; his face was completely drenched in red.

"Stop, Sy!" Ednon pleaded, but to no avail. Syros continued the pummelling. Thumnas was now emitting strange guttural breaths as he coughed out more and more blood. Ednon rose to his feet and attempted to tame his brother, but Syros appeared too lost in his exorcism to care. He began to cry, feeling utterly terrified, until a few adults from the village came, drawn by his loud hysterics, and forcibly restrained his brother.

A meeting was held in the village centre, where all parents and guardians came to discuss the problem that was Syros; even Amelia's parents, Abacus and Jernett, were present in an attempt to solve the ever-uncontrollable dilemma. Ira informed them all that he would do everything in his power to prevent such actions from happening again. The lad Thumnas survived the assault, although the scars and mental trauma were perhaps something that never left him. Ednon still saw him within the village from time to time even now, but it appeared something had changed inside him. He usually kept to himself, taking care of the farm animals, and never did he send a taunt Ednon's way again. He was not sure how he felt about this at the time, but the fact that he no longer had to deal with the constant abuse was something he was thankful for. However, looking back on it now made him feel sadness. Although the lad lived, breathed and even talked, it was as if something intrinsic in the boy's nature had left him and he was now a little less human.

After the meeting, the day turned to night; he

remembered his grandfather slamming the door of the cottage once the three of them had returned home. His grandfather very rarely got angry, but on this occasion the man was seething.

"What are you?" Ira directed his words towards Syros, who was sitting sheepishly on one of the chairs in the dining room. "Are you a beast or a man? You almost killed him, Syros!"

"He deserved it! He was attacking Ednon! All your talk of turning the other cheek, about not rising to aggravation, it means nothing when you're faced with real threat…"

Ednon idly doodled on a piece of paper; he had heard this argument between the two so many times, he knew each of the points that were bound to be made.

"If you're going to act like a beast, then perhaps I should treat you like a beast; you shall not leave your room for a minimum of two weeks. My goodness, lad, people are becoming scared of you."

"I hate you and I hate living here. I wish you had died instead!"

"You think I do not wish the same thing?" Ira paused, remembering this was a conversation that Ednon probably should not be hearing. He regained his poise. "Sometimes, Syros, I worry you truly are beyond saving."

"Good," Syros retorted. "As soon as I'm old enough, I'm going to enlist in the military and you'll never have to see me again."

The silence had returned. Ednon could feel the ever-present tension filling their surroundings.

His grandfather stood still, contemplating his next words carefully. "You are still too young to be making those decisions; one day, Syros, you will find that the only true conflict is the one that is happening inside of you."

Syros got up from his chair and stormed past them. Ednon in turn picked up his books and followed his brother.

"Ednon," his grandfather called. "Let Syros be by himself; you still have your studying to do."

"No, it's okay, I'll do it in my room."

"Okay... goodnight, Ednon."

Now alone in their room, Syros rummaged in his pockets and threw an object upon Ednon's lap. It was a pointed rock, stained with blood.

"There you go, Ed, you can have it."

"I don't want it..."

"Ed, I want you to know that what I did, I did for you."

Ednon studied the rock once more, before getting up to open the window. The curtains billowed as the cold air rushed into the room. He felt the weight of the rock in his hand as he raised his arm and hurled it as far as he could.

"Fine. Be like everyone else. You can hate me as well..." his brother grumbled, as he positioned himself into his bed.

"What would have happened if they did not stop you?" Ednon asked, his gaze caught by the sight of lights still visible in Thumnas's family cottage. "Would you have killed him, brother?"

"Go to sleep, Ednon," Syros responded, pulling the sheets over his head.

Ednon could not rest that night; his mind was on his brother, asleep only a couple of feet from him. And how, even at such a young age, he had only been moments away from taking his first life.

10

Human

The wretched feeling of dread followed Syros with each footstep that he took. He looked towards Mercivous, who was leading out in front. *Truly, was he not human?* he asked himself, watching the back of Mercivous's ethereal white hair as it swayed in the breeze. He had met many stronger and many fiercer, but never someone so terrifying. Something was not right, but he could not place his finger on it exactly. But whatever it was caused iciness to manifest inside of him. He no longer worried about the Alpelites and what they might do to him if he were captured. At least they would give him the sweet relief of death. His main worry was what the dead-eyed monster, who resembled so closely a human, was capable of, now that he had a little authority at his disposal.

Having already left their horses in a nearby military

encampment, the eight of them made their way up the mountains searching for the village that they had been ordered to detain, and only detain. The rumours were true; there were many squadrons who had made their way east and were now spread across the rocky wastelands.

Once they had stabled the horses, they straightaway headed towards their objective. He wondered what he would find there, how similar or indeed dissimilar was the Alpelites' way of life compared to his own. Raynmaher told them the chances of any level of combat was extremely low as Captain Simms' squadron had already dealt with the hostiles, leaving only unarmed peasants and farmers remaining in the village.

Reality had dawned upon him; he did not want to be here in these strange lands with these people. They were all dead inside. *But,* he re-examined, *that means I must be as well.* He wanted out, to return to Jovian and see his brother and grandfather once more. He was sure if he begged hard enough his grandfather would forgive him and welcome him back with open arms. Perhaps he would see Dashera too and ask for her forgiveness. He knew he did not deserve it, but he would ask for it all the same. But there was no chance of him ever being free. As Raynmaher had told him, defection was desertion, and desertion equals death. *Fuck!* He screamed so loudly inside his mind, he was certain his comrades beside him had also heard it. It was like a nightmare that he could not wake up from. Nightmares were horrid, but at least they ended. Life just seemed to drag on and on, and every waking moment was a hardship. Where had his anger gone? He missed it terribly. It had given him purpose; it made him long for the kill, not dread it like he did now. *What has happened inside of me? What changed?* Was it Ednon? His grandfather? Either Torjan or his ex-love Dashera? Or was it that moment he had shared beneath the moonlight with Saniya and the momentary feelings of bliss that he had felt, much like a set of sparks being set off inside of him. He speculated this was most likely it. Why was it that the emptiness was beginning to fill? And now, after all this time, he was finally starting to feel human.

"Syros…" uttered a timid voice.

He turned around to see Freckon standing behind him; Syros was completely shocked that the young lad had spoken, never mind to him of all people.

"Yes? What do you want?"

"You dropped your pin…"

He searched his military uniform to see that the golden pin had indeed fallen off. He tapped each of his pockets to see if he had placed it within one of them and had forgotten doing so. The fresh-faced lad, however, relieved some of his worries by stretching out his hand, revealing the golden article.

Syros took it from him. "Thanks."

"Sy…" Freckon continued. He appeared to be scanning the area to make sure no other members of their company could overhear them.

The rest of the unit had continued their path up the rocky mountain passes, leaving them both isolated some distance behind. They had trekked so far up the mountains, Syros was certain he had never been so high before. Still there was no sign of life, no Alpelites or indeed life forms of any kind; just their company alone with the rocky terrain, and the pure white clouds that grew closer with each step.

"What is it?" Syros asked.

The freckle-faced boy's face flamed with embarrassment. "I'm scared…" he uttered in a way that reminded Syros so much of Ednon. Syros did not know how to respond. He was also scared, but he was sure all members of the company felt the same. *Well, all except one*, he reassessed. He looked upon the lad, whose eyes remained fixed to the ground. *He is still only a child*, Syros thought to himself, staring upon the lad. However, he was old enough to have joined the military and, to Syros's knowledge, he had done so willingly.

"Ed—" he quickly stopped himself. "Freck," Syros restarted, trying to display true concern. "We all feel fear. It is good that you feel this; it shows your humanity isn't lost." He thought this over with Mercivous in his mind. "It shows that you're not a monster."

The lad's wide eyes still seemed terrified. It appeared that Syros's words had not calmed his anxiety.

"What scares you the most?"

The lad's eyes remarkably widened even further. And his head too, once more, scanned the location to check on their privacy. He took a few moments before uttering in an almost silent, petrified voice, "Mercivous… "

"Yes, he scares me too," Syros admitted. "But some words of advice…"

The lad lifted his head and, for what may have been the first time ever, he matched Syros's eyes.

"Do not show your fear. Even if that is all you feel, if it

116

is all that circulates around your being. Do not show your fear when you are around him; he will feed off it. Whatever happens, stay calm, and remember that Raynmaher and the others will return in the next couple of days."

Syros wondered if his words had had a positive effect or not. He could not gauge a response; it had probably made Freckon feel even worse. He was never one for words, especially those meant for comfort. At least he knew how to fight, but he was not sure what, if anything, Freckon could do – except pray and stay forever frightened.

"Oi!"

Koman was calling to them from a few hundred yards away.

"You two finished your make-out session yet?" he exclaimed in excited amusement. "The savages' village is just up ahead!"

With a long deep breath in, together Syros and Freckon made their way to rendezvous with the rest of the company who were all crouching behind thorn-covered bushes, viewing the Alpelite village. Syros moved closer and gazed down. It was remarkable; their homes were so like the cottages from Jovian. The way they carried around hay and other farm necessities, the way the young played with one another, all seemed so very human. The village was small – smaller than Jovian by quite a distance. There didn't seem to be many Alpelites down there. He only counted twenty or so out on the barren fields. This was his first time ever seeing the species, but he did not feel rage as he had once anticipated. He did not feel anything as he peered down upon them.

"Get off!" Narcisi shouted at Koman, whose hand was resting on her backside.

"So, what's the plan, Merc?" Deckard asked in a way that sounded unnervingly eager.

Mercivous's eyes were beginning to glisten. "We go down there and we make our entrance."

"What?" Steph sounded fearful. "We just walk in without a plan?"

Ignoring Steph, Mercivous stood up. Following an instruction, the others did the same and followed Mercivous as he walked calmly, as if with no care in the world, down the mountain pass and into the foreign surroundings. The Alpelites' heads all swivelled towards them as they walked closer to their homes, but they did not run or act overly concerned. Syros wondered how much understanding they had, as they congregated around the troop. The Alpelites all talked in hushed voices as Mercivous, as if conducting an orchestra, opened his arms out to them all.

"Does any here among you speak our language?" Mercivous called, his arms remaining outstretched. He seemed to be making fun of his recently received authority.

"I do," spoke one of the Alpelites; though rough and unpolished, it had, remarkably, just spoken Human as it moved out from the crowd. Syros was surprised how clearly it articulated his language. He never assumed for one moment that he could have a conversation with the monsters that he had fantasied about killing ever since he was a child. He perused the crowd. He thought he could ascertain a difference between the males and the females, as he matched the wide-eyed stares of the three-eyed life forms.

The males seemed taller, with smaller eyes and a sharper bone and facial structure, while the females were more hunched over, with softer faces. The young children stood around, holding onto their mothers much like human children did when frightened. These were not the ferocious monsters that he had been envisaging for so long.

"Oh!" Mercivous spoke with sarcastic surprise. "And what is your name, O Great Life Form of the mountains?" *He really holds no fear*, Syros thought. In fact, for him and some of the others in their company, this situation seemed to only breed confidence.

"My name is Deskkervel..." the Alpelite said as it stepped forward. This one was male and older than the others.

"Is it really?" Mercivous's manner was purely condescending. "I don't think I shall remember that... I think I'll call you *Foul* instead." Syros heard some of the other members of Zelta Squadron beside him begin to snicker.

The Alpelite appeared to become nervous, as it rubbed its dark brown-greenish hands together uncertainly. It remained standing, however, despite Mercivous's unsubtle attempt to belittle it. "And... what shall I call you?" it asked of Mercivous. A hint of fear, Syros noticed, was beginning to manifest in its voice.

"Sir will do just fine."

"Sir... " the Alpelite returned carefully, not wanting to provoke the dead-eyed monster staring it down. "Our village has already been inspected." Its grasp of the human language became harder to understand as it became visibly more nervous. "By a... Simms."

119

Mercivous nodded. "Oh yes. I heard of the visit Simms and company paid you, before you violently attacked them!"

The Alpelite shook its head furiously. "No… No!" it pleaded. "Not we… renegades… radicals… from Ankor…" Its speech was becoming almost completely unintelligible. In this moment, Syros saw that Alpelites, very much like humans, could sweat from fear. "This is a peaceful village…" it finished, gazing upon the stone-cold face of the last person in the universe with whom you would ever wish to be pleading.

"Peaceful?" Mercivous uttered with a bemused laugh. "Are you trying to lie to me, *Foul*? I can always sense a liar."

"No! No!" urged the newly-named *Foul*. "It is true… this village is separate… from all military doings… we are peaceful."

Mercivous tutted as he mockingly shook his head from left to right. "*Foul… Foul.* I feel as if you do not respect my authority. And if you don't, well, then how will the rest of you?" he said, once again opening his arms to the remaining Alpelites.

Deskkervel placed its two hands together in a prayer motion. "I assure you… you will have our full co-operation."

Syros feared the creature's pleas would go unheard. In fact, he knew they would. He had known it from the moment he had first heard that Mercivous was to lead this mission. The feeling had followed him ever since. He had known the inevitable outcome.

As expected, Mercivous gave it a menacing smile, before facing the rest of the company behind him. "I want this one dead," he ordered, and within a moment, despite yells and pleading from the on-looking Alpelite crowd, Koman and Deckard descended upon it. Koman, twice its size, punched it in the stomach, causing it to fall onto its knees, while Deckard unsheathed his long sword and placed it over the creature's neck.

"Merc…" spoke up the dark-skinned and thin-bodied Jamison, trying to be heard over the ensuing chaos. "Didn't Raynmaher say not to do anything rash before we rendezvous?

"Yes." Syros quickly backed him up. "This person does not deserve this."

"Person?" Mercivous uttered in bewilderment, his attention on Syros. "You consider these savages people? Such compassion, Syros. Maybe I was wrong… perhaps you were always the born hero."

"If I am a born hero," Syros stood tall as he gazed upon all his fear personified into one cold human vessel and its lifeless, yet somehow piercing eyes, "then that makes you a born villain."

Mercivous kept his eyes fixed upon the ground. Then, swiftly and viciously, he gripped Syros's head and brought it to only inches away from his own. Mercivous held on fiercely, but Syros did not care about the pain; complete and utter terror was all that overtook him. He struggled desperately, trying to break free, but Mercivous, much like a snake encircling its victim, did not release him. Then, he saw something that surprised him more than anything he could remember. Mercivous's eyes were filled with tears. He questioned whether it was true, but there was no mistake; the eyes an inch or two away from his own were unmistakably weeping. This scared him more than anything. Syros struggled violently until Mercivous willingly let go of him. He started breathing heavily, with no idea of how to interpret what he had witnessed.

Mercivous, on the other hand, walked away as if nothing at all had happened, before he stopped himself, seemingly struck by an epiphany. "I have an idea…" he turned his attention to Freckon, who was hiding sheepishly behind the tall Steph. "I want the small one to do it."

"What, no!" cried the young lad, as Koman grabbed him, bringing him over to where Deskkervel was kneeling still with Deckard's sword to its neck.

"Strike hard, you little cunt!" Deckard laughed, placing the sword into the petrified hands of Freckon, who instantly began to cry.

The sight was so horrible, Syros longed so much to look away. But with Mercivous continuing to stare at him, he gazed back, not wanting to show his fear. *Why was he crying?* Syros questioned to himself, as he considered the voids of Mercivous's eyes. Was that even possible? Or was he mocking human emotion? Was he that far removed from the rest of us? Or was it merely insanity that dictated his actions? He guessed that was it, as he broke their mutual exchange. He could not take it. The screaming. Freckon's crying. His own indecision. He wanted to do something, but what?

"Do it!" Deckard screamed into the ear of Freckon, whose entire body was rattling vigorously.

Syros shut his eyes at this moment; and as the Alpelites' shouts and cries intensified, he heard the thudding sound of a sword being swung. He reopened his eyes to see Freckon shaking, his entire right arm covered in blood. Mercivous, who was smiling, was still staring intently at Syros. The Alpelites moved forwards, with angered yells and violent motions. But they had no weapons and most seemed too old and meek, or too young. The other members of Zelta withdrew their swords and pointed them towards the crowd, attempting to silence it. Within this moment, Syros heard a loud roar from the hut beside him and out stepped an Alpelite, large and stocky, almost the size of his friend Torjan. It wielded a heavy battle-axe and ran straight towards him. Sensing the danger that he was in, Syros quickly withdrew his sword and parried the fierce blow. It had tremendous strength behind it, so much so that it knocked him to the floor with his sword flying out of his grip. Utterly defenceless, he looked up towards the Alpelite who had an expression of pure rage across its face. As it lifted its axe, intent on the finishing strike, Syros closed his eyes in anticipation of his death, before Steph quickly stepped in, slicing the Alpelite across its back, causing it to fall to the ground.

Syros stood up, breathing heavily. "Thank you," he told Steph, who was looking just as pale and panicked. At this moment, another Alpelite came charging out of the hut. This one was not as big as the previous one and wielded a halberd instead of an axe. As it made its way to within a couple of yards of them both, Mercivous stepped in and blocked the life form's path. *The speed of his hands is ridiculous*, Syros thought to himself, watching Mercivous engaging in swordplay with the creature, before he swiftly cut off the Alpelite's head.

Victorious, Mercivous moved towards Syros and Steph, wiping his blade as he walked. "What do we have here? You seem much more the warrior type."

With deep, growling breaths, the Alpelite uttered, "Human filth… "

"I bet you two were part of the group that attacked Simms' company, weren't you? You will be useful, and you speak Human, which is a bonus. Sorry about your friend… We will keep this one alive," Mercivous informed the rest of the troop.

"What do we do with the other ones, Merc?" Deckard smirked, anticipating the answer.

"Round them up," Mercivous ordered, the coldness returning to his voice. "Kill all those that struggle… " The others pushed their way past the crying Freckon, moving upon the hoard of Alpelites, who were now desperately trying to get away from the evil monster that was humanity.

"Let the cleansing begin," Mercivous murmured playfully, as the members of Zelta hacked their swords into the crowd. Yells and wailing were all that could be heard as death engulfed the once peaceful village, while blood stained its very air.

Syros could not prevent the blood lust. Instead, as the screams intensified, he watched the desperation within the eyes of the Alpelite who had come so close to taking his life. He observed the Alpelite trying to stand, but falling back down due to its injuries and the cries of anguish it made as the body stockpile of its fellow species grew. Syros was sympathetic and guilt also poured through him. His heart felt as if it had dropped inside his mouth and in this moment, he no longer cursed his existence because comparably he had it lucky. He prayed Raynmaher and the others did not take long rendezvousing with them, because if they did, then he feared for them all, be they Alpelite or human.

11

Oedipia's Temporal

In the silence Ednon heard the lucid voices as if from a scattered memory singing to him like a lullaby from times long past, "Come yonder, our empty vessel." He made his way out of the nothingness and into the black. He dared not disobey the voices, not after all that they had done for him. To be granted eternal life, for all this, truly he was blessed. He drifted through the darkness, searching. Searching for something that had existed far longer than even the universe itself. He had no idea how long he had been seeking, but it did not matter because, within this state of being, nothing mattered. He tried to locate his arms which were not there; if they had been, he would have outstretched them towards the eye as it came into his vision. In this tranquil reunion, he stopped and admired for as long as he could, before the light hit and he was, once again, back within the murkiness of existence.

Awaking in the blinding light, he found himself on the empty streets of central Asterleigh. Night must have descended as there was no one else in the vicinity. Not entirely sure he was even present there himself, he glided through the stony streets. The silence stood out to him, not at all how these streets would have been in his waking life. Finally, he had what he was pining for. A sense of calmness was all he experienced as he drifted to the shores of the Great Asterleigh Lake, where he found Medzu was already staring back down towards him from its clouds. Then, as he stood with arms raised, the tides of the lake swirled upwards. Medzu was illuminating as the waters reached the sentry God. The light continued to shine and his brain swelled; he had opened his mouth to shout when, without warning, the ground beneath him collapsed and with a silent scream he spiralled into the darkness.

Ednon woke with a panicked yell. He was in his new bedroom, in the home he was still not familiar with. He hoped he had not woken Amelia in the bedroom beside his own, or Abacus and Jernett in their room down the hall. *My dreams are poison.* Laying back onto his bed, Ednon closed his eyes. But it was no use, he could not escape the anxiety and images that haunted him, so he got up and paced in a circle, attempting a head-on confrontation with the thoughts. He remembered all his dreams clearly, as if they were not dreams at all, but rather they were his actual self. It was his waking life that he struggled to remember. Except for the horror; he could remember all that quite well. Especially the face of the young girl he had seen lying in the street only a couple of hundred yards from where he was now. He also remembered the smoke, the fiery scent of death, that he could swear followed him everywhere he went like an ever-present spectre. The city had been placed on high alert following the attack, but no culprits had yet been found. The fear of further explosions had caused the inhabitants of Asterleigh to become guarded and paranoid. Terror ran through the city, as if it were a virus being spread from one fearful soul to another. He wondered who would do such a thing. It couldn't possibly have been the Alpelites, it was not likely they could go unspotted in a city populated only by humans. So... who was responsible? For as long as he had grown up with Syros, his brother had always referred to the adversarial species as 'monsters'; he wondered what his brother would call the ones who were responsible for these attacks as, if his speculations were correct, they were most likely human. His grandfather rarely talked of the Alpelites, but when he did he spoke only of peace and coexistence with the life form. But he was not certain his grandfather had ever encountered any of the three-eyed creatures, so what experience could the man have been speaking from? Plus, on the night Ira had died, he had confessed to Ednon his true thoughts and feelings about the hatred he held for the Alpelites who had raided his village and killed Ednon's parents. So why had the old man leaned so heavily towards these ideals of love and acceptance? Had it only been a facade? Why love those who only hate? It all seemed like blind sanctimonious babble. He longed for Ira to be alive again to help guide his mind through these confusing times. He also wanted his brother to be back from the military, so they could all live on their old farm in Jovian once again. However, these outcomes were only to be found within his fantasies.

Walking around his room, desperately seeking a distraction, he saw a book on the right side of his desk. The title read *Poems from Worlds Long Gone*; it was the book that Ira had sent him to get on the morning before his death. *I never did give it to him*. He picked it up; the book was small and dusty with pages either torn or missing entirely. It must have been old, exceptionally old. He had read many books written hundreds of years ago, but Ednon estimated this one could be the oldest. Lying back down upon his bed, and not wanting to risk the chance of any more unpleasant dreams, he decided to open the pages and digest their meaning.

Daylight had come and the morning with it. Making his way out of his bedroom and down into the kitchen, he found Amelia and her parents already eating their breakfast. With pseudo joy, they bid him a good morning. He did not blame them for being false with their happiness – in fact, he admired it. The recent news of attacks and explosions around the city were enough to make even the most jubilant of optimists turn a little grey and colder. If he had not been feeling so separated from himself, he also would have attempted the joyous fallacy. But it was far too much effort with not enough consequence, so he instead decided to respond with a gloomy 'Morning', before pulling out a chair from the dining table.

"How was your sleep, Ednon?"

"Fine." He gave his usual response. He could not be honest with them. At least that was how he felt. He did not tell them his dreams. It was not like with Ira and Syros, when he would spend hours discussing them. He did not know what the future would bring or even if it was worth worrying about. *Does it truly matter? Any of it? If the world is genuinely nearing its end?*

Abacus peered over the top of his morning newspaper, filled with all its death and dreary reminders, and, seemingly sensing his mood, uttered, "Say, Ed... How about you come and see where I work? Like how you've been asking."

Ednon stared in silent puzzlement. He had never asked to see Abacus's workplace – in fact, he didn't know where Abacus worked and had never thought to question it.

"Okay..."

"It would be good to go out and get your mind off all the unpleasantness," Jernett added, as she cleaned a bit more violently.

"Can I come as well, Dad?" Ameila asked.

"No, sweetheart," Abacus laughed. Ednon noticed that he did not sound at all affected by recent events, because his laugh and upbeat attitude, unlike the others, did not seem faked. "You stay here with your mother. You will see enough of Ed when he comes home." Abacus turned back to Ednon. "So, Ed, do you want to go now?"

"Let Ednon eat some food, dear. The poor lad has just woken up."

"No, it's okay. I can just get something in the marketplace."

Abacus nodded as they both got up from the dining table. Ednon was wondering what this was about; was it to do with his grandfather and this Order that he had apparently been involved with? For the first time in ages, he was beginning to feel excited. He had not known much about his grandfather as a young man, but, from the way people spoke about him, it was as if he were some type of demi-god.

"Bye, Ed," Amelia smiled at him.

"Bye, Am." He responded with a smile of his own. It was fake, but for her he was willing to join the deception.

They travelled through the streets of East Asterleigh. From this distance, Ednon could still see Mundie's Tavern or at least what was left of it. There had been construction teams working on the place day and night ever since the explosion. Rumours were that they were going to erect a monument dedicated to the thirty-eight people who had lost their lives. Though he did not agree with the military's actions, he still mourned for the random act of violence that had not only taken the soldiers' lives, but also that of the young child whose eyes he could still picture, staring lifelessly. He wished he could forget her, but he couldn't; he suspected her image would most likely accompany him until the day he joined her in death.

The streets were packed as the weather, now unsurprisingly, was still scorching. This may have been his imagination, but he also thought that the suns looked closer than they had ever been previously – but he dismissed this notion as paranoia. There must be an explanation for the continuous heat, something logical. But he could not find one, other than pure luck and good fortune. They walked deep into the city's centre; old homeless men and women held placards while yelling about the world's end. It made him feel nervous; not because of the phantom's words backing their theories, but because now he questioned his own sanity. Would he be among them at their age? Ignored and mocked – homeless on the streets, preaching of a world's ending that never comes? Were they also haunted by phantoms who had once told them they were special?

"We're here," Abacus announced abruptly, stopping Ednon in his tracks.

He was surprised to see the building to which Abacus had brought him. It was a tavern, large and impressively structured, but still only a tavern. A golden sign read "Oedipia's Temporal" – *Strange name*, Ednon thought to himself.

"Isn't it a bit early to start drinking, Abacus?"

"Ednon, can you keep a secret?"

"Sure."

"I need you not to tell anyone what I am about to tell you, not Jernett nor indeed Amelia… Can you promise me this, Ed?"

Ednon gave a nod.

"Truth is," Abacus began, his hands rubbing together from tension, "I have not worked for many years and for this I have become a liar, even to my own family. Remember at Ira's funeral, I told you of an Order? Well, the Elders have decided it is time for you to be welcomed in, despite your young age."

Ednon had so many questions that he did not know where to begin. "What have you been doing for money all these years?"

"The Order takes care of all that… truth is, Ednon, I am now one of these Elders and that is the true reason for our move to Asterleigh."

Ednon was now more excited than he had been for years. The idea of secret Orders and Elders was certainly a more intriguing motive for moving to the capital than obscure work opportunities. However, he reflected, although it was impressive for a tavern, it did not look like the headquarters of anything too legitimate, especially compared to the number of grandiose buildings and temples that were spread throughout the city.

"Why a tavern?"

"It's not always a tavern," Abacus said, looking back towards the structure. "Our Order is large and reaches across not only Asterleigh, but our entire Empire. We have many friends, Ednon, many willing to offer themselves for our cause."

"What cause?" He felt as if this was probably the most important question, but was only now able to ask it.

"What else? Bringing an end to the war, of course."

"Why did the Elders ask for my help?"

"My lad, you are the grandson of none other than one of our founding members." Abacus was now displaying some excitement of his own. "Despite your lack of years, you have already shown yourself to be quite the visionary. You have much potential, lad. And the other Elders have also seen this in you."

Ednon took the compliment, but the only thing he thought of were the words 'one of the founding members'. He wondered who the others were; who had known and fought alongside his grandfather all those years ago? Were there many men like his grandfather? His line of questioning was interrupted by Abacus, who gave an indication for Ednon to follow him inside.

Ednon stepped through the doors of the tavern. It was like many others, dark and gloomy, with a bar to one side and dining tables to the other. The room was almost completely empty for this time in the morning, expect for two gentlemen sitting by one of the tables, along with the bartender, keeping to himself, cleaning the empty glasses. The two men glanced up as Abacus and Ednon entered the interior. With a nod, they both uttered in gritty voices, 'Abacus.' He had seen these faces before at Ira's funeral, but, having met so many new people that day, he could not remember either of their names.

"Ednon," Abacus said, as they made their way over. "This is Levy." He indicated the man on his right; a slightly chubby man with thin balding hair and glasses, and the younger of the two. He stretched out his hand to Ednon, who returned the welcome.

"You've got a lot taller since the last time I saw you, Ednon," said the man.

It's true, Ednon thought; he had gained almost a foot in height since Ira's funeral.

"And this is Jung." Abacus pointed to the older gentleman to his left. With long grey hair that ran down past his shoulders, this man seemed nearer Ira's age, except his face appeared more worn out, with additional wrinkles and tiredness. Unlike the younger Levy, Jung did not stretch out his hand to Ednon, instead opting to finish his beverage. With a slightly aggressive manner, he slammed the drink onto the table, and gazed up towards him.

"So, this will be the first meeting for the precious heredity of Ira?" the old man slurred his words, clearly drunk. "Well, lad, in a few years' time, when you have been to as many of these meetings as I have, you too will find that they only become bearable after getting utterly shit-faced." He began to laugh, but interrupted himself with a loud coughing fit.

"Do excuse my friend," Levy apologised, in a calmer, more intelligible voice. "I fear that Jung has grown cold to the world in his old age; despite this, he is still somewhat useful in these meetings after all these years."

Jung raised his empty glass to the sky. "You're damn right! I haven't been to a meeting sober in over ten years. Yet I am still the greatest mind amongst these pseudo-elite thinkers."

"Yes, your wisdom is unparalleled." Levy rolled his eyes. "Do you know the time, Abacus?"

"Should be almost nine. The meeting will be commencing soon."

Ednon looked around bewildered. *Was this truly it?* This Order that he built up so very high within his mind was the three of them getting lashed in whatever taverns were open at this time of the morning?

"Umm… will it only be we four, then?"

The three of them looked at each other and then laughed in unison. "Lord no, lad," Jung exulted in a rough voice. "We are only here to get a few drinks in us before it starts.

No, you will be much more impressed when we reach our true locale."

"Speaking of which," Levy got to his feet, "you know how Luther hates it whenever we are late."

"Luther…" Jung growled. "That arrogant, rich, good for noth—"

"Jung, watch yourself! You do not know who may be listening…"

The old man sighed, but, seemingly getting Abacus's point, refrained from continuing. It must be the same Luther he had met at Ira's funeral, Ednon speculated. *Was he also involved in this Order?*

"I think we are done," Levy called. "Lock the doors… " And with that the bartender came out from behind the bar, made his way over to the entrance, pulled out his key and, with a loud clanking sound, locked them both.

"Are we not going out that way?" Ednon asked Abacus.

"No, Ednon," Abacus said, giving him a wide grin. "For this meeting, we merely need to travel underground."

12

The Feast of Zelta

196 Days until the New Year

Syros sat alone in one of the abandoned Alpelite huts. He wished not to see anyone, human or other. He heard blood-curdling cries from the outside and tried not to imagine what grisly horrors Mercivous and his other comrades were putting the Alpelite villagers through. The screams had not stopped from the moment he had shut himself away from the carnage. All he wanted to do was stay here in his isolated loneliness until Raynmaher and the others arrived. He wondered what Saniya and Torjan were doing right now and whether their mission had been as blood-filled as his own. Were they also beginning to question what they had signed up for? He heard the young wailing and the old begging for mercy in broken Human tongue. He once again asked himself what the hell it was that he was doing here. This was not the vengeance he had envisaged. It was solely barbaric, lacking in anything that could remotely resemble compassion, neither soothing nor justifiable, only senseless destruction.

Mercivous had rounded up all the remaining Alpelites and tied them together as if they were animals. *Well,* he analysed, *I guess they are, but if the Alpelites are animals, then what does that make us?* He had never witnessed such pure delirium, not until he saw Mercivous's face as the slaughter commenced. No, best he stayed inside this place – this strange place that so closely resembled his old home in Jovian. It had beds, a fireplace, tables and chairs, even paintings on the walls of small Alpelite infants. Have they already been butchered and taken away from this world? Perhaps that was for the best. He only hoped Mercivous and the others did not prolong their agony. He sat in the corner of the small interior, surveying the hut's opening, hand on blade. If Mercivous and the others came for him, he was ready. He would cut them down or die trying. Sweat was pouring off him uncontrollably; he had not slept for the entirety of the two days that he had been in here. How could he, when bloodthirsty demons ran amuck outside? It was surely only a matter of time before they came for him.

"Syros?"

He held onto his sword firmly. He did not recognise the voice, but it did not matter. They had all taken part in the bloodshed, all of them had bloodlust in their gaze. He had seen it in their eyes, eyes to which he had never been able to connect, despite their years together in the military camps.

Syros sat up and withdrew his sword as the broad Deckard pushed past the hanging beads and walked into the hut.

"So, that's where you are!" The big-jawed Deckard smirked after he spotted Syros huddled in the corner. "You've been missing all the fun, Sy. Why not join us?"

"No," Syros held onto his sword tightly. "No, I think I shall stay here."

Deckard was much larger than him in both width and height, but he had faced him many times in the training courtyard back in Asterleigh. If push came to shove, Syros was confident he could take him. He searched his comrade's eyes for something to which he could relate; he was not sure there was anything going on behind Deckard's eyes at the best of times, but now he was certain they were nothing but cold and unfeeling.

Deckard rummaged through his pockets. "Suit yourself... a message came for you from headquarters." He threw a sealed letter to the ground.

"A message?" Syros reached forward and retrieved it.

"Yeah. A messenger arrived not too long ago."

"And what did this messenger say after he laid eyes on the village?"

"Don't know," Deckard declared with a shrug. "He's dead now, so I guess it doesn't really matter."

"You killed him. Why?"

"We couldn't let him return to camp and spoil all our fun, could we? If anyone asks, we can just blame it on one of the savages."

Ironic, Syros thought, as he watched the blood drip from Deckard's oversized hands.

The devilish expression had returned to Deckard's face. "Come and join us, Sy. We are about to have a feast and we wouldn't like to see our fellow comrade go hungry."

The further I stay away from them, the better, Syros thought to himself, watching the back of Deckard as he strolled nonchalantly away. However, his stomach was violently rumbling; he had not eaten anything since he had first entered the village. Despite how much he might now despise it, he was still a human being who needed sustenance. There was what could have been food within the hut, but it was of strange colours and textures. Who knew what would happen if he even attempted to ingest it.

Syros had not got along with his grandfather over the past couple of years, yet despite this, he found tears rolling down his face after he opened the letter and learned of his death. He cried for what had transpired between them and the fact that they would never be able to reconcile their differences. But mostly he cried for Ednon and how alone he must be feeling back at Jovian, without either of them there by his side. He wanted to get up from where he was sitting, in this vile, miserable, blood-soaked place, and return to him. But he knew he would be unable to. Raynmaher had said as much back in his tent, that he was bound, until death, to the military. He could run away, but he did not know in which direction. All he could do was sit here and reflect solemnly, thinking of all his mistakes. "Keep safe, Syros" had been his grandfather's last words to him. Well, he certainly hadn't taken those words to heart; he was currently the furthest thing in the world from being safe. *What else did the old man tell me?* "I fear I will not be the one who ends up saving your halo that now seems so lost within the dark." Ira had always been one for dramatic speeches, but appeared to be right on this occasion; Syros's entire life had been plagued by darkness. He certainly was not Ednon, that was for sure.

He had woken up one night when he was a child, in the darkness of their shared bedroom. Though Ednon was only a couple of feet away, asleep in his own bed, he looked very much like a distant star, coming in and out of focus. Ednon's whole body was illuminating, pulsing through different stages of brightness. Syros wondered whether it was real; perhaps he was only dreaming. He asked Ednon the following night to watch him sleep to see if he too shone like a star. "Was I shining, Ed?" Syros had asked after Ednon woke him. The disappointment Syros had felt as Ednon indicated that he hadn't had been astronomical. *Why? Why am I never the one who is special?* He sat up into the night. *Why is he always the perfect one?*

"Syros?"

Quickly wiping the tears away, he sat up to see who it was that wanted his time. He was surprised to see young Freckon walking through the hanging beads and into the hut.

"Sy?" he repeated quietly after scanning around to locate him.

Syros did not respond. He did not want Freckon here, not now, not when he had so many tears still inside him fighting to get out. The newly blooded killer made his way over apprehensively, sat down on one of the empty beds and

141

looked over towards him, a haunted expression across his face.

"It's horrible, isn't it? I never knew this was what military life would be like, I never thought…" he stuttered nervously. Syros noticed he was trying to open up. "I never wanted to join the military," Freckon continued feebly. "My father grew sick after my mother died. I needed to get away from everything, but I never thought…"

"Freckon."

"Yes, Sy?"

"Fuck off."

And with that, Syros stood up. Ignoring the hurt across the timid lad's face, he made for the open door and out into the village. He was sorry. Truly sorry. He had not meant to hurt the young lad's feelings, but it was true, he could not care in the slightest. In this world, his not caring was the least Freckon should be worrying about; he could, for example, be like one of these dead Alpelites, Syros thought, noticing the bodies that had been lazily tossed to the side of the walkway. This village was death. This world was death. Humanity was death. Existence was a man endlessly burning on cinders, while death was the sweet relief of a tsunami pulling him out of his misery. He felt enmity as he made his way through the rows of Alpelite bodies, not for his comrades who had butchered them, but for existence itself. He craved to no longer have independent thought, to cease being the angst-filled orphan boy from the war-torn planet of Vena. To be like the Venians. *Although, we have even managed to make the Venians hate us.* At the centre of nature and all those organisms within her reach, there is inherent cruelty. Life was nothing but a struggle for survival; everything else was irrelevant. Survival is the only thing that matters in this world. He was not a pessimist; he merely saw things clearly.

He knew where his comrades would be holding their feast as there was only one hut that had joyous sounds emitting from it. He did not expect anything less, or indeed more, from his comrades. This was life, death was a part of life, so who could blame them for trying to enjoy it? But the look of pure ecstasy across Mercivous's face as the deaths ensued, was something that he could never understand. There wasn't a star in sight in the sullen night sky – for some uknown reason, this made the whole situation feel even more depressing. The rain was also beginning to fall for the first time since Sechen's passing all those months ago.

He heard something as he walked on, different to the laughter from the biggest hut on the outskirts of the village. He realised the noise was coming from the closest hut on his right-hand side. It sounded muffled, mixed with frantic thudding. He reached the opening, peered inside and saw the large Alpelite, who had come so close to killing him, chained up to the wall. Beaten and bloodied, with the central of its three eyes completely blackened, the Alpelite shook itself violently, trying to break free from its chains. *You should have killed me,* Syros thought to himself as he walked past, moving closer towards his comrades' location. *You should have killed me… and made everything so much easier.*

Wandering up to where the feast was taking place, the sounds of joyous laughter now in clear earshot, and without anything else to lose, he walked inside. The chatter abruptly stopped. Even Narcisi, Keenan and Koman, who were having sex in the far corner, and who had previously been all groans, stopped and stared at him. The rest were all sitting around a wooden table, eating a meat that Syros did not recognise, and at the table's head sat Mercivous. Although the youngest teenager among them, he looked very much like a king entertaining his adoring subjects. His blue eyes, so bright that they seemed completely white, fixed on Syros as he stepped forwards.

"The white knight joins us!" Mercivous elated to the others, who began to laugh. "Sit down, Syros, we were wondering when we would be seeing you once more."

Obeying his command, Syros sat down in an empty space next to Jamison at the opposite end of the table. He picked up the meat and studied it. It was burnt, but it did not smell like pig, cow or any other meat common to him.

"You hungry?" Mercivous motioned to the platters of meat. "There is plenty left, Syros, plenty to last for days…" Syros placed the meat down and started to breathe heavily, feeling dizzy and faint. The room laughed once more, with Mercivous's crazed howls carrying the loudest.

"What's wrong?" Mercivous demonically hissed. "Are you not hungry? What about Narcisi, would you like to sleep with her? She may not be as pretty as your dear Saniya, but she seems very eager. She keeps asking if she can have you… No? That's sad… perhaps you could put yourself to good use then. That big fucker we have locked up, we need to keep it alive for Raynmaher, as it knows of the radicals' movements. But it seems ever so angry. I'm not sure why."

He mocked, as he took another bite out of the meat. "Go take watch over it and be of some use."

Gladly, Syros thought as he stood up. *Coming here was a mistake.* He should have waited alone, away from the delirious silver-haired madman and his legion of brain-dead puppets.

"And Syros," Mercivous called after him. Syros turned back round, to see an expression so manic and deranged he was certain it would forever haunt his nightmares. "Stay virtuous…"

Syros made his way into the hut where his would-be killer was chained up. Its two remaining eyes followed Syros as he sat down against one of the walls and gave out a deep sigh. *This is like a nightmare…* he thought to himself. No, even his nightmares were never as dark as this – this was reality. If only he were indeed dreaming, how he would love that. *I'm sorry, Ira. I should have listened, and now everything is broken and evil.* He began to feel tears once more; he would never see him again and from the way things were heading he would never see Ednon either. He placed a hand in front of his eyes, trying desperately to stop himself from breaking down entirely.

"Human…" the chained life form spoke quietly. "Can you tell me what has happened to my people?"

"I'm so sorry," was all Syros could return, in a voice that shattered like glass.

"They were nice here," the Alpelite continued. "They took care of my wounds even when they knew the danger it may have brought them."

A moment's pause followed; the rain fell through the cracks in the flimsy rooftop, dropping silently onto the ground. He could also hear the wind pick up pace, causing the hut to gently shake from side to side. The Alpelite's face was bloodied, with parts of its body missing entirely. Syros spotted in particular that two of the creature's twelve fingers had been removed completely. After a moment of silence, its eyes lifted to him. "I watched you. You did not take part in the slaughter. Why is this?"

"Because I still have humanity," Syros responded, now not entirely sure what the term meant.

"Humanity?" the chained Alpelite uttered with a faint scoff. "Look around you, boy, to this village and the young whose lives are now over before they had even started… this is the extent of your humanity."

"An Alpelite raiding party attacked my village, killing both my parents…"

"The same thing happened to me when I was young," it said with a slight shrug. "We cannot change the wrongs of the past, or indeed present, for we are merely individuals playing a part in a much larger game." The disparate life form's voice was deep and rough, yet Syros still could make out every word that it uttered. "We may not have evolved from the same mammals or indeed originated from the same planet; we may not even have the same colour of blood flowing within us. But we are both comprised of the same stardust and matter, and perhaps that may be enough. Medzu teaches us not to hate, yet we ignore his teachings so blindly."

"You speak our language well," Syros said, taken aback

by the Alpelite's articulation of the tongue that was not native to it.

"I feel that we made more of an effort to understand your language than you ever have ours…"

"What is your name?" Syros asked the once three-eyed organism.

"Bora," it responded, after another moment's pause. "I was born and raised in the volcanic dead wastelands of Ankor. You are not like the others." It strained its back to sit upright. "You are not cruel, not like the one with the silver hair. It comes in here and cuts its blade into me slowly, while singing gently into my ear, telling me the atrocities it has done to my fellow species. But you are not like this; you have compassion. I thank you."

Syros felt shock, *after all we have done to this village, how could it possibly be showing so much magnanimity?*

"Don't thank me. I didn't do anything to help. I could only stand by and watch."

"I do not expect you to risk your life for us, human. Survival is one of the only things that matters in existence. But you feel sadness for us and this is why I thank you." The Alpelite, though having the appearance of being strong and ferocious, seemed to have a gentler side to it, which reminded him so much of his friend Torjan.

"To protect what one holds dear," Bora continued, its breathing heavy, "is also one of these important treasures in life." Syros touched his scarred hand after it had said this and thought of his vow with his friends as they lay underneath the moonlight. He also thought of Ednon; they were, truly, all that mattered in life.

"It's uncanny, isn't it?" spoke a cold voice.

Syros quickly turned his head to see Mercivous standing by the entrance of the hut; his white eyes were gleaming within the stygian night. The sound of thunder suddenly roared in the distance, as a slight smile grew across his milky-pale face.

"Just how like us they are," Mercivous continued, making his way into the room. He crouched in front of Bora who had returned to complete silence. "The way they beg for just a few more seconds of momentary existence." He pulled out a blade from his belt, before stopping to admire its sharpness. "The way the young cry to their mothers for help…"

He buried the dagger deep into the side of Bora, who let out an anguished yell, before twisting the knife in the Alpelite's side. "It's all so very human…" It was from an entry point that would not kill the creature, but Syros was sure that Mercivous knew this already, as he watched the delirium grow. *Just kill him…* Syros put his hand upon his sword's grip. *Just kill him…* Decisions were weighing in his mind, they were flying at such a pace that they were hard to focus on. *Just kill him…* He knew what he wanted to do, but the ramifications of such an act he was certain would bring into his life only future darkness.

"So… very… human."

As quick as thunder, Syros unsheathed his sword and plunged it through the back of Mercivous. And there was silence once again. Heart pounding and mind cracking at the seams, and after a moment of stillness, he withdrew his blade from his comrade, who turned to look at him. Then, swiftly and viciously, Mercivous gripped Syros's head and brought it to inches away from his own. His eyes seemed full of shock, as if he could not process what was happening. His long fingernails, sharp as arrowheads, clawed at Syros's eyesockets. The grip, just as before, was fierce, yet Syros could feel it faltering. Mercivous gave a single cough and gore splattered into Syros's face. Through the red mist he sensed Mercivous growing weaker and, as they continued their mutual exchange, they both knew he was going to die. Blood gushed onto the floor like a king spilling his wine at a grand feast. *Die... die... die...* Syros pleaded, as he watched his adversary fall to his knees.

"Perfect..." was the last word that Mercivous uttered, as he finally collapsed, a puddle of red circulating around his cold, unmoving corpse.

13

Dissonance in the Underground

Ednon travelled through the vast underground network of tunnels and corridors. It was dingily lit, with small vermin scurrying in every direction as the four of them wandered onwards. Ednon guessed they must be close to the sewers, as something slimy from above dripped onto his head. A foul smell was permeating the air. Not at all what he had expected, making his way to the headquarters of such a supposedly prestigious Order. The bartender at Oedipia's Temporal had led them to a secret passageway in the back of the tavern underneath an array of various ale and wine barrels. They had been walking for what felt like hours, through bland darkened corridors that seemed to stretch on for miles, intersecting in every direction. Ednon was surprised by just how easily the Elders weaved their way in the underground web. He was certain if he were ever left here alone, he would be forever buried beneath the golden city. Levy and Abacus led the group out in front, while Ednon found himself in conversation with the utterly drunk Jung, who was telling him stories of long ago in a slurred, mumbled manner.

"Then there was the time at your grandfather's bachelor party," Jung chuckled happily, as he reminisced. "We had gotten so drunk that night that they found your grandfather passed out naked upon the top of Kymous's shrine!" He laughed while taking a sip of ale that he had taken, without the bartender's knowledge, from the back-stores of the tavern. "Simpler times, Ed, much simpler."

Ednon listened to the old man tell his stories in disbelief. Could this really be the same Ira he had known? The idea of his grandfather drunk, upon a shrine of any kind, was almost impossible for him to imagine.

"Did you use to drink with my grandfather a lot?"

Jung nodded his head. "Oh my, yes. But I knew him when he was much younger, and a lot less wise. Anyway, that all changed after he married Orla."

His grandfather had rarely talked of his grandmother; she had died many years before Ednon was born. All he knew was that his grandfather had loved her dearly, drawing many sketches in an attempt never to forget her face. From all the stories and depictions, she appeared to have been an exceedingly beautiful woman.

"Did you know my grandmother well?"

"Only that her beauty caused trouble; your grandfather was always very smitten. I remember it was me, Ira and Fergus…"

"Fergus?" Ednon quickly interrupted. "The same Fergus who was at Ira's funeral?"

Jung pondered thoughtfully. "Yes, he may have been there. I don't remember seeing him myself, but I had quite a lot to drink that day. Err... where was I? Ah yes... I digress," Jung snapped, suddenly annoyed. "It was me, Ira and Fergus. We were in a tavern in Asterleigh when she walked in, her long golden hair swayed as she took each footstep, her eyes radiated life, her..." Jung coughed uncertainly, "other features... that was when your grandfather turned to me and said that was the girl he was going to marry. And then, lo and behold, a few months later, they were."

"That's a nice story," Ednon said, feeling a little warmer.

"Aye, it's a nice story. Almost enough to actually make me have some faith in this shit-stained mundane existence." He spat as he downed his bottle of ale, before throwing it behind him, causing rats to scurry and squeak viciously. "Fucking vermin!" he shouted, watching the bottle smash upon the ground.

"Perhaps if you were not such an old misogynist, you would have one of these stories of your own," Levy said, giving Ednon a slight wink.

"Bahhh, I've known plenty of women in my day, but none I could stomach for more than a couple of hours."

Levy shook his head. "I trust you know the correct way to treat a woman, Ednon?"

"I think so..." he said, eyeing the back of the smiling Abacus out in front. His true desires and wants had begun to feel entombed ever since the day that Ira had died, but as time passed by, and after hearing his grandfather's love story, the chains of uncertainty felt as if they were beginning to loosen and he knew what it was that he craved above all else – and that was Amelia.

They continued to walk through endless corridors until they reached an intersection, one gloomy passageway leading to the right and another to the left.

"We go left, don't we, Abacus?" Levy asked with unease.

"I believe so…"

"Why is this place so deep underground?" Ednon asked the three of them.

"It needs to be hidden," Abacus replied. "The military above all else must not know of our location."

"Does the military not know of these underground networks?" Ednon asked, thinking that in all the times he had previously visited Asterleigh, he had never heard about this place's existence.

"No. There are only a select number that know of this underground world. That is why, Ed, when we resurface, you must never tell a soul about this place."

"I won't," Ednon promised.

"It is so hidden," Abacus chuckled, "that apparently even I cannot remember its location."

"Then what do we—" Ednon began, before a new, deep, fourth voice interrupted him.

"Abacus. Jung. Levy." From out ahead, in the darkness of the corridor to the left, walked a tall man, bald-headed with black skin and wearing dark shades even though there was no sunlight to disrupt his field of vision. Ednon recognised this man. It was the one who had been standing next to Luther on the day of Ira's funeral; the one who had given him the sweet.

"And even the prodigal son, young master Ednon." The man was enormous and intimidating, with no warmth coming from his exceptionally sonorous voice.

"You are late!" he snapped, his attention on the rest of the Elders. "The meeting started over half an hour ago."

Levy twitched uncomfortably. "Sorry, Memphis. Time must have escaped us."

Memphis gave a snort as he spotted Jung, who was struggling to stand upright and whose eyes were noticeably going in and out of focus. "I think I could hazard a guess as to why you are late." He pointed a finger at the old man. "It's that one there, the one who embarrasses us whenever he finds it fitting, the old drunk."

Jung swayed back and forth. "Ha! You do not intimidate me, you trained dog, and neither does your master! Ira and I were planting the seeds of this Order while you were still sucking at your mother's sagging tits!"

"You planted the seeds," Memphis agreed with a nod. "But now it has moved far and beyond both yours and Ira's comprehension. You are now old and decrepit, and no longer belong here among us."

"Decrepit!" Jung lunged forwards, only to be restrained by the much younger Levy. "Come fight me, cretin, so we can see just how decrepit this old man is!" Ednon admired the man's bravery, but he was certain if the exchange did come to blows, Jung would stand no chance against the younger, fitter and larger Memphis.

"Are you really so uncivilised, Jung?" Memphis uttered, as a sinister smile grew across his face. "Anyway, I do not fight foolish old drunks."

"Jung, calm yourself!" Levy and Abacus continued to restrain the man.

Jung brushed himself down. "Ha! I have better things to be doing... you can tell the short prick that he can blow me!"

"What are you saying, Jung?"

Jung spat upon the ground. "I'm saying I quit this facade of an Order! I should have done it long ago, when it first started to be infested with this type of parasite!" He pointed aggressively towards Memphis, whose smile had not wavered. Jung began to walk away, but before doing so, placed a hand upon Ednon's shoulder.

"If Ira knew what had become of his teachings, he would be turning over in his grave... " Jung murmured, levelling his head down to match Ednon's eyes. "I pray that when you find out what we are, what we have become, that the nightmares do not forever haunt you. As they have with me..." and with that he stumbled, banging into the walls, making his way back the way they had come, singing drunken old songs, with nothing but the darkest of sorrow emitting from his trembling voice.

"Well, gentlemen, we have a meeting to get to and the others are waiting," Memphis said, undeterred by the scenes that had occurred.

"Is he going to be okay?" Ednon said, apprehensively, looking over at the sad sight of Jung's distant figure.

"I wouldn't worry too much, Ed. Jung has always been one for theatrics."

"It doesn't sound much like theatrics… he seems genuinely sad."

"Gentlemen!" Memphis uttered assertively, once again gaining their attention. "We really must be going. Luther gets quite displeased when he is forced to wait…" and with that he began leading the way down the corridor to the left, with Abacus and Levy following suit. Ednon gave another glance to see if he could spot Jung, but the singing had completely died away and he could no longer make out his figure. With deep breaths in, he followed Memphis and the others.

His thoughts lost in the continuous intersections and corridors, Jung's words echoed in Ednon's mind. He was beginning to feel uneasy about what it was this Order did. Why would the way they were now cause Ira to turn over in his grave? Questions ran through his brain; they were racing so fast that he tripped over his own feet after not paying attention to his footsteps. Why did Ira never tell him of this place? If he was so proud of what he had achieved throughout his lifetime, then why not tell him? At least once? He considered the fact that he had not known a great deal about his grandfather, not the man he used to be anyway. *Something does not feel right*, he thought to himself, looking around the damp, bleak, vermin-infested area. This was not where he would expect members dedicated to pacifism to meet. Something about this place, so far underneath Asterleigh's surface, seemed evil, intimidating and far from welcoming.

After walking a few hundred yards more, they came across a locked door. As Memphis was leading, he knocked on it with three loud thuds. After a moment of silent waiting, the door creaked open and another unfamiliar face was staring back down at him. The stranger peered down at Ednon before uttering, "This way, gentlemen." Nerves jangling, Ednon followed Memphis and the others inside.

The room was large and lit by candles upon each of the walls. Strangely marked red flags hung from the ceiling, dangling above an enormous round wooden table where the other Elders sat. All their eyes fixed upon him as he timidly made his way over. There were fourteen of them, including the three that he was with, each older than the last. It appeared that beside himself, Abacus was the youngest among them. In the most prominent of seating positions sat the especially small Luther, who, much like Memphis, was wearing dark shades even though there was no natural light to be found within the murky room.

Luther stood up, only gaining an inch or so in height. "Master Ednon! We were just talking about you. How have you found life in the capital?"

Awful, he thought silently. "It's fine," he responded, worrying over just what they had been saying about him.

Luther nodded his head. "Good… good… do sit." He motioned towards four vacant seats around the table.

"Jung has gone home, Luther," Memphis informed him, sitting down in the empty seat to Luther's right side.

The short man continued to grin. "Perfect. We do not have to fetch a seat for young master Ednon then… "

"Sit down beside me, Ed," Abacus whispered, as he pulled out two chairs directly opposite Luther.

"I will talk to you both afterwards." Levy gave Ednon a slight pat on the shoulder.

He knew some of the faces as he gazed around the room. Stall owners from the Asterleigh market, teachers, and even a face he recognised as being that of a priest were all staring towards him as he nervously sat down, in anticipation of finding out what this secret Order's aspirations truly were. However, it appeared he would have to wait, after Luther stated to the group, "As this is Ednon's first meeting, why don't we let him take the floor…" and he could feel all eyes upon him once again.

He cleared his throat in nervousness and calmed himself for a moment. "I think we should assist the people of Asterleigh as much as we can after these recent attacks, and do everything within our power to try and find those responsible."

A stunned silence engulfed the room. All eyes were no longer upon him, as the Elders looked at each other in bewilderment. It did appear, however, that he had said something quite humorous, as the room began to laugh; even Abacus beside him was in loud hysterics.

"Oh, young master Ednon," Luther chuckled, trying to regain his poise. "You are quite the comedian! This is something, I am sure, that Ira did not pass down to you."

"I'm serious," he said, not understanding what had caused the ruckus. All laughter died down as each of the members saw from Ednon's eyes and demeanour that he had, truly, not intended his last statement to have been taken as a joke.

"Ednon?" spoke up the man he recognised as being one of the priests of Asterleigh. "You do know what the Order's goals are, don't you?"

"Yes, to stop the war." Each of the Elders looked at him and, within a moment, he came to an inner realisation. "You did the attacks…"

The eyes of the Elders shifted nervously and, unlike previously, they would not make eye contact even for an instant.

"Why?" he asked, turning to Abacus. He then faced Levy, whose eyes represented shame.

"Ed, do you know what it means to be a pacifist, a true pacifist?" Luther asked, all previous amusement having escaped his voice.

"I'm sure you're going to enlighten me…"

"Pacifism is doing what we can. No…" The fat, short man rethought his statement. "What we… must do, to end the hardships brought about by war and conflict. So the innocent may flourish in a world that does not know these types of horrors."

"That girl was innocent!" he shouted, his mind on the image of the dead child he had seen lying in the streets outside Mundie's Tavern. "She was only five years old."

Luther sighed. "Ah, yes… the young girl was a misfortune… caught up in the wickedness of this world."

"Not the wickedness of this world. Only the wickedness of your actions."

Luther, not being able to think of a rebuttal, stayed silent, giving Ednon time to address the entirety of the room.

"You are terrorists," he told them firmly. "You are terrorists and nothing more."

"Ednon," Levy addressed him sadly. "We are doing what we must to make this a better world."

"Killing children makes this a better world?"

"You must consider the bigger picture, Ed. We have a plan to end all of—" Abacus began, before Luther interrupted him in a booming voice.

"We are the fifty per cent!" the pear-shaped man exclaimed, rising to his feet. "There are reportedly over eleven million of us inhabiting this planet! A great divide has begun, boy! A divide started by men like your grandfather. We represent the other half!"

"What is it that you plan on achieving with these bombings? How could this possibly end the war?"

"It's simple," Luther continued, the drama still in his voice. "We attack the military while they are weakened: most squadrons have made their way east, dictated by the whims of the Supreme Leader. Whilst they are gone, we attack the bases, barracks and the taverns that the military frequent. Then, when the time is ripe, we rise and force the Supreme Leader out of hiding. And then we start planning for the future of the human race."

"Which is what?"

"All the Alpelites desire is Asterleigh, young innocent Ednon. After we hand over their city, there will be no more need for bloodshed. There is plenty of land here for us, all the Alpelites wish for is to return to their home underneath the clouds of their watching God."

"My brother is on that campaign east. What will happen to him?" Ednon asked, feeling apprehensive.

"We have friends throughout this land," Luther continued, not directly answering his question. "In Lowton, Roxton, Brascote… in all villages and towns neighbouring the border. When the time comes, we shall take control of the borders and lock the military campaigners outside these lands. They can submit to our new rule or die in the wilderness." The short man sat down, impressed by himself, for the way he had quietened Ednon's verbal attack. "Do not worry, lad. As I told you before, the New Age is coming. As our dissonance reaches its most violent and bloody, it shall come, and then a glorious light shall engulf these lands and peace will be known. Led by people who have been entrusted with safeguarding understanding and co-existence."

"People like you…" Ednon stated, staring into the blackness of the man's shades.

Luther gave a shrug. "Why not? All previous members from the golden generation of our Order have either retired, drunk themselves into a stupor or died. Someone has to lead humanity into its glorious future, so why not me?" And with that, he leaned back into his chair and removed his dark-tinted shades to reveal his eyes or, perhaps more precisely, his lack thereof. His eye sockets were sewn completely shut; whatever had happened to the man's eyesight appeared to have happened under the bloodiest of circumstances, as they were mangled and torn, as if they had been viciously burnt.

"In this life, you reap what you sow," Luther continued. "The New Age will soon arrive… and with it… our salvation."

Is this what you wanted, Ira? Ednon thought, gazing around the room of old self-proclaimed Elders and murderers. *Is this what you would have wanted from me, to be a part of this world, so hidden underneath the surface? Did I truly know you at all, or were you always fake in my presence?*

Fake, like the compassion of a short, chubby, blind man, preaching a New Age of a world already long gone. The fate of which was out of all their hands, be they belonging to a pacifist or anyone else.

14

The Forlorn Angel

"Morning," said Bora, looking up after washing its face in a nearby stream, having sensed Syros's presence. The suns were out once again; the storm from the previous night had only lasted a short while. Songbirds were filling the air with blissful sound while the two of them found themselves in a secluded, grassy, life-filled area in the depths of the mountains.

"Morning…" responded Syros, sitting down underneath an adjacent oak tree, overlooking the wounded creature.

"How was your sleep?" Bora asked, standing up on its feet. Sensing the gloomy mood emitting from Syros, it continued, "Nightmares?"

Syros scoffed. The nightmares did not bother him anymore; he was used to them, for they had come in an abundance over the last couple of days. What scared him was that when he awoke from his sleep and entered into the realms of reality, he seemed to still be within one.

They had escaped in the middle of the night, stepping over the lifeless corpse of Mercivous, whose eyes, even though dead, Syros could swear followed him as he escaped from the blood-filled hut. He never would have expected that the first life he took would be one of his own species. And now, due to this, he ran a traitor, in a constant hope of escaping the insanity that had once plagued that small Alpelite village. Moving through the darkness, the wounded Bora leaning on his shoulder, they had found a small cave. And in the little sleep he'd had, he dreamt of horrific images and blood-filled scenarios. He dreamt of his old home in Jovian aflame and walking inside the smoke-filled interior to find his brother's body lying motionless, his eyes, much like his ex-comrade's, never failing to leave him.

"Do not worry, human," Bora said, crouching over the rapidly flowing stream while it continued to wash its face. "I had some nightmares of my own."

"You dream as well?" Syros asked. He had never thought about this much. Bora had appeared to have been sleeping soundlessly after he had awoken. Having failed in leading his own mind down more peaceful paths, Syros had instead stayed awake, newly bloodied blade in hand, watching the entrance of the cave, waiting to see what type of horror would befall him next.

Bora's expression indicated that it had been insulted by Syros's questioning. "Of course I dream, human." It stood and outstretched its muscled limbs. "We all dream."

"I do have a name… "

The creature, ignoring what he had said, started to make its way towards him, limping slightly but very noticeably. "So, human. Where do we go now?"

"Does it matter?"

"Of course it matters. You want to live, don't you?"

Syros thought this over; he wasn't too sure any more. He was leaning towards the idea that perhaps death truly would be what was best for him. Everything had left him; Ira was dead, and his friends Saniya and Torjan were far away doing their own mission. And Ed – he had no idea how his sibling was doing, how he was feeling, how he was coping with life after their grandfather's death, if he even missed his older brother. Perhaps it was better he was out of Ednon's life. He had only been a disappointment; he should have been a better sibling. But now he wouldn't have the chance, for if he returned he would surely be executed for the murder of Mercivous.

The Alpelite had a look of worriment upon its face. "You know, human… I have only known you a short while, but you seem like a most moody type. Why not try cheering up?"

Syros looked at it, bewildered. *Was it joking?* "What is there to be happy about?" he asked the once three-eyed Alpelite.

"You should be thankful that you are living at all. Existence is worth the struggle. There are many who die while still inside their mother's womb, many who will never experience what life is and the beauty that there can be."

"Are all Alpelites so positive?" he asked, surprised at the

creature's optimism. "If your race is so evolved, then why do you fight us to retake Asterleigh? Is it merely because of all the pretty buildings?"

Bora's face clouded with anger, so much so that Syros felt worried for a moment. Even though the Alpelite was wounded, it still dwarfed him by almost two feet. Despite its talk of understanding and adulation for life, it had only a few days previously brought a heavy axe down upon him, forcing him to act quickly to parry it, or he, much like Mercivous, would also be dead.

"You humans steal our home and expect no repercussions?" It gave a slight scoff of derision. "There is a mysticism surrounding Asterleigh that you humans know nothing about... We should have known what your race was like when you first arrived here; what has the human species ever done but destroy your own planet? And now you come to destroy ours?"

The creature was making sound points that were hard to argue against; instead, his mind went to something that he had wondered about relentlessly ever since he had first set foot in the grand capital. "How does the statue of Medzu stay stationary on the clouds?" he asked, his curiosity piqued. "How did the Alpelites ever achieve something so inconceivable?"

The Alpelite had a look of puzzlement on its greenish-brown face. "Statue? That is no statue, human. It is Medzu's empty shell."

"If that's its shell, then where's its consciousness?" Syros responded, displaying his own bewilderment.

Bora gave a slight shrug. "Perhaps it left to get away

from this world that is so barbaric. Tell me, human, if you had the opportunity to leave this world, would you not jump at the chance to do so?"

He turned this over within his mind, but he did not need to for very long. Yes, he would. In a heartbeat. Without any hesitation or second thought.

"So, human," Bora continued, "where do we go? I'm sure when the rest of your kind find out what you did to the silver-haired one, they will come searching for us."

Syros thought it over. "How about we join the Venians in the forests? I have heard stories of humans running from battlefields to join them, seeking sanctuary away from the war."

Bora sounded unconvinced. "Bahhh... the Venians, though pleasant to the eye, are quite a boring species." It looked Syros over speculatively. "Do you drink?"

"What?"

"Drink." Bora repeated. "Do you drink wine?"

"Yes..."

"I think you shall like Ankor then. There are other humans living there. More than you might think, deserters from throughout the years who have joined our cause in retaking our homeland. Yes," it continued, "I think you shall enjoy Ankor."

"How do I know you won't kill me the moment we walk through the gates?"

"You saved my life," Bora reassured him, giving a low bow. "In our culture that means a great deal."

Syros watched over the bowing Alpelite, unsure of what to make of the whole situation. Truth be told, he was not sure why he had saved the creature's life. When he had retrieved his blade and pierced it through the back of Mercivous, it had felt as if something unworldly was in control of his actions. If he could replay the moment, he was not entirely sure the same outcome would reoccur.

"And what would I do in Ankor? How would I spend the rest of my life with you and your people?"

Bora lifted its head back up. "Well, that's up to you, human. As I said, you have saved my life; once I tell the officials in Ankor of your deed, I'm sure they will look upon you favourably. You can choose to join us in our fight for Asterleigh and our God for whom we have been yearning. Or you can settle down. I'm sure we can find a pretty human mate to bear your children."

This actually did not sound too bad to Syros, as he visualised what kind of future Bora was speaking of. But it was not what he wanted, not really. He wanted to return home to Jovian and live on his old farm once more, with his brother Ednon. He wanted Torjan and Saniya to be there, so they could live out their vow and die as old people together on the same day. But what he longed for the most was for the endless nightmare that life had become to finally end, and to wake up having forgotten all of the horror that had befallen him in his life up to this point.

"Okay," Syros agreed. "We shall travel to Ankor."

Bora gave him a slight smile. "Good. We shall leave after I enter into my nothingness," it said cheerfully, before making its way past Syros and to a rock on the edge of the clifftop. Syros watched it, bewildered. *Its nothingness?* Bora climbed upon the rock and entered a stance that he had seen many times throughout his life.

"Care to join me?"

"No," Syros responded, not moving from the shade of the tree. He had not meditated since he was a small child. To clear his mind of everything, at this moment, was surely nothing short of impossible.

"Suit yourself," Bora called, stiffening its back. The suns were out once again and the weather had returned to a state of extreme humidity. Syros watched Bora silently, as its body obstructed the rising suns behind it. The minutes passed; other than the chirping of a few songbirds and the slight rustling of the wind, it was a moment of pure unadulterated silence. Syros leaned his head back upon the tree and closed his eyes.

"Please," he silently begged, to whatever it was that might have been listening. "Please... no more hardships..."

He experienced a surprising feeling as he sat under the shade of the blossoming tree. It was a sense of calmness and serenity, but he didn't expect it to last. So when the newborn silence was disrupted by the sound of galloping horses approaching their location, he did not feel surprised in the slightest. He got to his feet and withdrew his sword.

"Bora, they are here."

They stood and watched the mountaintop, as the noise grew louder with each second that passed. After a moment Syros could see four figures heading towards them. He squinted his eyes trying to identify the riders. As they came into his vision, he determined the figures belonged to the oafs Deckard and Koman, as well as his friend Torjan; even Captain Raynmaher was among them, leading out in front.

The horses slowed down as they neared their location, just a mere ten yards away. Deckard and Koman, along with Torjan, dismounted, while Raynmaher stayed on horseback, looking over at him with sadness in his eyes.

"Hello, Sy," Torjan said.

"Hello, Torj."

"I've heard some disturbing stories." Raynmaher's eyes shifted to the large Alpelite standing beside him. "Very disturbing, Syros. I did not believe them, but after they showed me Mercivous's corpse... well," he said solemnly. "I never expected that you, of all people, would turn traitor against your own kind."

"I am a traitor," Syros responded, looking into the eyes of his once mentor and Captain. "But all the same, I could not let Mercivous have his way with the village; I plunged my blade into his back and for that I have no regrets."

"Koman and Deckard told me what happened in the village. How you led the others into the massacre of the Alpelites, how you grew so mad with blood-lust you killed Mercivous, before making your escape with this... cretin..." he continued, motioning his hand towards Bora, who was standing perfectly still, its eyes nervously shifting between the two.

"They're lying!" Syros snapped, gesturing towards Deckard and Koman, who had smirks growing across their faces. "Who could believe such a story, concocted by these two morons?"

Raynmaher sighed. "All the same... the facts are clear. You killed Mercivous, your own comrade and brother-in-arms."

Syros nodded his head. "Aye, I killed Mercivous. He was a sadistic bastard. My only regret is that I did not prolong his suffering." He gripped firmly onto his blade, as the four of them made further steps towards him. The mountain cliff on which Bora had been meditating was steep, seeming to go downwards for miles. Perhaps the fall would not kill them and even if it did, did it matter?

"Where is Saniya?" he addressed Torjan. "Is she safe?"

"She's doing okay, Sy. Of course, she hasn't stopped crying since she heard the news."

"Tell her I'm sorry."

"I will."

"Put down the blade, Syros," Raynmaher urged. "Put the blade away, come with us willingly and give up the creature. It is not worth your death."

"What will happen to me if I do?"

"You will be sent back to Asterleigh and await trial. Who knows, you may live long enough to return to your village an old man, to be with your brother."

Syros searched Raynmaher's eyes. He could tell he was lying. He knew in this moment that they had come here to kill him. He continued to clutch firmly onto his blade; Bora was strong, but was wounded with no weapon. The Alpelite was not going to be much help.

"There are only four of you. I feel as if you may have underestimated my abilities, Captain." He tried to emit an aura of confidence, but he knew he would stand no chance, not against all four of them.

Raynmaher shook his head. "I liked you, boy. It's a shame, a damn shame," he uttered, before motioning to

Torjan, Deckard and Koman. "Kill him and the savage that he has foolishly aligned himself with."

"Sy…" Torjan whispered, as the three of them inched closer towards Syros and Bora. "Do you remember our vow?" A slight, surprising smile had found its way onto his face.

"I do, Torj." *Why was he smiling?*

"Well…" Torjan continued, as the three lads, with swords drawn, stood only a foot away, readying themselves for combat. "It won't be today."

Syros looked at his friend in shock. Then, within a moment, Torjan lunged at Koman and Deckard, knocking them both to the ground, their blades flying off into the distance. "Run, Sy!" Torjan yelled as Deckard and Koman quickly rose and began to restrain him. Syros realised the drop behind him was truly the only way they could go. He gazed back at Torjan. His mind was racing; he could not just leave his friend.

"Tame the beast!" Raynmaher ordered, as Koman withdrew a small blade from his belt and plunged it into the back of Torjan, who gave a loud cry of anguish. Koman brought down the blade again and again. Torjan now had blood pouring from his mouth and it looked as if at any minute he would lose consciousness. However, just as the fourth blow was about to be struck, Torjan quickly manoeuvred around, knocked the blade out of Koman's hand and plunged the dagger through his comrade's eye.

"Run, Syros!" Torjan shouted, as Raynmaher moved steadily towards them, his long blade glistening in the sunlight.

Syros gave one more panicked glance, then, without

hesitation or second thought, grabbed Bora and jumped off the mountain cliff.

They tumbled for what felt like an eternity, the pain growing with each frantic passing second. Eventually, they fell into a mass of thick verdant bushes. Facing upwards to the mountain top where they had been, Syros let out a deep pained yell. Breathing heavily and heart pounding, he checked Bora beside him, tangled in the soft branches.

"Are you okay?" he asked the battered and torn creature.

"Praise be to Medzu! I think I was wrong," Bora uttered after a moment of pure silence.

"Wrong about what?"

"You have now saved my life twice… Perhaps I was wrong; you may not be a human after all… but an angel, sent here to watch over me."

I'm no angel, Syros thought to himself, gazing towards the sun-filled blue sky. Angels do not leave their friends to die alone. Nor do they literally shit themselves from fear at the prospect of jumping off the edge of an enormous cliff.

15

Temple of Yashin

Ednon was drifting through the streets of Asterleigh, which were, just as before, deserted of all life; only he and Medzu were present in the golden-laced city. Behind him, he was aware of the monumental statue illuminating, shining even more brightly than it did on a normal day when he wasn't in the bliss of his dream state. The sky behind the effigy was red, blood red; Sechen was passing through the cosmic firmament. He did not focus on the stars for too long, his eyes remained fixed upon the ground, the stone-cobbled streets on which he walked. He was moving out of the city and into the meadows, which, much like the city itself, were vacant entirely. Contact with his senses had been lost somewhere in the esoteric allure; something was pulling him in. The wind was howling, even within this dream state he could feel it rippling against his skin, but it was like the knocks on a door of an empty house and not enough to wake him. He glided across the grass, up the verdant hills, heading towards the crimson night sky. He stopped and admired the view, but not for too long. The city was beautiful from this location; golden temples rose far above the ground as if the buildings themselves were trying to reach Medzu, sitting motionless upon the clouds.

Ednon turned around to see a figure standing before him, naked in the rain. He opened his mouth to ask its name, but no words manifested. The figure's eyes were pure unadulterated darkness, like the emptiest of voids. It looked human, but how could it be? No human glowed with an unworldly brightness, nor did they have what appeared to be red veins twirling round to forge patterns, which for some unknown reason resonated somewhere deep inside of him. The glowing figure moved closer; the redness of the sky grew darker as the entity raised its hands and the plains were suddenly engulfed in shadows. The ground beneath him collapsed and, for the second time in as many dreams, Ednon felt the sensation of spiralling. Awaking in the stillness, he saw the kaleidoscopic eye form before him, before the orb of vision parted to immerse him in the endless ethereal light. All fragments of fear, joy, sorrow and love he had ever previously held were lost as the light continued to shine. He heard a distant voice, as the lucent reached its celestial brightest.

"Ednon…" A hand gently nudged his shoulder.

Ednon opened his eyes. He was sitting in the hall of the Grand Library. He found the hand that had awoken him belonged to the elderly Ageth.

"Ed, I'm sorry to wake you, but there is a man here looking for you."

"A man?" Ednon asked languidly, wiping the sleep from his eyes. "Who?"

"He did not give a name. He arrived at the entrance and asked whether you were inside. What shall I tell him?"

A man? Ednon once again questioned, now only to himself. *Who could it be?* Who would come here searching for him; was it someone from the Order? Who would even know he was here, in the darkened depths of the Grand Library?

"Tell him I will see him," Ednon told her, eager to find out who this visitant was.

"Okay." She gave him a worried glance. "I will bring him here. Do not move from this spot, Ed."

Ednon had fallen asleep while reading one of the books on Vena's ancient history. He had come here after learning of the Order's intentions, unable to get out of his mind how wrong his perception of his grandfather had been. *Why couldn't he have told me? Why would he teach me these ideals of pacifism, knowing what his fellow Elders were planning?* Ednon thought back to what his grandfather had told him on the night of his death and how he was more of a hypocrite than Ednon knew. *This must have been what he was alluding to,* he deduced, standing up and having a stretch. *Still, why could he not have told me?* He felt as if he would have had a clearer understanding if only the words had come out of Ira's mouth, instead of Luther's.

Ednon's eyes searched around the halls. He was half expecting the phantom to be here once again; that accursed shadow whose words had condemned only horror and despair into his life ever since he had the misfortune to hear them. However, in the five or so times he had returned, the spectre had not reappeared. He was beginning to question whether he had truly seen it. Perhaps all it was, all it ever had been, was a daydreaming mind's overactive imagination. He liked to think it so, as that would mean the world's ending was also only a fantasy he had concocted in his mind. He prayed that this was the case.

Ednon sat and waited at his table, anxiously anticipating who needed his audience; perhaps it was Abacus, come seeking a reconciliation. He had not spoken to Abacus since their meeting in the underground had finished, instead opting for avoidance and circumvention. He was surprised, however, to see it was not Abacus who had come to find him but the old man Robles, whom he had met in Jovian's cemetery, along with the blue-eyed woman, Ethna.

"Good day, master Ednon." The old man spoke in his usual formal tone.

"Hello," Ednon replied. Robles was, much as before, dressed both formally and elegantly. Ednon looked at the belt around the man's waist and saw he was once again carrying his sword.

"I have never been in this building." Robles glanced around at the shelves of books, while giving his grey moustache a twirl.

"Not a keen reader?"

Robles pondered for a moment. "I think I would have been. But you see, I never learnt to read."

"You never learnt to read? If you don't mind my asking, why is that?"

"My father was a military man. As was his father before him. Military life was all I knew, hence, no time for reading."

"You've served in the military then?" Ednon was beginning to feel a smidgen of apprehension, once again directing his eyes towards the man's sheathed sword in his iron-studded belt.

Robles placed his hands behind him and puffed out his chest. "Yes, Sir! Over forty years of gallant service, Sir!"

"How did you come to be in the employment of Ethna?" Ednon asked, wondering why the man had not sought retirement in his old age; did he not have a wife and children to care for?

"When duty calls, Sir, you must answer."

"A little tamer than fighting in wars."

"You'd be surprised, Sir." Robles cleared his throat. "Speaking of Lady Ethna, she has asked if you would accompany me to visit her within the Temple of Yashin."

"Why? What is it that she wants?"

"She did not say, Sir."

"What happens if I refuse?"

"I'm afraid this is an order, Sir."

And with that Robles stood completely still, his arms remaining behind him as he continued to stare at Ednon, who gave a loud sigh. Judging by the man's character, he was not going to leave until Ednon had agreed to accompany him back to the temple of the forgotten God.

"Fine..." he murmured, collecting his rucksack.

"Very good, Sir." Robles smiled faintly, before making

his way, now with Ednon trailing behind, through the long stretching halls to the exit of the Grand Library.

They journeyed through the crowded streets of Asterleigh. Ednon kept his distance from the elderly Robles, who turned his head every hundred or so paces to make sure he was indeed still following. The man's insistence on calling him "Sir" was starting to make Ednon feel uneasy. He had asked Robles to call him "Ed," which for some reason gave the man a bewildered expression as if he could not register what it was Ednon had requested. They walked deeper into the centre of Asterleigh. Ednon had not visited this part of the capital much; this was where the wealthy and powerful resided. The houses surrounding them were massive and beautiful, rising far up into the sky. The streets were also much less populated; there appeared to be some unwritten rule that the poor and homeless could not frequent this part of the capital. He had heard stories that the military patrolled this location at night, arresting any homeless they found lying in front of the gold and diamond encrusted gates. *Surely there is enough wealth to go around?* Ednon thought, gazing at the towering buildings and ancient temples. In a city so filled with gold and diamonds, how could there be so many people going hungry and homeless? When the Alpelites populated this city, did they also have these problems?

"Master Ednon," Robles spoke, still insisting on the title. "We have arrived."

Ednon lowered his eyes to a sight he thought could only exist in fairy tales. The Temple of Yashin was astronomical, larger than any building he had ever seen before in his life. The courtyard leading to the temple was pure green and held many golden fountains, with ponds the size of Eos Lake. And straight ahead, surrounded by high golden railings, was a pathway leading over one hundred yards to the entrance of the building, which resembled a normal temple although the size of a palace. A huge marble dome was covered in copper-plate, which reflected the glow of the suns, and tall towers stood at each corner of the structure, protecting the sacred area within. That woman whom he had met by his grandfather's grave truly lived here? He had heard rumours of this place, but never had he seen it. The class divide this side of the border did not seem to be affecting her in any negative way. The entire acreage of this place alone was probably bigger than his old village.

"Wow…" Ednon marvelled, as Robles retrieved a key from his pocket and unlocked the impressive golden gates. He stood there, holding the gate open, silently motioning for Ednon to walk through. Ednon had never seen a place like this; he had passed many mansions throughout Asterleigh, but had never entered their grounds. There were workers spread across the enormous gardens, tending to the beds of flowers, shrubs and trees. Robles led him all the way down the stone pathway and to the entrance of the temple and gave him another quick glance, before unlocking the wide gilded doors and walking through.

Ednon followed Robles. From inside, it did not resemble a temple – there were seemingly no shrines or any place of worship – but was more like an oversized house albeit with a richer and more opulent decor. Intricate glass chandeliers hung from the centre of the wide main hall that connected many different rooms. The walls were mostly a rich red, covered with numerous paintings and artistically styled sculptures. Robles led him to the end of the central hall and to the door that was the furthest away from them. He walked briskly, with Ednon once again dragging behind. Still coming to terms with what kind of fantasy dreamland he had entered, Ednon followed Robles into the next room and was shocked to see the elderly Jung sitting at a long mahogany table with Ethna opposite him. The old ex-Elder looked almost presentable compared to the last time Ednon had seen him in the underground network. He had cut his long hair, shaved his beard and was not looking utterly intoxicated. Jung seemed just as surprised to see Ednon, as he was returning his look of shock.

"Ednon!" Ethna stood up to greet him. "Do have a seat with us. I believe you already know Jung?"

"I do," Ednon responded, unsure of what to make of the situation. Robles slipped behind him to whisper something into Ethna's ear. She listened intently before motioning the man away.

"I think I shall be leaving," Jung said, steadily rising to his feet.

"Ah yes, thank you, Jung. You have done your species a great service."

Jung gave a loud snort before uttering "My species... to hell with my species... to hell with it all." And with that he walked past, trying his best to avoid eye contact, leaving Ednon, for the second time in as many days, watching the back of the sad old man as he trudged away.

He turned his attention to Ethna and to the subservient Robles standing behind her.

"What is it that you want?"

"Do not worry about that yet, Ed. Won't you sit down?"

He slowly obliged, taking out one of the chairs. Something did not feel right, yet, as he lifted his head to look into the fierce yet attractive face of Ethna, he could not place his finger on what it was.

"Would you like some tea, Ed?" Ethna smiled, her eyes still not wavering from his own. *She really is very beautiful,* Ednon thought to himself.

He felt the nerves growing inside his stomach and his face suddenly flamed red. "No... no... I'm fine, thank you... " His eyes darted to Robles, who was standing behind her, his hand resting on the handle of his blade. *What was Jung doing here?* The last time he had seen the old ex-Elder, he had been making his way drunkenly back through the darkened corridors of the underground network, so what was he doing here of all places?

Ethna motioned to Robles behind her, apparently not paying attention to Ednon's answer. "Bring us two cups of tea, Robles."

"Right away, ma'am."

"How are you enjoying life in Asterleigh, Ednon?"

"It's okay... I heard this place was a temple, but I do not see shrines or anything relating to Yashin whatsoever."

"Yes, well, we had them removed many years ago. We do not worship the primitive savages or indeed their false gods... "

But what about Medzu? Ednon thought only to himself,

deciding not to aggravate the woman further. *Surely you cannot deny his existence, not when he looms over us all from the clouds?*

"Horrid business, all these bombings." She quickly changed the subject. "I hear you moved into a home quite close to Mundie's Tavern. I'm glad to see that you are doing well." Robles returned holding a silver tray, carrying both biscuits and the cups of tea. He gave one to Ethna, before offering a cup to Ednon, who thanked him.

Ethna took a deep sip from her cup, before carrying on with the conversation. "A young girl died in that explosion. I knew her… she was the daughter of someone who had worked under me."

"I'm sorry," Ednon sympathised, holding up his tea, but failing to take a sip from it. He now knew why he had been brought here, why Jung before him had also been here. His suspicions were finally confirmed when Ethna asked him calmly, "If you knew anything of these attacks, you would tell me, wouldn't you, Ed?"

It was an interrogation, a calm and subtle one, but an interrogation all the same. He sat for a moment in silence, contemplating his response. What could he say? Should he tell them the truth? The Order had killed many different people throughout the city, including the young girl. He felt himself sweat. What had Jung told them? Did they already know?

"I would…" Ednon spoke, after a period of drawn-out silence.

Ethna leaned in closer. "Good… so, Ed, what can you tell me of this underground Order?"

Ednon was shocked. *She already knew?* Did that mean she also knew he too had travelled down there yesterday?

Ethna noticed his surprise. "Do not be alarmed. Jung has already told us everything. We are only wanting you to reinforce his claims. You are only a child, Ed; do not worry, you will not be held accountable. But these are some very dangerous men that you have got yourself involved with. Now… what can you tell me about the man, Luther?"

He thought of his brother Syros, and what Luther had told him yesterday about the Order's plan to lock out all the military squadrons from this land. To save his brother, this could be his only option. Conceding defeat, and finding no other path, he decided to tell them what they wanted to know. "He is a short, fat, bald man," Ednon informed them, newly filled with guilt. "Late forties, around the same height as me, wears black shades to hide his blindness while he uses a stick to move around."

"Do you know his second name?"

Ednon shook his head. "Please," he said, thinking of both Abacus and Levy. "Not all of them are involved with the attacks, you must know this."

"Do not worry, Ed, we are only after Luther. The others shall remain unharmed. All we want is for the bombings to end."

"Could you please talk to the others and make them stop the attacks as well?"

"I will do everything that's in my power."

The room once again returned to silence, apart from the frantic scribblings in a small notebook emitting from Robles who was writing down all that had been said.

Ethna took another sip, before gazing back at Ednon. "Thank you, Ed. You have been most helpful."

"I can go?"

"Of course. As I told you before, you are not responsible for these men's actions." And with that, she motioned to Robles standing beside her. "Show Ednon the way out, Robles."

As he followed Robles back up the long stony pathway to the wide golden gates, he questioned what he had done, the possible repercussions and the severity of what might happen. He worried about Abacus and Levy, but mostly he was afraid for Amelia and Jernett. He also lamented over his grandfather; *what would you think of what I have done, Ira? Would you have praised me? Or would that only have come from the version of you that I thought I knew? Were you in actuality more of a Luther, ready to kill all those threatening your dream? Would you have killed me for what I have done?*

Ednon walked out of the gates; he glanced at old Robles, who gave back a cold and indifferent look. "Goodbye, Ed." He slammed the gates shut, leaving Ednon alone, staring at them, the harsh sunlight reflecting from their smooth and golden surface.

16

The Endless Dreams

146 Days until the New Year

Syros and Bora journeyed through the vast mountain landscape, travelling to Ankor. What Syros would find there he did not know, but this felt like the only option he had left. He suspected that he would never be able to return to the human territories, for now he knew for certain that he would be executed for Mercivous's murder. He touched his scarred right hand each time they stopped to rest. *I hope that you are okay, Torjan,* he thought, replaying the moment on the cliff over in his mind. *I should have stayed and fought alongside you, but I'm a coward.* He did not know whether Torjan had survived his stab wounds, but surely even if he had, they would have executed him for helping in their escape. He tried not to think about it too much, but failed often. He also thought of Saniya and her pain at losing them both. *Our vow was utterly meaningless*, he grieved silently. In the end it had meant absolutely nothing, just naivety and wishful thinking – and now he wandered through the emptiness of the mountains, travelling to a city where he would be a stranger to everyone. Everyone except Bora, of course. The Alpelite had tried numerous times to cheer his mood, telling him humorous stories from its childhood and ribbing him playfully. He could not deny that the Alpelite was beginning to grow on him; it was intelligent, compassionate and, most surprisingly of all, fun to be around. When he first left Asterleigh all those months ago, this was the most unlikely thing he could have ever envisaged befalling him.

They had been travelling for at least a month underneath the incandescent suns and insufferable heat, when eventually they made their way off the mountain track and onto a long stretching stony path.

"It will be only a day's walk from this point onward," Bora informed him. *Great*, Syros gloomily thought to himself. He still had no idea how they would be received at the volcanic capital of the Alpelites. Bora had told him that because Syros had saved its life, the officials of the city would look on him favourably. Nevertheless, he still felt nervous. What if the creature was lying to him? It wouldn't be too hard for Bora to hand him over to the city officials to have him executed, or tortured for information on Zelta Squadron and the plans and movements of all the other squadrons that had been sent east. But he had no choice other than to accept what the life form had told him. He would have liked to have thought that having spent so much time with Bora he knew its true character, but he could not be certain, not entirely. The demons in the back of his mind had only grown more insistent over the past couple of weeks. He was so paranoid now that he hadn't slept for the last few days. He needed to stay ever vigilant, if he wanted to cling onto survival.

After walking a few more miles, his feet beginning to become unbearably sore, they came across five Alpelite corpses surrounding a cart, presumably once heading towards Ankor. Bora moved closer to inspect the bodies while Syros stayed back, cautiously watching over the situation.

"What killed them? Do you think it was the humans?" Syros called uncertainly. *Could they have already made it this far east?* He wiped the sweat from his forehead. *Is it me that they have come searching for, Raynmaher and the others, looking to enforce justice for Mercivous's murder? But how would they know we were travelling to Ankor?* He scanned their location; he could not see anyone else here, only himself and Bora along with the dead Alpelite bodies. Only empty wastelands and a few sizeable desert palms.

The Alpelite lifted its head and stared back towards him, with a look of sheer puzzlement. "The human military have never made it so close to Ankor." Bora motioned to Syros to come nearer; reluctantly, he agreed. As he walked closer, he could see that the dead Alpelites did not appear to have stab wounds or entry marks of any kind. What they did have were stiff expressions that almost resembled smiles across their cold, motionless faces.

"No entry points," Bora marvelled, crouching down

to get a closer inspection of one of the bodies. "No blood, wounds or signs of any kind of struggle."

"So what killed them?" As the nervousness inside Syros grew, the palm behind him gently swayed in the wind.

Bora looked back, just as perplexed. Then, a hand, from what Syros had assumed was a corpse, grabbed Bora. Syros jumped in shock, heart pounding. It faintly spoke into Bora's ear. Bora had taught Syros some of the Alpelite language, in an attempt to quell the boredom of the constant travelling, but he was far from expert and the almost motionless Alpelite was murmuring so quietly that Syros could not properly ascertain its words.

The dying creature's voice faded and its body returned to stillness. Bora stood up; Syros would never have expected to see this, but the greenish-brown life form's skin had just turned a little paler.

"What did it say?" he asked Bora hesitantly, unnerved at seeing the ever-optimistic creature in its current state.

Bora shifted his attention to the now certainly lifeless Alpelite. "It said… the ones that rise up from the ground…"

After Syros helped bury the bodies, using a shovel they found on the supply cart, they continued their walk to Ankor. The suns were going down; the night was fast approaching as they came across the grand capital of the Alpelites. Stone walls contained the city; they were so high that he could get no impression of the buildings within. They walked up to the gigantic entrance; the walls and the gate did not seem to be made from stone, but to be part of the rock-solid ground itself, making them appear very much one with the mountains that surrounded the city on each of its sides.

As they walked closer, the gates opened, allowing Bora, along with the more apprehensive than ever Syros, inside. Alpelites swarmed in the streets; even though this was merely the outskirts, there must have been thousands of the three-eyed creatures staring back at him. Ankor in many ways did not appear very different to Asterleigh, although the marketplace was filled with unfamiliar substances and items. There were no golden temples, but instead what resembled shrines made from solid rock. One thing that was different to Asterleigh was the fact that the Alpelites, of all shapes and sizes, were peering over at him speculatively.

"Do not worry, human, they won't hurt you."

"How do you know?"

"Because I won't let them. Your life is in my hands now. You are not the first human to ever come here, yet it is still something that is unusual for them."

Just how many times does this happen? Syros questioned himself. *How many humans over the years deserted the military to come and live with these people?* He soon discovered that Bora had in fact not been lying to him, as his eyes fixed on another human being. He looked like an old man, in his late sixties; it seemed weird to Syros to see only two eyes in a sea of three. He was part of the vast Alpelite herd as if there was nothing unusual about it whatsoever. The man stared back at Syros, who did not slow down to talk as he needed to keep up with Bora, who, despite the weeks of travel, was still moving at a steady speed through the crowd.

"Where are we going?"

"We are heading for the Palace," Bora informed him. "We need to seek permission from our leader for you to live here among us."

"And what happens if your leader refuses?" Syros questioned, his mind unable to focus on anything, as he swivelled his head distracted by the sights.

Bora did not answer and continued with its fast-paced movement. As the two made their way deeper into the city, Syros could see that Bora had not lied about Ankor being built upon volcanic lands. He spotted a volcano, looming over the northern edge of the city, as the Medzu shell did over Asterleigh. He had never seen one before, only read about them in Ednon's books. Legend had it that there was also an inactive volcano buried far beneath the surface of Asterleigh, but it had long been covered up by the movements of time. Bora had told him that the one outside Ankor was inactive, yet he could see the reason why the Alpelites longed so much for a return to Asterleigh, as waking up underneath a sleeping God must be a hell of a lot better than sleeping underneath a dormant volcano. He did not stare at it for too long, as it made him feel uneasy. The city's buildings were well constructed, rivalling those the Alpelites had built in Asterleigh. But the sight of the imposing mountain every morning was something he could live without. Still, he could not be too picky; as the creature had told him, he should be thankful he was living at all.

They proceeded to the long stairway leading to the palace doors. Despite this being the palace of the Alpelites' capital, it stood much lower than many buildings he had seen in

Asterleigh, although it was still a grand sight to behold. They halted in their tracks, awestruck by the fantastically ornate structure.

"A word of advice."

"What?"

"Don't speak much. Just nod politely and keep repeating 'Thank you, Your Grace'... understand?"

"Yes."

Bora nodded. "Good. And tell him how you killed that human, he will like that."

And with that, Bora made his way up the long steps towards the Palace's doors. Syros gave another worried glance at the enormous black volcano that rose so high it almost touched the clouds, took a deep breath and followed Bora. Alpelite soldiers standing still within a sentry unit flanked the path as they strode to the gates of the Palace. With a nod, the Alpelite standing next to the entrance gave a shout in its native tongue and the gates opened, allowing them both inside.

The Palace's interior was impressive; there was a single hall, wide and magnificent, filled with Alpelites carrying swords, shields and axes, and dressed from head to toe in suits of silver armour. As they went further, a chubby Alpelite, sitting upon a throne of silver, and the only one not dressed in armour but instead in silver silk, stood up and moved upon them both. The number of Alpelites carrying weapons was not helping Syros's paranoia and the single figure moving swiftly towards him was also not calming his nerves. However, he was shocked to find that instead of hitting or attacking him, the Alpelite brought him into a warm embrace.

"Thank you," the round Alpelite told him, holding him close. "Thank you for bringing my son home to me." The Alpelite's human tongue was not as good as Bora's, yet none the less the words that Syros thought he heard startled him. Bora had a wide smile etched across its face. *Its son?* But Bora had told him that its parents had died after a human military campaign attacked its village. The wide creature finally let go of Syros, moving from that deep embrace to entwine the much taller Bora.

"Hello, father," Bora said in its native language. Syros didn't know many words of the three-eyed species, but Bora had taught him this particular phrase while they were travelling through the mountains together. The two continued to talk to each other until the chubby lord's attention moved back to Syros; its eyes were wide and seemed to hold warmth.

"Thank you," it said again. "My adopted son is home."

That settles things, Syros thought. He was glad that the creature he now considered a friend had not in fact lied to him.

"Thank you, Your Grace," Syros answered as previously instructed. But then finding the fortitude and sensing the grandly dressed Alpelite's cheerful mood, he asked, "So you adopted Bora as a child, Your Grace?"

· The creature gave a nod of the head. "Yes," it answered in a deep, rough voice. "I have adopted many children… war makes many orphans… thirty-four." The eyes of all the sentry Alpelites were upon them. Syros wondered how many of them spoke the human tongue and how they felt about their lord using it – the two species were at war after all. The lord gave out a bellowing laugh and indicated for Syros and Bora to follow it as it waddled back to the throne. Syros felt the Alpelite guards staring once more; they did not act as pleased to see him as their lord professed to be. Bora and Syros joined the grandly dressed Alpelite in sitting down on the chairs beside the throne. With a loud shout from their lord, wine was instantly brought over. He watched the cup in front of him fill up; it was not like any wine he had ever previously experienced; its texture was lumpy and brown and resembled mud more than it did wine. With a motion for a toast from the happy creature, Bora and Syros lifted their mugs and he tasted the strange substance. Surprisingly, he did not find the taste too bad – in fact, it tasted better than most wines that he had ever previously tried.

With a joyous groan, the lord of Ankor spoke to him. "If there is anything you wish for, human, ask for it, and I will attempt to make it so."

This startled Syros even more. He had not been expecting this reaction; he had envisioned pleading for his life. He did not understand why Bora had been so apprehensive about this meeting and why he had been warned not to speak much. He stared back towards the creature, unsure of what to say. If he could have anything in the world, what would it be? He genuinely had no idea.

"I would like to have a bath, if that is okay, Your Grace?" Syros replied, having thought of nothing else.

The lord let out a deep laugh, and even Bora beside him began to chuckle. "Yes, human, you may have a wash. Afterwards, you can tell us what you know of your species' movements in our lands and then we can sort out your living arrangements here among us."

Syros felt worried; he did not what his fellow species were planning. He assumed that Raynmaher had purposely kept them in the dark on what their true motive was, as they travelled from their barracks in East Asterleigh.

"I…" Syros began, before he was interrupted by a loud shout from one of the Alpelites on garrison duty near the entrance. He did not understand much of what the creature said, apart from one word, because it was the same in his own language – the word "Venian". With that, the previously cheerful Alpelite lord stood upon its feet, confusion across its face. It gave a shout back that very much sounded like an order and the doors opened.

"What did it say?" Syros inquired.

"It said Venian ambassadors have arrived from the forests, seeking an audience with our lord," Bora responded.

"Does that not happen very often then?" Syros probed, trying to understand the collective shock that had engulfed the room.

"It has never happened before…"

The doors to the throne room were flung open and in stepped six thin-bodied emerald-eyed creatures. This was only the second time Syros had seen the flower-like organisms and now there was a group of them, gliding their way across the room. Bora and the lord of Ankor stood up to make their way forward to greet the sentient life forms. The Alpelites on guard all firmly gripped their swords. Were they really expecting a fight from the thin-bodied flowers? They did not seem frightening. In fact, they were nothing short of beautiful, with their large sparkling eyes and bodies that twinkled gently. He could not understand why the Alpelites seemed so on edge.

"Human… " a quiet voice whispered behind him.

Syros turned to see an extra Venian with its head sticking out from the ground beside him. He knew this was the way the creatures travelled because he had seen it once before, when the Venian that he had met in the forest with Torjan had left, once it had led them back to their comrades.

"Human." Its eyes glistened as it caught his attention. "What are you doing here, so deep within the mountains?"

It spoke as if it knew him; could this be the Venian he had encountered that night with Torjan? "Are you the same Venian who helped me after I got lost in the forest?" He wondered why this one was not with the others or why it was speaking to him in a hushed manner, as if not wanting to be overheard.

"No," the Venian informed him. "I am not of that exact body, but as you were told on that night, our race is one, sharing all experiences and thoughts. Where is the fat one?" It scanned the room.

Syros presumed it was speaking of Torjan. He didn't answer; he still felt so much guilt about how that whole situation had played out. Sensing Syros's pain, the Venian smiled, "Do not worry, human. Salvation is nearing…" it finished softly, before receding back into the ground.

Syros watched the creature's head slowly disappearing. *What did it mean?* The last time he had talked to a Venian it had also spoken of salvation. He was not entirely sure, but, much like the Alpelites, he too was beginning to feel apprehensive. He stood up from his chair and made his way over to Bora, standing stiffly behind the lord of Ankor, who opened its arms to address the life forms.

"Welcome," it said, causing the Venians to each give the silkily dressed Alpelite a low bow. "Never before have you decided to come here to Ankor. May I ask why you have chosen to do so now?"

The Venian in the centre moved forwards out of the group, giving a glance around the room towards the row of Alpelite guards, who had not ceased their firm grip on their sheathed swords. "We are here to end the war, Alpelite." It spoke so softly that Syros queried just how he could hear the words as clearly as he did. The flower-like life form's eyes made him feel separated from himself, as if he were in a dream.

"Ah!" The lord of Ankor happily beamed. "So, after all these years you have finally decided to join our cause and aid the species with whom you have shared this planet for so long. Is it only now that you have begun to feel this kinship between us?"

The Venian who had stepped out in front did not answer straightaway, as it thought over its response. "I do not believe kinship is the right term, Alpelite," it said, outstretching its long thin hands. "We watched you grow before us upon our surface; we watched your evolution with our very eyes. We have seen your hardships, along with all your horrors. We are your mothers. Your existence within this universe is down to our doing, both our benevolence and our conscientiousness. We have looked away during your war with the humans, but now the stars have fallen and the flow of fate moves in a

197

different direction. We are the mediums for this everlasting change."

"So, you mean to help us return to Asterleigh?"

"Yes. Something like that…"

"Good. With you by our side we shall overthrow the humans and retake Asterleigh." The lord of Ankor tried to smile at the Venians, but failed to do so. Syros noticed the atmosphere within the room had not changed. The Alpelites were still unnerved by what was happening before them and by the six Venians whose glee had not lessened.

The Venian gave a slow shake of the head. "You do not understand." Its wide eyes grew even wider. "Your race has never understood. We have watched you weep, all of you. We have eyes everywhere, even here within the mountains. What makes you so sad?" Its voice tried to display sympathy, but fell short. "Is it your longing for home and Medzu that makes you cry? Or is it your own stagnation, here in the mountains, which depresses you so?"

The Alpelites were becoming very apparently heated by what the Venian had said; even the lord of Ankor, who had previously been all smiles, now had anger upon its face. The Venian let out a strange sound that Syros, much as the time before, recognised as a laugh. It continued this noise for a full minute; the entirety of the room kept silent, waiting for the creature to regain its composure.

After a moment, the Venian did manage to control itself and looked down at the short Alpelite lord. "But do not despair," it continued, mouth wider than Syros had ever seen before on the life form. "We have brought you a gift from the stars."

The Venians parted and Syros could see a cloaked figure walking up the steps and into the throne room. A strange sensation swept over him as he watched it moving closer towards their location, one that he had never felt before, as if all air was being sucked from the atmosphere, as if space and time were warping. The visitor removed its hood, as it made its way past the Venians, leaving Syros able to see its face for the first time. It appeared human enough, with a bald head and face covered in strange markings. However, the one aspect that did not seem human was its eyes, two black sunken eyes that appeared to have no light within them whatsoever. Its skin was a tone of colour he had never seen before, a type of light grey azure, with red veins visible on the outside, curling, twisting and forming patterns. Syros even noticed that its whole body was illuminating, pulsing through different stages of brightness.

Syros and the others stood perfectly still, shocked by what the Venians had brought them. *Is it human?* Syros marvelled. *No, it can't be, but if it isn't human then what is it?* The lord of Ankor had taken a step back as the Alpelites standing on guard all withdrew their swords. *What is going on here?* Syros again questioned, staring at the Venians, whose smiles had widened even further. *Why have they brought this illuminating being and where did they find it? Can it be as they said, it truly came from the stars?*

"What are you? Where… are you from?"

The Entity did not answer straightaway, as it continued its lifeless vacant staring around the Palace. When it did respond, it was with a voice that sounded distant, as if not coming from the room that they were in. "From worlds far away…"

"Y-y-you seem human," The lord of Ankor's body was shaking. It pointed its finger towards Syros, who was standing just yards away. "You look like our friend here."

Within this moment, the blank sunken-eyed Entity locked eyes with Syros. It was only for a second, but seemed to last an eternity; Syros gazed back into the most vacant of all voids. It was as if he were staring into Mercivous's eyes once more, only he was certain that this body had only the darkest of presences, so unworldly, like nothing he had ever before experienced. The Entity broke its stare away from Syros, who let out a deep gasp as if he had arisen from the depths of the ocean. Nothingness was all that was running through his mind; no fear nor surprise, only nothingness.

"I was human, once," the Entity said, its two empty voids back upon the fat, shaking Alpelite. "But having wallowed within the endless dreams, I have become something much more."

"What are you now?"

"I am the burning star," it uttered, and at that moment Syros heard a yell from one of the Alpelites on guard. He turned and saw a Venian had appeared behind it, its long leaf-like arm had become sharp, piercing through the Alpelite's back.

"Wh—" the lord of Ankor began, when a Venian rose from the ground behind it and too pierced its sharp arm through the creature's back, before withdrawing it, leaving the lord dead on the floor.

Bora let out a roar and withdrew its blade. The Alpelites on duty also unsheathed theirs and charged towards the Venians. Syros grabbed his sword, but it was too late. More and more Venians rose up from the ground. There now seemed to be hundreds of them within the throne room. Syros caught the eyes of an Alpelite guard as it swung its axe towards one of the intruders, but the botanic being's body was nimble enough to dodge the attack. The room continued to fill and now the Venians outnumbered the Alpelites by at least five to one. Like a virus attacking its host, the Venians swarmed the Alpelite guards. Syros watched in shock, but suddenly his attention was drawn to the glowing Entity that had locked onto him. It steadily moved forwards; he could not do anything, except run once more. He ran so fast past the Alpelite guards, whose bodies were piling up on the ground, that he forgot about the long winding steps outside and fell down them, plummeting to the very bottom.

Head dazed and heart pounding, he looked upon the manic, stricken city. Buildings were ablaze in the pandemonium – it appeared they had already been attacked. The Venians were everywhere, in every corner, killing all males, females and infants that they came into contact with. Loud, blood-curdling screams filled the air as the desperate Alpelites fell beneath the relentless onslaught. Syros searched for his blade, but he could not find it. Mind spinning and panting heavily, he sensed something behind him. He turned in time to see a Venian rising from the ground, its emerald eyes fixed on his own. It brought its hand back, readying to pierce it through him. *This is it*, he thought to himself, *my death*. He prepared himself for the blow. However, the creature did not kill him, instead gliding straight past into the frantic city. *Why didn't it kill me?* Syros marvelled. *They seem to be killing all others they encounter, so why not me?*

His mind raced over this for a moment, until he felt a presence coming from the entrance of the throne room. The glowing Entity stood there, its arms wide open. Then, to Syros's amazement, it began levitating, ascending so high into the sky that it blocked out the two suns. The unworldly life form lifted its hands and a sound like the roar of thunder echoed around the blood-soaked capital. The ground beneath Syros started to shake, causing him to fall violently upon the rocks. He looked up and saw that the volcano looming over the city was now spewing smoke into the air, while molten lava streamed down its blackened slopes, heading straight towards the city. He struggled to his feet and gave one more glance to the chaos happening around him, before outstretching his hand as a single black ash fell into his open palm. He silently watched it for a moment, before it slowly disintegrated into the nothingness.

17

Asterleigh's Burning Star

Ednon's mind was still on his latest encounter with Ethna and the aged Robles. He did not know what the two of them would do with the information he had given, but he felt uneasy. He walked through the crowded streets of East Asterleigh with these thoughts plaguing his mind; he also could not stop thinking of Ira, and what his grandfather might have felt about his grandson's latest actions. He doubted whether he would have been proud; well, he might have been, but there was no way of knowing. *How long have the Order been carrying out these types of attacks against the military?* Were they happening when Ira was at the helm? Was the old sickly man who had brought him up for almost all his life a killer? It made him sad to think it possible – in fact, it made him feel nothing but sorrow. Was Ira watching from wherever he was? Could he also see the doleful expression that had not left his face, ever since that moment many months ago? The days flew by at such a pace that Ednon could not hold onto them. Time itself was slipping through his fingers. He had not found a way to bring back his brother and now it looked as if time was running out. He still had no news of Syros and now, after all these months, he no longer asked for it. Chances were Syros had probably died out there in the wilderness, his hatred along with him. *It's okay*, Ednon lied to himself. His brother longed for death; he had pretty much told him so. Everything was slipping, the clocks were ticking and there was nothing he could do to prevent it.

"Boy..." A gruff voice caught Ednon's awareness.

It was one of the homeless on the streets, an old man with long unkempt hair and a beard, with dirty unwashed clothes, sitting upon the floor with an equally shaggy-looking dog.

"Boy, do you have any coins for an old lost wayfarer?"

"Of course," Ednon replied, as he rummaged through his pockets; he did not have much. He had originally planned to get some food from the marketplace, but his latest meeting with Ethna in the Temple of Yashin had caused unwanted pains to form in his stomach, so he doubted whether he could eat anyway. He threw the few loose coins he had into the man's bowl.

"Thank you, my burning star..." The way the man phrased his words stopped Ednon dead in his tracks. *My burning star?* He had heard these words so often over the last couple of months; could it be a coincidence this elderly beggar also used them? He gingerly gave one more glance at the tramp. The man's eyes were unadulterated darkness and were staring at him intently, not breaking their gaze. They were the same eyes from his dreams, two empty voids sucking in his entire being like endlessly spinning black holes. He stared back, his mind completely blank – *was this real?*

"Ed!"

Breaking his trance, he saw Amelia running towards him. He swiftly glanced back at the old homeless man. His eyes had returned to normal. Ednon let out a deep sigh. It must have been his mind playing tricks on him. Y*es, that was all it was, daydreams of a naive mind*, he reasoned uncertainly.

"Hi, Am."

"Ed," she repeated, giving him a worried look. "Where have you been all day? I haven't seen you since you left to see Dad's new workplace."

He quickly thought over his response; there was so much he could not tell her.

"I went to the Grand Library and helped Ageth around the place, before crashing out on one of the chairs in the hall."

This was half true; after Abacus had shown him the underground networks and after his latest encounter with Luther, he had felt so much anger with them all that he had stormed off, spending most of the day by the great Asterleigh Lake staring up towards the Medzu statue, contemplating his newfound knowledge of the Order and their actions. When night came, he still felt too enraged to return to the house to see Abacus, so instead he had entered the Grand Library through a secret entrance, before quietly falling asleep after reading a book on the Venians' evolution through time. So when Ageth had awoken him earlier this morning, he was surprised she had not yelled at him for breaking into the place.

"Oh," Amelia spoke hesitantly. "Are you hungry? I was about to go to the marketplace and get something to eat."

He had not had anything to eat for more than a whole day, but the unsure painful feeling was still lingering in his stomach. "I don't have any money," Ednon answered, remembering the old beggar.

"I'll pay."

"Thanks," Ednon replied, holding his stomach in an attempt to quell the aching.

They both set off down the street. Ednon gave one more glance at the aged vagrant behind him, who was continuing to stare right back. *I'm going insane; that is the only logical answer for what I saw. The black voids of my dreams manifesting into the realms of reality, but what does it mean?*

Ednon continued to query this as he and Amelia reached the Asterleigh market. He was only half paying attention to the things she was telling him; his mind was on subjects and thoughts vastly more important. *How would she react if I told her about Abacus? Would she be angry? Cry?* He couldn't tell her, it would only make her upset, and that was the last thing in the world he would ever want to do.

"What creature is that?"

Ednon and Amelia, along with the rest of the packed marketplace, turned to see what had caused the commotion. The yell came from a young stallholder, who was pointing a finger towards a small creature that had buried its face into the man's produce. Ednon recognised the life form; he had wondered when he would be seeing it once more. Along with a swarm of passing Asterleighians, they made their way closer to the stall and nearer the transparent organism. There was a collective gasp as the creature revealed its face to them for the first time. Sounds of bewilderment and hushed awe were all that could be heard from the gathering throng – even Amelia was admiring the strange animal in a state of pure wonderment. Much as had happened on the two previous occasions, the spiral-marked life form trudged towards Ednon, its two flippers caressing the ground as it moved. The crowd dispersed as it gathered pace; it was small, only rising a foot above the cobbled street, but to Ednon it seemed many feared the unfamiliar species. The Asterleighians parted, leaving a passage for the creature as it continued its slow stumble towards him. When it reached his feet, it once again gave a small joyous squeak, before, unsurprisingly to Ednon now, beginning to rub up against his shin.

"Ahhh…" Amelia cried, overcome with its unworldly cuteness.

Ednon knelt and started to pet the creature on its forehead. *Why does it keep appearing? What is it about me that attracts it?* The mass around them appeared to have lost some of their initial shock and started to close in.

"Child." A voice spoke up from the crowd. Ednon lifted his eyes away from the creature and towards a tall, skinny male in his mid-thirties, who had moved upon them both.

"Yes?" he responded, as the small transparent organism shifted closer towards Ednon.

"That creature, I have never seen a species of life quite like it. I would like to buy it from you."

"Buy it… Why?" Ednon replied hesitantly, as the

creature wrapped its flippers around his leg, holding onto him tightly.

"Who knows how many creatures of that kind are left upon this world? I would like it for research. I will pay you a handsome price."

The creature had completely buried its face into his leg and did not seem to want to go with the man. *What kind of research or experiments would they conduct on it?* It locked its scared wide diamond-shaped eyes with Ednon's own.

"No," Ednon answered firmly. "It's not for sale."

"Child," the man repeated, showing a little firmness of his own. "I don't think you understand. I work for the State. One way or another, you will hand the creature over."

"All the same." He pulled out his rucksack and picked up the shining life form, placing it in the bag. "You cannot have it."

The man had a look of pure rage as Ednon placed the rucksack around his shoulders.

"Am, let's go!"

"Okay, Ed…" she responded uncertainly, as the two of them began to weave their way through the crowd. He half expected someone to stop him, to physically force him to hand it over, but no one did. All they could do was stare as Ednon, alongside Amelia and the unworldly glowing life form, gradually made their way out of the busy marketplace.

The two of them all but ran back to their home in East Asterleigh. Abacus and Jernett must have gone out, as the house was completely empty. In the kitchen, Ednon opened his rucksack, allowing the sparkling life form out. It beamed warmly, before waddling over towards a bowl of fruit upon the kitchen table. Ednon and Amelia stood still, watching the strange species as it grasped one of the apples, before taking small bites out of it.

"Whatever it is, it has quite an appetite." Amelia leaned her head only inches away from the creature, which was giving joyous squeaks as it continued to munch on its meal.

She isn't wrong, Ednon thought to himself. On the night of Ira's death, the creature had not appeared to stop eating. Even after he had given it all the grain he possessed, even after he had placed it in the barn with the farm animals, the creature's hunger had not subsided, as it had instantly begun to eat their food also.

"What's its name?"

"I'm not sure it has one," Ednon replied, watching the animal devour the remnants of the apple before moving on to a second one.

"Well," Amelia said, smiling, "what do you want to name it? If this creature has appeared to you three times, I think it's safe to say it has some sort of bond with you."

Ednon contemplated the transparent organism. "I'm not sure. I don't even know what gender it is."

Amelia continued her close inspection of the little animal, before replying, "I think it's a female."

"How can you tell?" The creature didn't appear to have sexual organs of any kind, nothing whatsoever that would help them determine its sex. The only features he could see were its two wide diamond-shaped eyes, two large flippers and the strange spiral-marking upon its forehead.

"I'm not sure. I can just tell."

Well, if it was a female, he knew what he wanted to call it. "Orla," Ednon answered, taking out a chair.

"After your grandmother?"

Ednon gave a nod, then reached out to pet the life form on its forehead. The creature stared back and as Ednon's hand made contact, its diamond eyes started to glow, the spiral on its forehead rotated and Ednon found himself engulfed within the brightest of ethereal lights.

Ednon was floating through the black; shooting stars and comets flew by within the cosmic darkness. *Am I dreaming?* He didn't feel as if he were; he felt very much lucid and awake. His body was numb, yet he still felt wild sensations course through him. He was travelling closer towards a black hole, which had now obscured all his vision. Stopping for a moment before contacting the cosmic tunnel, he realised it was not sucking him in – in fact, his movements were completely free. He stayed motionless, adrift and at peace, gazing upon the hole as it spiralled; then, the hole started to disintegrate, changing into the kaleidoscopic eye that he was now familiar with. The eye parted and he was once again immersed by the unworldly light.

Ednon opened his own eyes to find himself standing upon slow-moving tides. *Where am I?* This place seemed so familiar. It had the appearance of Eos Lake, but something felt different. He marvelled at the sky; it was pure purple. *Purple? Is this truly Eos Lake?* Was he even in his own dimension? Ednon continued to scan his location and what he saw shocked him more than anything he had ever previously witnessed. He saw Ira, Syros and himself playing upon the shores; it must have been many years ago as each of them resembled their younger selves. Ira still had his long brown hair, and he and his brother were still children. He made steps across the water. He did not know why he moved forwards; it felt like the only thing he could do. Suddenly, the young child he recognised as himself pointed a finger towards him, and in this moment the purple sky blackened, and the stars within it started to fall. They crashed into the water, making him lose his balance. He shot his gaze to where he, Syros and Ira had once been, but the figures had completely faded. As the stars plummeted around him, he examined the waters below, seeing his reflection for the first time. His eyes were completely black. He continued to stare in utter incredulity until he sensed something large and ever-burning crash on top of him.

Ednon gave a loud yell. He was back in the kitchen. Amelia was standing still in astonishment. He surveyed the room; the small creature had vanished.

"What happened?" Ednon asked, panting heavily.

Amelia continued to stare at him, an expression of utmost bewilderment still very much apparent. "It was like…" she began, after a moment of pure silence. "You disappeared; you just vanished completely…"

They continued to stare at each other. His mind was racing with so many different pieces of information that he could not focus on just one and, as he stared back at Amelia, he could tell that she too had no idea what to make of the situation. However, the startled silence between them was quickly disrupted when Ednon heard the front door open, and in walked Abacus and Jernett. They exchanged a quick look as they moved into the kitchen and placed down their newly-acquired shopping.

"Good afternoon, you two," Jernett addressed them both. "Ednon, you did not return last night. Are you okay, dear?"

"I…" Ednon began. He did not know what to say, his mind was still racing out of control. Should he tell them of what had just happened with the small life form? Would they even believe him?

"Ed… " Abacus gave a slight cough, which saved Ednon from his moment of indecision. "Could I have a word?"

Ednon gave Amelia one more glance as he followed Abacus out of the kitchen. *What is it that Abacus wants? Is it something to do with the Order?*

Abacus dragged him into the hallway and started to speak in an unusually hushed tone.

"Ed," he began, sweat forming on his brow. "I don't have long. I just wanted to sa—"

At this moment, the front door behind them was violently kicked open with a loud bang and in charged six men, all dressed in military uniform. They lunged towards Abacus, knocking over a nearby vase in the process, causing it to break upon the tiles. Abacus fought back, punching one of the men square in the face and elbowing another in the stomach. However, there were too many of them and they quickly subdued him. The noise attracted Jernett and Amelia, who both let out loud screams as the men viciously smashed Abacus's face to the floor.

"Abacus," uttered the oldest of the military men, and

the only one not physically restraining the struggling Elder. "You are hereby arrested for acts of terrorism against our kind. You will soon be sentenced and hanged for your crimes. May you suffer eternal torment for your treason against our proud race."

And with that the five men hauled Abacus to his feet, bound his arms and placed a black bag over his head. As quickly as they had entered, they proceeded to push him out of his broken front door and onto the streets where a small crowd had already gathered, leaving Ednon alone with Amelia and her mother, along with the sharp broken glass edges spread across the entirety of the now desecrated hallway.

18

Stars of Dusk

How much longer until we die? Syros thought to himself, gazing over the Alpelite horde. It was surely only a matter of time. Death was a certainty; the only question was when it would come. Yet, despite the utterly dire circumstances, they still clung on to survival. But how could they possibly survive against an enemy that could, without warning, rise from the ground to kill them all? If, of course, the hunger did not kill them first or the toxicant the Venians released, which could at any moment manifest into the air, leaving them cold and stiff. The Venians had expelled chemicals into Ankor, choking all Alpelites that had the misfortune to breathe in the vapour. This was not a war they could win. *No*, Syros reassessed, *this was no longer a war at all, but a genocide.* If the Venians wanted them dead, then Vena itself truly longed for their extinction. The Venians were sad proof of a reality that even flowers can kill when pushed to the extreme. They could not fight against them, or indeed that strange unworldly Entity with the powers of a god, who caused the ground to shake with a single lift of its hands. It claimed to be from another world, although seemed almost human, but how could one human have such abilities of complete and utter devastation? And why was it fighting alongside the Venians to wipe out the Alpelites? The Venians were supposed to be pacifists – that was all he had heard about the species ever since he was a child. Could it be that this Entity, whom they claimed fell from the stars, had managed to convince the Venians to join the conflict? If so, then this terrified him more than anything. Even if by some miraculous chance the Alpelites managed to unite with the humans, there was no likelihood, even with their two forces combined, that they could ever hope of defeating the Venians.

Bora turned away from the Alpelite mass to Syros. "We should stop to rest soon. The old are becoming fatigued."

Syros studied Bora. It seemed to be indestructible, not only had it sustained torture from his old comrade Mercivous, but it had also survived the bloodbath that had taken place in the palace of Ankor with only a few minor wounds. In fact, Syros speculated, they all appeared to have escaped Ankor far too easily. Not only had the Venian that had arisen behind him not followed through with its piercing blow, but their frantic escape out of the city's gates had also not been hindered. *If the Venians truly want us dead, then why not kill us?* And why had the botanical beings appeared in Ankor at the exact same moment that he had? So many questions were within his mind, yet he had so few answers.

Syros and Bora were standing upon a nearby cliff, watching the Alpelite multitude as they journeyed through the mountain pass. There must have been thousands of them, of all different ages and sizes. Many of the surviving Alpelites had instead chosen to head east, while this swarm, led by Syros and Bora, were travelling westwards. Most had found their endings within Ankor, either bloodied from the piercing sharp arm of a Venian, or left lying still with the stiff expression caused by the flower-like life forms' deadly poison. He had seen more death than he could have possibly imagined, but it no longer left him feeling scared or mournful. It made him feel only hollow.

"Do you still mean for us to travel to Asterleigh?" Syros asked.

Bora gave a nod of the head. "Yes, human, it should only be a few more weeks until we reach your borders."

"Why?" Syros challenged callously. "Even if the humans do not just kill us as soon as we reach the border, does it truly matter where in the world we go, when the Venians travel from under the ground? Would Asterleigh not just be their next target?"

"As I told you before, human, there is a mysticism to Asterleigh that your species knows nothing about. The Venians cannot arise there, the ground beneath is too dense, plus in Asterleigh we have Medzu to watch over us."

"And where was Medzu in Ankor! When the infants choked and the elderly were butchered? Why worship a god that has no interest in you? As you told me before, Medzu's consciousness left this world many years ago, so why do you continue this blind worship?"

"Habit, most likely. Truth be told, the only difference between us and the gods is that they are large while we are small."

"Then why…" Syros continued, staring intently at the wounded Alpelite, "do you still hold hope that Medzu will save us?"

Bora gave a long pause, gazed back down to its fellow species below them and spoke in a voice that shattered like glass. "Because it's the only hope that we have left…"

Syros stopped himself. He should not be attacking Bora, not at this moment; the Alpelite clearly had much love and affection for its people, so the recent slaughter and threat of complete annihilation must be weighing heavily on its mind. Despite the current circumstances, perhaps it would be best to portray himself as being optimistic.

"The humans will kill us as soon as we reach the border…" Syros could not fake it; they were all going to die. All of them. His own fallacies would not change this inevitable fate, so why even bother?

"If we die, then we die," Bora said, still surveying the Alpelite crowd as they continued to move through the steep-sided ravine. "But at least our fate will be in our own hands."

Syros did not respond and solely joined Bora in a silent watch over the thousands upon thousands of three-eyed life forms passing below them. *There are so many of them*, Syros thought, as he witnessed one of the elderly pick up an infant. *Each with their own lives and stories.*

"Human," Bora said. The creature was standing a little taller, a new glint in its eyes. "There is only one God. It's a God we have all been worshipping ever since life first appeared in the universe and its name is Survival. We will survive this; we shall all survive this."

Syros stared back silently. He appreciated Bora's attempt to lighten his mood, but the truth was they had only lived this long because the Venians had allowed them to do so, and at any minute they could reappear. Furthermore, who knew what other powers that strange Entity possessed? Syros and the Alpelites had hardly any weapons, next to no food and no horses. Despite this playing in his mind, he gave Bora a sturdy nod. "Yes, we shall survive this."

"Good. Now let us join the others in the canyon."

Syros could feel all of the Alpelites' three eyes staring up at him as they steadily headed down the rocky path to the mountain road. He was still not used to them; even after all the time he had spent with Bora, the Alpelites felt like strangers and many treated him as such. He seemed to be the only human within the horde travelling west and most of the Alpelites did not speak his language, so Bora was the only one with whom he ever truly conversed. He missed human beings, he could not deny it. Despite the last couple of encounters he had had with his own species, he could not lie about feeling less on edge with his own kind than he did with these three-eyed ones. Who knew how they really felt about him? Syros questioned, as he stared round the gathering. He was sure many of them must hold anger for him in their hearts; their two species had been at war for thousands of years and they were all collectively starving, so what would stop them from…

Syros's thought process was interrupted as he felt something pull on the back of his shirt. He turned to face an elderly, hunched-over female, a silk shawl across its face to help shield it from the intense sunlight. The old Alpelite was carrying a newborn sleeping gently in its arms. The weathered life form spoke in its native tongue, while searching Syros's eyes.

"Bora… what is it saying?" Syros called, provoking the Alpelite to see what caused his discontinuance.

Bora gave a smile. "Thank you for helping us…"

Syros felt his face redden. *Please don't thank me*, he thought, as he gazed back into the elderly female's eyes. He wasn't any different from the rest of them; he wasn't helping, not really. The only reason he was here was because of circumstance, nothing more.

"Thank you," Syros answered, in the little of the creature's tongue he knew. The elderly female let go of his top, then joined the others as they made their way down the rocky passageway.

I hope you survive, Syros thought to himself, as he and Bora watched the back of it moving further and further away. *If Medzu is truly watching over us, and if it has an ounce of compassion, it would save you both.*

The darkness of night was approaching; the once bright sunlight was disappearing and with it the rocks of the mountains. They were entering the grassy meadows and deep forests, which stretched ahead for as far as they could see.

"We should set up camp and restart our travelling in the morning."

"Here in the meadows so close to the trees? What would stop the Venians from killing us as we sleep?"

"As you said before, human. If the Venians truly wanted us dead, they would have done so already."

They sat around the campfire, now the only thing illuminating the complete darkness. He, Bora and two other large-bodied Alpelites sat up on guard duty as the others tried to get as much rest as they could within an abandoned encampment that they had stumbled across when they had entered the forest. It appeared to have belonged to humans, but there was no sign of anyone else in their proximity. *What happened to them?* Syros questioned, swivelling his head round the deserted camp. *Had the Venians already come? If so, then where were the bodies?* His worriment did not appear to be shared by Bora and the other two, as they laughed and joked with each other in their native language. Syros could only understand a few words of what the creatures were saying to each other. In this moment, he missed Saniya and Torjan greatly. He wondered where they both were. He assumed if Torjan were still alive, Raynmaher would have sent him back to Asterleigh to await trial for treason. And Saniya, he had no idea where she was, or the rest of Zelta Squadron. He prayed they had returned to Asterleigh and that she was safe. He remembered how beautiful she had looked that night underneath the moonlight. *I should have kissed her,* Syros thought to himself. He had seen Dashera's naked body a few times back in Asterleigh and he wondered what Saniya's looked like compared to hers. He imagined both of them kissing underneath the moonlight while caressing each other's bodies and the moans of pleasure both girls made. And then, after that, they would turn their attention on him. They would treat him like a god, not just one god out of five, but the greatest of all the gods. He fantasised not only having Dashera and Saniya fall for him, but every girl on this planet and on any other worlds as well.

The flames on the campfire began to flicker, and Syros's eyelids along with them. It was the early hours of the morning and there was only so much listening to an unfamiliar language he could take. It was a cloudy cold night, no stars nor moonlight, only the blackness of space. He closed his eyes and began to imagine, imagining himself on distant planets trillions of lightyears away from this one. A new life, a new outlook and a new destiny – perhaps what Torjan had told him was true, when the three of them had sat there gazing up to the stars together many moons ago, that this is what happens after death. *How much longer?* he questioned weakly as his eyes shut, and his body and mind grew numb. *How much longer until I finally…* A loud noise from the bushes promptly alerted his senses.

"Bora!" he shouted, rapidly withdrawing his sword.

Bora and the other two Alpelites got to their feet, also drawing their weapons, and pointed them towards the bushes. Had the Venians already come for them? He continued levelling his steel in that direction. The leaves parted and his disbelieving mind saw Saniya's face emerging – *Is this real or am I dreaming?* Their eyes matched and it was as if for a moment he had forgotten himself entirely.

He continued to stare back; *I must be dreaming*, he told himself. However, it appeared his eyes and mind were not lying to him, as she swiftly moved out of the bushes and entwined him within the deepest embrace that he had ever previously experienced.

"Syros! I thought you had died. Oh Sy… they killed everyone… Raynmaher, Freckon, Steph… we were the only ones who made it." She hung on so tightly he could feel her trembling.

Syros surveyed the bushes from which she had emerged and saw Hurus leaning on Petula's shoulders. From head to toe, he was covered in blood, his eyes were also completely glazed over – it appeared Petula was doing all she could to keep the lad upon his feet.

"What happened?" Syros held Saniya's head firmly to his chest. His heart was pounding. He could not process what it was she was telling him; the only thing that mattered was that she was here with him, in his arms.

"The Venians attacked us a few nights ago." Her voice was almost unintelligible with grief. "Oh, Sy, this all seems like some horrible nightmare."

"It's okay." It wasn't; he knew it and she knew it, but what else could he say?

"We will nurse your friend," Bora told Petula, as the three Alpelites gently picked up the now unconscious Hurus.

"Please take care of him!" Petula pleaded.

"Do not worry, we will give him the best medical attention that we can." With that the three Alpelites lifted up Hurus between them and carried him off into the campsite. Some of the other Alpelites were emerging from the tents to see what the commotion was.

"Sy, I've missed you so much…" Saniya spoke again, her cries intensifying.

"It's okay." He kissed her on the top of her head and brought her in even closer. "We're alive…we're both still alive…"

The hours passed and the darkness grew. Syros was lying beside the campfire, head on a log as a makeshift pillow, with Saniya gently sleeping on his lap. All the others had either gone to bed or were attending to Hurus's wounds in a nearby tent. But he could not sleep; there was too much adrenaline running through his body and too many thoughts occupying his mind. Instead, he sat and stared into the fire for what seemed like an eternity. The commotion had finally died down and silence had descended upon them, apart from the scurrying of a few woodland animals moving through the forest.

"Has she finally fallen asleep?" Bora whispered, appearing behind him.

"Yeah," Syros responded, as he gently played with Saniya's hair.

Bora let out a deep yawn, stretched out its limbs and lay down beside them, eyeing the shimmering blaze.

"How is Hurus doing?"

"Not too well," Bora answered solemnly. "We must wait until morning to see whether he lives, but I wouldn't hold out too much hope."

Syros did not respond and merely joined Bora's quiet

staring into the fire. They were all dead, all of them, Mercivous, Captain Raynmaher, even sweet innocent Freckon. Only five of the original members of Zelta Squadron were still living, if of course Torjan was even still alive, wherever he might be.

"Human... can I tell you something?"

"Of course."

"I know you are not helping us out of honour or kindness. Who knows? Perhaps deep down you do not truly care for us. I know the only reason you are here is because if you were anywhere else you would most likely be dead..."

Syros eyed the Alpelite wearily. Why was it telling him this?

"For all that," Bora continued, still fixated by the burning embers, "there is too much hatred between our species. Even after you saved my life and we first began to travel to Ankor, I wanted you dead. And that is because I have been designed throughout the entirety of my existence to want you dead; even now, I can feel it in my very being. Even with Medzu's light guiding me, I can feel its cold abyss. It's pure hate. It has always been there... I suspect there it shall remain until the end of my life. I have a wretched feeling deep inside me... we're not going to survive this, none of us will... and you know what? I think we may have deserved it." The Alpelite leaned backwards and placed its hands over its eyes. "Silly, isn't it, how our lives have played out."

"Yes, but we're friends now, aren't we?" Syros smiled.

"Yes, human... we are friends." And with that it stood

224

up, gave another loud yawn and started to walk away. "I'm going to bed. We near your borders with each day; we will need our strength."

"Okay, good night, Bora."

"Good night, Syros."

Syros looked down at Saniya and played with her hair once more. As he continued his gentle stroking, her eyes opened to match his. He smiled at her as she regained consciousness.

"Hi." She sleepily raised her head from his lap.

"Hey."

They stared at each other silently, the clouds above parted and the moonlight of Vurtus began to shine down upon them. He continued to search her eyes, her bright pale eyes, searching, searching for something to which he could relate. Was she also doing the same? What was it she was searching for within him? Moments passed, silence lingered and the wind began to gently blow. Whatever it was she wanted, she appeared to have found as she broke their shared elongated period of nothing.

"Syros…" Saniya got to her feet, grabbing his hand and pulling him upright.

"Yes, San?"

"Come with me…"

With that she led him, still clutching his hand, drawing him away from the glow and the silently sleeping three-eyed creatures, to deep within the forest. She steered him far into the placid woods, not making a sound, with the moonlight guiding their way. Eventually they reached a clear, deserted area within the trees; a small stream ran past them, the moon from above was on full display as she faced him. After a few more moments of silent nothing, she slowly undressed, until she stood completely naked in the moonlight. Syros watched her, his mind blank, feeling very much like he was within a dream.

"San…" he started. "We shouldn't… " before she moved closer and kissed him. The trees around them gently swaying and the light from above illuminating them, he finally started to lose himself and, with that, all thoughts of death. He clasped her firmly, returning her love, as the still night sky above them slowly filled with eternal, ever-burning stars.

19

Brother

10 Days until the New Year

Ednon sprinted through the streets at such a pace he tripped over his own feet. Wincing slightly, he picked himself up and, ignoring the concerned glances from a few onlookers, started to run once more. He knew where he needed to go. His mind was racing and the pain was growing, but he could not stop running. He accidently collided into a couple, causing all three of them to topple over.

"Watch yourself, kid!" the man shouted, as Ednon rose to his feet and regained his previous pace. He could not slow down – for the sake of Amelia, he couldn't. However, his eyes did indeed catch something that managed to slow his charge. He spotted a poster upon a wall and a face he was now all too familiar with.

WANTED: THE MAN KNOWN AS 'LUTHER'
FOR ACTS OF TERRORISM
AGAINST THE STATE
PERCEIVED AS BEING
EXTREMELY DANGEROUS –
DO NOT ATTEMPT TO DETAIN WITHOUT
MILITARY PERSONNEL PRESENT.

Underneath was a sketch of a man with a bald head, dark-tinted shades and a baleful grin. Ednon stared at the picture in dismay; *how long have these been here?* He studied other walls as he continued onwards. The posters were everywhere, on the sides of taverns, shrines, shops and even on schools, each showing the same depiction of Luther. The other Elders must have been arrested along with Abacus. However, it appeared that Luther had managed to elude the military's clutches. Taking a deep breath in, he tore his eyes away from the posters and started to run once more.

At last, he reached his intended destination and, panting heavily, Ednon banged upon the golden gates. There was no response, so he hammered on them once more. *They must be in*, he pleaded to himself. *For the love of Medzu they must be.* He studied the barrier to see if there was a way for him to climb up. The gates were at least fifteen feet tall and he could see no footing to lift himself over. He could wait until someone came by to open them, but who knew how long that would take? The military man who had burst into their home said Abacus was to be hanged for his acts of treason, but did not give a specific time or place. His mind drifted to Amelia and her mother. This was his fault. How could he live with the guilt if he could not prevent the execution from taking place?

"Ira…" He dropped to his knees in defeat. "Ira, please help me…"

Leaning back upon the golden gates, he placed his head in his hands. Ever since Ira's death, everything had gone so wrong. His family had been ripped apart; he could not let the same happen to Amelia's. He began to cry and hated himself for it; he was still such a child, weak and helpless. He wished he were more like his brother; he had never seen Syros cry, not in all the years they had grown up together. He could pray to the gods to ask for their help, but that now seemed like a most pointless endeavour, for the gods had never answered his prayers.

"Yashin, Kymous, Quirina, Medzu and Pia," Ednon said, looking up from his book to face his brother. "Apparently, these are the five gods who have been charged with watching over all life within the universe."

"Gods aren't real."

"How do you know? The Medzu statue in Asterleigh is as tall as a mountain; how could that exist without the help of divine intervention?"

He remembered Syros shrugging. "They say Medzu loves us. Well, if that's the case, then why did it let our parents die?" Ednon kept quiet and searched his mind for a rebuttal, but could not find one. "We are alone, Ednon. Nobody is coming to save us."

"Young master Ednon, returned to visit us so soon?"

Robles's face was peering down at him, leaning over the top of the gateway with a curious expression.

"Robles!" Ednon stood up, feeling relief run through him. "Robles, I need to speak with Lady Ethna!"

"I'm sorry, young master, but I'm afraid madam is not here at present. Perhaps you should come back in a few weeks from now."

"Where is she?"

"She has journeyed north to Roxton, to conduct an urgent meeting. I am sure whatever you feel is so important to bang so violently upon these gates can wait until her return."

Ednon stared at the old subservient man; he knew Robles was lying to him. The only times he had previously seen the fiercely blue-eyed Ethna, Robles was always trailing behind, like an old dilapidated shadow. If she had truly travelled north to Roxton, there was no way Robles would not have accompanied her. Nevertheless, even though he knew the man was prevaricating, it did not make his entry any easier. He needed to say something to break through the bushy-moustached man's false pretence.

"I know where Luther is…"

He waited for a response that did not return immediately, although Robles's steely eyes had widened.

"You truly know of Luther's whereabouts?"

"I do."

Robles looked back down upon him while giving his moustache a stroke. Seeming to have accepted Ednon's supposed information, he eventually answered, "Wait here… I shall return in a few minutes."

Please, Ednon silently begged, as he watched Robles's head disappearing behind the closed entry. *Please just open these gates.*

He waited and, as promised, the old man finally reappeared. "Very well, master Ednon, you may come inside." And with that the gilded barrier opened, and for the second time in as many days, he entered the prodigious grounds of the Temple of Yashin.

Instead of leading him the paved way to the doors of the temple, Robles led Ednon around the side of the massive Alpelite-built structure. There were many in the extraordinarily green gardens, doing various odd jobs. They all watched as Ednon and Robles walked swiftly across the immaculately cut grass.

Eventually, they found Lady Ethna, who was watching a few workers cut down a huge oak tree. She fixed her piercing eyes on Ednon as he approached, a fierce almost terrifying expression upon her face. However, it immediately changed as Ednon made his way to within a couple of feet from her.

"Ednon!" she beamed. "Come to visit us again. Why do we not go inside, out of the heat, and Robles can make us som—"

"I need your help to release Abacus!" he declared loudly, still panting from his running only moments before.

Her face became cold and ferocious. "And why would I do that?" she retorted, as if what he had said was the most ridiculous thing she had ever heard. "The man is responsible for the deaths of many people throughout these lands and is a known traitor to the human race. Why should I help you allow him to escape justice?"

"Please… he does not deserve death."

"I have met many people throughout my life, child. Some good, some bad. Some like angels fallen from the sky; others like the darkest of cretins, only upon the world's surface to enact their own evil ways. Despite this difference, death comes for them both. Death is unbiased, for sooner or later it takes us all."

"Please, if you could talk to the military, I am sure they would listen to you."

"My sweet innocent child." She shook her head. "I am the military. I am the state, the empire and the sovereign. I am our species' future and its last dying hope. The traitors will be executed before too long… The common folk shall see what happens to people who turn against their own kind. We shall hang an Elder in every city across these lands to remind them what treason brings. It's not their fault though, Ednon, it's the fault of your grandfather before you, preaching of a world of co-existence with those vile creatures. So, little one, the next time you journey to his grave, tell him the deaths of hundreds of innocent lives are on his hands. The executions of the ones responsible will bring some justice; of course, all except for that rat Luther, who scurried off into the sewers like the vermin he is…"

"I—" Ednon began. He did not know what to say as he stared back into the young woman's eyes. *Can it be true? Could she really be…*

"So, Ed, if you tell me the location of Luther, I shall allow you to visit the murderer you long so much to see."

"He, um…" He desperately tried to work his brain to find something to say. "He is most likely down south." Ednon paused, giving himself more time. "He used to talk about how many supporters he had in Lowton and the surrounding villages. If he is anywhere, he will most likely be around those parts."

Ethna stepped closer, her eyes like those of a hawk as it surveys its prey. "I hope you are not lying to me, Ed. You do not strike me as the kind of boy who tells lies."

"I'm not…"

"Good." Ethna gave him a wide smile, before addressing the old Robles. "Robles, did you write down what Ednon has told us?"

"I have, ma'am," Robles responded with a nod, his pen and notebook in hand.

"Now, Ed, for being a co-operative boy, I shall allow you to visit that pseudo-pacifist you so desperately want to see. Robles shall escort you to the dungeons."

"What day will the execution take place?" The fear and anxiety in Ednon's stomach had grown to such a level that he felt as if he were about to puke.

"Not until after Sechen's passing most likely." Ethna appeared distracted by the workers cutting down the oak tree. "Ednon, as I told you before, we are not the enemy," she continued, sensing his jittery state. "We are both human and in this world, that is all that truly matters. Especially now as we increase, making our mark upon this planet, as the Alpelites' numbers begin to dwindle and as the glorious future of the human race finally begins…"

Ednon followed Robles as they walked through the streets of Asterleigh. He was not sure if it was genuine, but he had an ominous feeling that this would be the last time he would ever see Abacus. There seemed to be no way whatsoever he could prevent the execution. But he suddenly remembered the phantom's words in the Grand Library, so perhaps it did not matter. The night of Sechen's passing was soon approaching and when the star and the moon crossed each other, all their endings would come.

As he continued his journeying through the streets, his mind instead went to his grandfather and the words Ethna had spoken about him. She was right, Ednon gloomily conceded to himself. *All Ira's teaching had ever done was cause more conflict and death.* Ednon had never met an Alpelite, but he assumed they were just as blood-hungry as humans. Perhaps his grandfather was not the great man he had once thought. His brother may also have been right all along; a world of two different species co-existing could be a fairy tale that has no place in the real world. Also, maybe Ethna was right to put the Elders to death; they had, of course, committed endless murders, including that of the young girl that he still, even after all this time, could not get out of his mind. It was all wrong, down to its very foundations. Just a bad circumstance to be born in such a place at this moment in time, and because of this star-crossed misfortune, they were all truly cursed.

They had made it into the depths of the cold, darkened dungeons. Robles waited outside, giving him his private meeting with Abacus. There was hardly any light, apart from a few lanterns helping him on his path. Ednon walked down the spiral steps to where the prisoners were held. There were about ten windowless cells in total, all on his left-hand side; to his right, lanterns spread across the old granite walls. He moved down the line of cells, until he eventually found Abacus lying upon the dusty ground. His hair and beard were unkempt, and newly acquired bruises were marked across his face. His eyes seemed full of frailty as he looked up after hearing Ednon approaching.

"Ed…" he uttered in a faint gruff voice, determining who it was that had come to visit him. He struggled to his feet and moved closer to the metal bars, only to be stopped by the chain across his ankle, causing him to give out a loud curse. Ednon watched as the man violently pulled on this tether to try and create more space for movement, but, having failed, he instead slumped back against the wall, an expression of defeat across his battered face.

"Ed…" Abacus repeated, his lips dry and throat rough. "I do not wish for you to see me like this."

"I had to." Ednon tried as hard as he could not to divert his eyes from the once proud Elder. "It's my fault you're here."

Abacus shook his head, only half of his face visible in the light emitting from the lanterns, the other half completely consumed by the shadows. "My boy, it's no one's fault but my own. My actions and they alone have led me to my current state. I have brought this not only upon you, but my wife and daughter. I fear I have failed Ira, and before too long I am sure he will tell me what he thinks of my failings when I meet him in the great beyond."

"How have you failed him?"

"The morning before his death, he told me what he was planning to do. He showed me the poison in his hands. I prayed and I begged, but he had already made up his mind – he told me he had many years ago." His voice was fainter than the winter suns; despite this, Ednon listened carefully. This out of everything was what he needed to hear the most. "He told me to care for you. To watch over you to my death. And to never bring you into our Order. But I failed; I was never one to keep promises."

Ednon leaned forwards intently, feeling the cold ice of the metal bars on his face. "Why did he not want me to join the Order?"

"He knew what we had become. He knew we had been transformed into nothing but old hypocrites, sitting upon our high horses, our every action a direct contradiction to what we spouted. Your grandfather left our Order soon after he heard the news of what happened to your parents. Something changed within him that day; he was no longer the charismatic hero I knew as a young boy when I used to hang onto every one of his words. It was as if his wings had fallen off and he was human once more."

"My grandfather had a lot of hate in his heart. He told me that on the night he died," Ednon said quietly, remembering there were other prisoners down here who might be eavesdropping on their conversation.

Abacus attempted a smile. "Who can blame him? There is one simple flaw with pacifism, Ed, but it is a most important one. We are human beings and we hate. No matter who you are, how holy or progressive you may feel. Deep down, you hate. It's the sad reality of who we are. That's what our race is, what it has built its foundations on. We will always find one to take the assault of our hatred. If it was not the Alpelites, we would most likely be hating each other."

"What do you hate, Abacus?"

"Myself right now…" Abacus said with saddened disdain. "For the pain I have brought upon my wife and daughter. Ed… " He suddenly spoke, straightening his back and clearing his throat. "Tell them I'm sorry. For all I have done. From now on, you sha—"

"This isn't the end. There is still hope, Abacus…"

Abacus gave a shake of the head. "Of course this is the end, lad. The military will never allow my release; the dates are set. I will be joining Ira soon."

"I know who the Supreme Leader is…" Ednon blurted without thinking. "I can go talk to them an—"

Abacus's eye widened to such a degree it was almost comical. He nervously gave a low hushing sound before his visible eye searched around the darkened room. "Ed…" he said in a voice quieter than a whisper. Like a wild animal hopelessly attempting to break from its leash, he tried to move closer to Ednon. "Ed. Who is the Supreme Leader? You need to tell me."

"I'm sorry, Abacus, I can't."

"Ed…" his voice sounded panicked. "I need to know their identity. Please, lad."

Ednon gave a shake of the head. He knew what telling Abacus Ethna's identity would do. And that was to only bring more death to this world.

Abacus appeared to be thinking over his response. Ednon was not too sure as he could no longer gauge the expression of the man whose face was now completely engulfed by the shadows. "Lad…" Abacus replied, his voice sounding as strong as it had for the entirety Ednon had been down here. "We can change the world. We could bring forth peace… all you need to do is tell me the name."

Ednon took a step back. This was not the man he had known for almost his entire life. He seemed dark and threatening in a way Ednon had never previously experienced. He felt his hair stand on end as if a demon had risen from the rock-hard surface and crawled its way into Abacus's shell.

"It may be the only way to save Syros…" tempted the voice from the shadows. The hallway was growing darker; the lanterns upon the wall were fading.

"I need to go, Abacus…" Ednon said, feeling his forehead sweat as he stared aimlessly at the outline of an obscured figure slumped against the wall of the darkened cell. "It's getting late, I need to get back and—"

"Syros?"

He turned his head quickly, but he could not see who this voice belonged to. Feeling somewhat relieved, he made his way over to the wall behind him, got on his tiptoes and outstretched his hand to retrieve one of the lanterns. Now with a source of illumination in his hand, he made his way over to the cell where the new voice had come from. *He must be the largest person I have ever seen*, Ednon thought, gazing upon the man. With black skin that showed marks of beatings, a completely shaven head and arms each the size of large ale barrels, unlike Abacus who had one chain across his ankle, this man had three; one to the ankle, another around the waist and the last chaining his neck. He positioned himself upright as Ednon cautiously inched closer.

"Who are you?" Ednon asked. "How do you know my brother?"

"Your name's Ednon, isn't it?" The calmness of his voice surprised Ednon, who was expecting something much more rough and guttural. "Of course," the man continued, giving a wide grin. "You're exactly like him, same brown eyes and same curly hair. Yes, it must be you. My name is Torjan," he continued, trying to act as dignified as possible, despite his current circumstance. "I was travelling with your brother east, as part of the mass military campaign. We were in the same squadron together."

Ednon's heart pounded. "You travelled with Syros? How is he? Where is he?"

"The last time I saw him he was with an Alpelite, travelling east; I was ordered to track him down and kill him, but when the time came, I couldn't do it. And that's why I'm here," he said, motioning his head around his cell, giving a faint smile, but a genuine one. "But do not worry, the last time I saw him he was still very much alive."

"He was travelling with an Alpelite? Why would he be doing that?"

Torjan shrugged. "I'm not sure. Perhaps he had a change of heart when confronted with the true horrors of war. Or perhaps he is a natural survivalist. Who knows what truly lies beneath the exterior of our brother."

"Our brother?"

Torjan lifted his hand and opened the palm, revealing a

scar covering the entirety of its length. "He used to speak of you." Torjan put his hand back down to his side. "And your grandfather also… as far as I'm concerned, he is as much a brother to me as to you. Making you my brother as well." A sudden cold rushing wind gushed through the dungeon door, blowing out the lanterns' flames, leaving them all in complete blackness. "Do not worry, Ednon!" Torjan called, assuming this was the signal for Ednon to make his exit. "You will see your brother once more; it's not in our blood to let people down! Plus, if he does, he will have me to answer to!"

Ednon blindly felt his way across the wall until he found the door of the dungeon. Knocking on it violently, he waited for Robles to open it for him. Panting heavily, he stepped out from the dungeon and emerged into the light. Robles was staring at him intently. However, instead of saying anything, he merely walked up the spiral steps. Ednon assumed he was supposed to follow suit and started to trail behind, his mind not only on his brother Syros and how he was still very much alive, but also on his new brother, three times his size, whom he never before knew he had.

20

Dawn

In the gloomy hours of dawn, the rain drizzled down. The moon had disappeared and all the stars along with it; grey clouds now stretched across the morning horizon. Syros sat awake, watching the rain drip from the leaves. He glanced down to Saniya, who lay bare, sleeping in his arms underneath a large oak. He let out a sigh and continued to contemplate the open landscape. He had a wretched feeling inside him, so much so he felt like crying. *What is it she sees in me?* he questioned to himself, as he felt Saniya gently moving. He did not understand. He was nothing but broken, so what was it? The feelings of depression grew and the anger along with it. *Would it please you, my love, if I could fix whatever it was that was wrong? But would that even still be me?* Death had come so frequently over the last couple of months that it no longer felt real. *When we die, will we still be together, or is that just foolish thinking? How can I enjoy the time I have now, when the empty void lingers so closely? In death, we are alone.* But now he was awake and cognisant, he also felt alone, he always had. *There is no point*, he solemnly reflected. *None whatsoever.* The world is ever-changing. *Eco systems, relationships, people, even the caterpillar changes into the butterfly,* he thought to himself as he watched one crawling on the branch beside him. Everything changes, apart from the emptiness he felt inside himself each day, because that was always there.

"Morning…" Saniya's eyes were now open, her silky hair wet from the rain, her pale eyes full and radiant, her smile both warm and welcoming.

Syros did not respond and solely continued his idle staring out into the open forest. He didn't even glance at her as she calmly raised her head from his midriff.

"Have a good sleep?" Saniya continued cautiously, unnerved by his lack of response. Noticing his absent expression, she added, "I used to watch you all the time when we were together in Asterleigh, when it was you, me and Torjan. You were always so sad. I would ask Torjan what we could do to make you happy, or seem happy at least. I felt something change inside me as the days passed by and as I continued to search your eyes for some sign that inside you felt alive. And now, whenever I look at you, I don't know what's real." She gave an embarrassed laugh, her face suddenly flushing crimson. "I love you, Sy. I have always loved you. And I will continue to until the day I die," she whispered, as she gently stroked his arms. "Oh Syros." She sighed, softly kissing his chest. "What do I have to do to make you happy?"

"I want to die," he said, revealing to her a knife in his hands. "Please San, you have to do it…"

She stared back at him in shock and attempted to forge words that her mouth would not allow her. They continued their silent staring, until he heard thudding footsteps approaching their location. It was Petula, drenched in rain, which almost covered the fact she was crying.

"San," she spoke desperately, undeterred by their nakedness. "Please come… it's Hurus…"

"What's wrong?"

"Please…"

Swiftly, they reached for their clothes and together followed Petula through the woods and back to camp. The fire had burnt out; many of the Alpelites were awake and drying themselves off, getting ready to break camp for the long arduous journey to the United Human borders. Petula moved through them assertively, as Saniya and Syros followed behind her. He could feel Saniya's eyes on him as they walked, but he could not return her gaze. Petula led them to a tent where Hurus lay upon a blood-soaked bed, his eyes shut and face as grey as the rainclouds filling the sky above. Lit candles were spread out throughout the tent's interior, flickering weakly. Two old Alpelite females, whom Syros assumed were caring for Hurus, stood over him with herbs and medicine. Syros moved forwards and crouched down beside his bed, as Hurus slowly opened his eyes.

"Sy…" Hurus spoke faintly, after he determined the identity of his visitor; his voice was distant and afraid.

"I'm here, Hurus."

"I think I'm dying, Sy…" were the last words Hurus uttered before all light in his eyes disappeared.

Petula let out a wail, as Saniya cradled her in her arms. Syros did not feel anything as he continued to grasp onto Hurus's hand. Nothing ran through his mind except for the words, *Lucky for some.* All that could be heard was Petula's fierce weeping, along with Saniya's breaking words of attempted comfort. He continued to consider the lifeless corpse of his dead comrade until he heard a frantic voice calling to him from the outside.

"Where is Syros? Is he here?"

Bora was peering through the tent's opening, eyes both wide and panic-stricken. "Syros…" it panted. "They have come…"

Feeling so very hollow, Syros let go of Hurus's hand. And, once again ignoring the desperate appeal from Saniya, he made his way out of this place of sadness and death to the outside, filled with just as much of both.

"The Venians?" Syros asked Bora, as the two walked away from the gathering crowd of curious Alpelites.

Bora gave a wide-eyed nod. "They said they want to speak with you."

"Me?" Syros asked, as they walked into the depths of the woods. "Why? Did they tell you?"

Bora shook its head. "They said to keep walking into the forest and they will appear before you."

"Okay," Syros said, sheathing a loose sword into his belt.

"You're going to go now? Without a plan?"

"As you said before, Bora," Syros shrugged, "if the Venians truly wanted us dead, they would have done it already," he finished, before pushing past the thick branches, entering the darkness of the trees.

Syros journeyed far into the once placid forest; the forest that had always brought him wonderment as a child and that was most likely now to be the place of his death. The rain had picked up in strength; he was drenched in the torrent that fell from the trees. He continued to push past branches and leaves. He did not know where the Venian would appear, but he guessed it didn't really matter as they could rise from the ground at any time. He clutched firmly on to the top of his sword's grip; if he had to fight he was ready, even if there was no chance of victory.

He walked to a clearing that seemed familiar. Was this where he had been only moments ago with Saniya? It appeared the same, but how could it be? He was certain he had not travelled in that direction. *It must be the same location*, he thought. It was, of course in the darkness of early morning that he had come here, led by Saniya. The sweet pure-hearted Saniya. One of the only people in this world who had ever truly cared about him. *I must be a monster*, he reflected, as he sat underneath the same tree where they had been the previous night. He heard birds starting their morning chorus above him and watched a young fox cub run past. Laying his head back upon the tree's bark, he closed his eyes and waited. If the Venians truly wanted to see him, they could appear here. He was done with acting upon the whims of another. He placed his head in his hands and started to cry, more fiercely and uncontrollably than he had ever previously done in his entire life. *Oh god, I'm such a piece of shit… San… I'm so sorry.*

"Human, why are you crying?"

"Because I'm a monster…"

"Yes, you are… but no more than the rest of us."

Syros opened his eyes to see the face of a Venian peering down at him; much like his first encounter with the species, its face stuck out from the tree only a foot or so above him. He stood up and stepped back, allowing the tree to part, and watched the Venian emerge.

"Morning, human."

"Morning," he returned, eyeing the Venian claw its way from the opening.

The Venian stepped out and gave him a smile. "I have always enjoyed these parts of the woods… very… romantic." Its emerald eyes twinkled as it spoke.

Syros began to feel unnerved. Had the Venian been watching him last night with Saniya?

"Don't be so surprised," it uttered, its extraordinarily thin mouth stretching. "As I told you on the first night we spoke, we have eyes everywhere, in the biggest trees and in the smallest blades of grass; we see everything. You have no secrets, not from us, human."

"Why have you not killed us?"

"We wanted to, but we were ordered not to."

"That's nice of you… I thought you were supposed to be pacifists, anyway?"

The Venian nodded in agreement. "We were… however, blind pacifism is foolish, especially when true opportunity for change presents itself so miraculously."

"That glowing Entity who destroyed Ankor?" Syros thought back to the moment he watched the unworldly demi-god type figure ascend into the air before setting off the huge volcanic eruption. "He was the one who ordered you not to kill us?"

The Venian gave a slow, approving motion, its wide eyes becoming even wider, as if it were growing in excitement.

"Why? Why does he want us alive?"

"Us?" The Venian sounded bemused. "Our Lord and Saviour does not want the rest of your company. Only you."

"Okay," Syros restarted, his mind working at the speed of light. "Then why does your Lord and Saviour want me alive?"

The Venian appeared to give a motion that reminded Syros of indifference. "He says he sees something inside you."

Syros could not process what he was hearing; he felt so tired; he had not slept all night or eaten a proper meal in weeks. And now the Venian was delivering upon him this type of information. He had only met eyes with the unworldly Entity for a fraction of a moment within the Palace. Was it possible this strange being had looked into him in that short period of time. Into his very soul?

"The night of Sechen's passing is soon upon us..." the Venian continued, its apparent growth in excitement not quelling. "Come find us on Yima's Fields, we shall be waiting for you, human."

He knew Yima's Fields – they stretched open for miles to the west of Asterleigh. Surely first they would have to make it past the border – but how would that even be possible?

"What's going to happen on Sechen's passing?" he asked, fearing the answer.

The Venian stared back, its eyes emotionless and refusing to flicker. It slowly started to recede into the ground. "You already know what is going to happen... Our Lord and Saviour has promised us salvation in the stars. And to do so, well... I feel the expression you humans use, out with the old and in with the new, is suitable?" It smiled as its face became one with the muddy terrain below it.

"Wait!" Syros yelled helplessly. The rain now fell harder than it had all year round. He slumped to his knees, utterly defeated. *It's over*, he gravely contemplated. *The world was going to end and there was no way to prevent it.* Water fell from his long uncut hair, streaming down his face. If he hadn't already expelled the last of his tears earlier, perhaps they too would be pouring from him. *Salvation in the stars*, he thought staring skywards, *sounds pleasant.*

"Yes?" a voice caused him to jump, completely startled.

The Venian's head had appeared once more, "I can't stay for very long, human... I must admit I do hate the rain."

"We can stop this from happening!" Syros pleaded franticly, stumbling towards the head sticking out from the ground. "We can make this a better world for all of us. Our species can live together in peace, I know we can! Please, just give us one more chance!"

The Venian had a look of sheer annoyance across its face. "You truly called me back for this? This day has been far too long overdue, human; I fear this moment has been coming since before you first entered into existence. It has been destined ever since your kind first arrived here."

"You have compassion... I've seen it," he told the

creature, desperately searching its eyes. "You could have left me and my friend in the forest to die the first time we met. Please, you can still help us…."

"Compassion?" the Venian responded, as if he were nothing more than an insect wallowing in dirt. "How do you think you have survived this long? Who do you think caught you when you and the Alpelite jumped off that cliff, falling to your certain doom? We have shown far too much compassion already. Where has your compassion been for all these years, when the Alpelites and the humans butchered each other upon our soil? You insult us, you insult this entire world that has brought you in and kept you living for all these years, as if you were our very own. We loved you like you were our children. And you broke our hearts."

"What did happen to our home world? Did the first ancestral humans ever tell you?" Syros asked, both broken and quiet, resigned to his loss.

The creature pulled a face as if it were reminiscing, much as a human did, on the years of its youth. "Surprisingly, they didn't. Perhaps even they themselves did not know. Maybe a situation like this one occurred and that old world you inhabited also wanted you gone. Or perhaps you just got lost in the clouds and forgot how to land. Either way, human, you have taken far too much of my time already…" it finished, now with an air of sadness, before beginning to recede once more.

"Are you truly going to abandon your home world?" Syros shouted, as the head became one with the soil. "After you were born in the very heart of Vena?"

"As long as we survive, Vena shall live through us!" the Venian responded, its face now disappearing entirely. "Come and find us on the night of Sechen's passing!"

Syros sat alone in the muddy dirt of the planet that was never his home. He wondered what the humans' home world had been like; was it a little less war-stricken than this one? Or was it even worse? Did their gods also stand by as the innocent died in droves? Did the very world itself seem like it wanted our deaths for what we had done to it, just like this one? He wondered how life would have been if he, Ednon and their parents had been born there. Would they have been fortunate or unfortunate to live in such a place?

Syros stumbled his way back through the forest, his body soaked and mind rampant, his stomach empty and feelings dissipating. In this moment, he felt very much designed as if all of his life had been predetermined. "We do what we must for humanity's sake, Syros..." He recalled Captain Lars Raynmaher telling him these words in his tent. *You old bastard, see where your humanity got you... you're dead now along with the rest of them. All the others you managed to blind with your bullshit. How many were senselessly killed over the centuries? To have a sense of pride in one's own species. To become a useful cog for humanity. Well, I don't want to be buried underneath the weight of your humanity any longer. You've cursed me with it... I want out... I want out... I want out...I want out...*

Walking back into camp, he saw Saniya and Bora standing outside the tent in which Hurus, only a few moments ago, had died. He moved upon them, before reaching out to Saniya and bringing her into an embrace.

"Syros… it's Petula, she… she's gone… I couldn't stop her…"

"What happened?" Syros asked, his heart feeling as though it had dropped to the bottom of his stomach.

Saniya could not respond, instead opting to place her hands in front of her streaming eyes.

Bora's stare was fixed upon the ground. "It's not just the girl… Many of the Alpelites have also taken their own lives."

"Well…" Syros said, in a voice so distant and emotionless it scared even him. "Let's bury the dead."

"Oh, Sy, please… I don't want you to die."

"I'm not going to. And neither will you. None of us will."

"How?" Bora asked, raising its head to match his. "What did the Venian tell you?"

"We need to reach Asterleigh as soon as possible," he said, deciding against telling them the specifics of his meeting with the Venian. "Tell the Alpelites we need to break camp immediately."

Bora gave a nod, then proceeded to make its way round the camp, telling them all the news.

"Is there a chance that we're not going to die, Syros?" Saniya asked him, still engulfed within his arms. *My true delicate flower*, he thought caressing the top of her head, *sooner or later we all die.*

"Keep holding on to me, San," he told her. "Just keep holding onto me and everything will be okay."

Days became nights as they continued to travel westwards and, as instructed, Saniya had not left his arms. Much like the Venians, it was now as if they were one. When they slept, they did so in each other's arms; when they ate, they did so side by side; when they went to relieve themselves, they even did so in each other's company. She held onto him as dearly as he held onto himself and his own state of mind. But now he was more scared for hers than he was for his own. Options weighed in his psyche like a ship's anchor, causing his travel across the waves of time to desist. What was he to do? Join the Venians in the stars? Or stay here in this desolate place, but die alongside the woman he loved? He hoped when the time came he would make the correct decision, but an ominous feeling now gripped him, so dark and apparent it was all he felt aware of.

Out of the forest, they could see the stone walls of the Human Empire's borders. The walls were high, stretching skywards for over fifty feet. The night was late, so Syros could not tell if any guards lay sentry upon its gates. The company walked towards the large drawbridge over an empty moat. There were now only a couple of hundred of them; many of the Alpelites had either died before making it to this point or instead had had a change of heart and decided to head back east to try and find some salvation there. Syros stepped forwards, Saniya still entwined with him, and gazed up to the drawbridge. *What were the Venians planning?* he asked himself as the rain continued to fall. At any moment, the drawbridge could lower and the human military could rush out to slaughter them.

"I had a dream last night, Syros. Want to hear what it was about?"

"Tell me about your dream, San…"

"Well, it's the same as every night." She spoke quietly, gazing at him from his chest. "I dreamt that Medzu was crying tears of blood – even without eyes, I could tell it was crying. The sky behind it had parted. And the tears fell upon us like rain, until it took us all, like a wave hitting against the rocks. What do you think it means?"

Nothing good, he thought. "Do you want to know what I dreamt about?" he said, giving her the best smile he could. "I dreamt you and I grew old together. We got a farm on one of the islands off the mainland. We had children. A boy and a girl. And Torjan was there with us also. Wouldn't that be wonderful?"

"It would be. But that's never going to happen, is it?"

He stared back wordlessly, before a voice saved him.

"What's the plan, Syros?" Bora asked, stepping forward. Its once strong body had become skinny and weak.

"I—" he began, before he heard a loud clanking sound. Shocked, he noticed the drawbridge lowering in front of them.

What happened? Had the humans decided to let them in? Warily, the horde moved forwards. Human bodies lay across every inch of the interior. There must have been at least fifty dead humans, all dressed in military uniforms, and above the carnage stood the Venians, their large emerald eyes as wide as their malevolent grins.

"You didn't have to kill them," Syros told one of the Venians directly near him.

"No," the Venian agreed, its expression becoming delirious. "No. We didn't…"

The throng behind had joined them inside, their faces shocked. Yells could be heard as they saw the Venians along with the piles of dead humans.

"The night of Sechen's passing is approaching," the Venians whispered, beginning their journey downwards. "We shall be seeing you soon."

"What do they mean, Sy?" Saniya said, looking up at him.

"Nothing," he returned, his stomach feeling violently ill. "Don't worry about it."

"What do we do now?"

He knew what he was going to do. *I'm going to find Ed*, he thought to himself. *I don't care if I have to search this entire land. I'm going to find Ed, even if it's the last thing I ever do.*

The Golden Generation

Ira sat alone upon a boat drifting across the slow-moving tides of the great Asterleigh Lake; sighing to himself, he reeled in his fishing rod. It had been close to four hours, yet he was still to catch one fish. He gave a glance down to the bucket – bait was quickly disappearing and night was fast approaching. It was now or never. He searched skywards to the Medzu statue. The stars had begun to appear behind the effigy in the clouds; the celebration of Sechen's passing was going to be beginning soon. *They can wait,* Ira reasoned to himself. *There is always time to drink.* He had hired a small boat and rowed out here by himself. He liked the water; he enjoyed its calmness and he appreciated the time he got to reflect. Plus, the scenery was unbeatable. The night was in its twilight stage. There was no better time to cast a gaze towards the great God in all its miraculous wonder. Kissing his knuckles, he raised his fist to the air and prayed that Medzu would bring him luck.

As Ira rowed back to shore, he could make out a figure in the distance waiting for him. After he made it to the silky yellow sand, he could distinguish who it was.

"Any luck?" Fergus smiled, after Ira planted his feet upon the golden particles.

"None," Ira grieved. "Not one damn fish."

"Oh well." Fergus moved forwards to embrace his friend. "Perhaps your luck will come later. I hear Jung has arranged quite a spectacular night for us."

Ira laughed. "If I know Jung, then I'm sure whatever he has planned involves a plethora of alcohol."

"I'm sure that it does," Fergus chuckled. "Well, you've deserved it, friend. It's been a very strenuous year." He studied Ira for a moment before continuing, "What do you think about?"

"What do you mean?"

"When you're off on your own… what do you think about? You have always enjoyed your privacy. Even when we were growing up in Madale. At first, I thought I was just bad company, but even after we moved to Asterleigh, and even now that we have made so many new friends, you always make these arrangements to be by yourself."

Ira kept silent, which gave Fergus enough time to continue.

"Thinking about how you can save us mere mortals?"

"Sometimes I think that it's all for nought," Ira admitted. "That our teachings are falling upon deaf ears. There still seems no end in sight to the war, even after all we have done."

Fergus gave his short brown goatee a caress. "The people hear you more than you may think. Many are coming around to our way of thinking. We have planted the seeds into their minds. They now know this doesn't have to be the way things are. That their children don't have to be sent to a war that shows no sign of ending, to face an enemy many have never met. Your message is persevering, friend. You have become famous in this city."

"Yes, well, we don't do it for fame, do we, Fergus?"

"No," Fergus agreed, "of course not. Who needs to give the military more reasons for beatings, eh? That's the problem with becoming a prophet, there will always be those who wish to silence you." Fergus grabbed him by the shoulders. "Come now, Ira. Tonight shall be a time to forget all that. Let's go; the others are waiting for us."

They walked through the streets of Asterleigh; people swarmed the streets in a joyous party atmosphere. As Ira and Fergus moved down one particularly narrow alleyway, a group of military personnel, who had previously been all smiles and drunken laughter, became silent as they noticed the two men walking towards them.

"Watch out… this may be trouble…" Fergus advised quietly.

As Fergus and Ira moved past, the stockiest of the military men violently pushed against Ira with his shoulder, knocking him to the ground.

"Coward! Friend to the savages…"

Fergus lifted him back to his feet. "Come, Ira… just ignore them."

However, Ira had been in this situation plenty of times before, so he knew that a beating was soon to take place. The men had a mixture of rage and disgust across their faces, but to his surprise the group carried on, moving past them and into the centre of Asterleigh. *This must be my lucky day,* Ira thought to himself, watching the men as they sauntered down the stone-cobbled street. Perhaps his prayer to Medzu had not been in vain.

They eventually reached a tavern known simply as Oedipia's Temporal. *Strange name for a tavern,* Ira pondered to himself, whenever he saw the golden sign. With a slight push from Fergus, the doors opened and in walked the two men. The tavern was busy and rambunctious with loud hearty laughter, with men and women in each corner of the bar. It was not hard to find Jung, as like most drunken evenings, and even in a room filled with so many people, his voice carried the loudest by far. Jung noticed them as they entered and, with a beaming smile, he moved forward to embrace them both.

"Happy New Year, dear friend. Sorry to say I did not wait for you. I must admit I have already had a few…"

"Settle down, Jung." Ira chuckled. "The night is still young; one day you may find that your drinking gets the better of you."

"You are very wise, very wise…" The full-bearded man staggered back and forth as he nodded. "Your words have never been lost on me. Not like those pricks over there." Jung gestured to a group of men wearing red military uniform with gold braid, sitting together at one of the tables on the opposite side of the room.

Ira shook his head. "My dear Jung… what kind of message does it send if we go around getting into fights? How will that help our cause?"

Jung growled. "Bahhh… out of respect to you, my brother, I shall keep my distance…"

"Thank you. Now, let us drink and be merry."

Hours passed by inside the tavern; Ira was surprised by just how many people came up to him to offer their words of praise. There were now many who sat at his table – it had been as Fergus said, it appeared he had become quite the celebrity within the golden-laced city. Then, Ira noticed her; a woman had walked into the tavern, her long blonde hair swayed with every footstep, her eyes so full and radiant that in this moment Ira knew that she was the girl he was going to marry.

"Who is she?" Ira marvelled, watching the woman as she walked to the front of the bar.

"Are you okay?" Jung laughed, as the men at the table searched for the woman that Ira had spoken of. "I don't think I've ever seen you like this. How are you feeling? Perhaps it's best if you went home to bed."

"She is beautiful…" Fergus uttered, as his eyes too locked on the woman.

"That's the woman I'm going to marry."

"Not if I marry her first."

Ira turned to Fergus. "We're in quite a predicament, friend." He brought out a single golden coin. "Well, what do you say, brother? A single toss of the coin to determine our fates. Heads I talk to her, tails for yourself."

As he searched Fergus's expression, he could tell the man was worried. "Okay," Fergus replied after a moment. Tossing the coin into the air, Ira felt relief run through him as the golden piece landed upon the table, head side up.

"Yes!"

"It's just as always…" Fergus grimaced, taking a deep sip of ale, before slamming the empty glass back upon the table. "The great Ira always gets his way… all of the recognition… all of the luck…"

"Better luck next time, friend," Ira smiled, giving Fergus a pat on the shoulders, before promptly getting up from the table.

The unknown woman was standing alone. Ira was surprised at how no other suitors had moved in. Not wanting to waste any time, he quickly made his way over.

"May I buy you drink?" he asked.

The woman's deep amber eyes locked on his own. "Why yes, Ira, you may."

"You know my name?"

"But of course, who does not know of the great Ira, traitor to his own kind and sympathiser to the savages."

"I've heard worse."

"Yes, so have I. I was merely being kind."

"What is your name?"

"Orla."

"A very beautiful name, if I may say so."

"I hear you are a strange man," Orla studied him from head to toe. "A strange man with strange ideals. It appears you are completely loathed by some and utterly adored by others."

Ira grinned. "What side are you on?"

"I'm not sure," Orla returned his smile. "I've only just met you…"

"Well then, how about we do this again, say this time nex—" A loud crash and angry yells caused everyone in the tavern to stop in their tracks. Ira turned to see that Jung had one of the military men caught within a headlock and an enormous fight had broken out between the two groups.

Ira let out a sigh. "He told me he wasn't going to do anything…"

"Friends of yours?" Orla's eyes widened, shocked at just how violent the exchange of blows was becoming.

Ira shook his head. "Sadly, yes… if you would excuse me, I must sort this mess out."

"Until next time, friend of the savages."

"Yes, until next time."

As he made his way over to the brawl, he heard the tavern doors shut. It appeared that Fergus was no longer here among them. He reached in his pocket, retrieved the coin and studied it before giving one last glance towards Orla. He wondered just how lucky he had truly been this night.

A full year passed by and, as Ira had predicted, it was the day of his wedding to Orla. He watched the guests arriving and was saddened to see that his oldest and dearest friend had not come.

"Did you send word to him?" Orla caressed the back of his shoulders.

"I tried… but I have no idea where he is."

"I'm sorry, my love. But we best not let it spoil our day."

"No. Best not."

"Anyway, it appears that somebody else wants your

time…" Orla gestured to a young, short, pear-shaped man who was waddling his way down the hall wearing what Ira assumed was an exceedingly expensive black suit. As the man got to within a couple of yards, he fell nervously to one knee.

"Ira…" The man spoke in reverence, keeping his stare fixed upon the ground. "It is an honour. Forgive me. But to meet one's heroes, a man who could truly be called an equal of the five great gods of mythology. I'm afraid I am awestruck."

"Get up, Luther," Ira pleaded. "You're embarrassing me."

Luther lifted his head and awkwardly got to his feet. "It is an honour to meet you as well, my lady," he said, facing Orla.

Orla laughed. "My lady? I am not royalty, young man. I work in a bakery."

The short chubby man's face reddened. "Ira, I must confide something in you. Your teachings, they mean a great deal to me. I lie awake at night thinking of what you say; the world is a wicked place, filled with wicked people, sometimes I feel like I can't take it. The sorrow, I mean, it follows me constantly, like a shadow being cast from an eternal sun."

Ira placed a hand upon Luther's shoulder. "Do not despair, friend, for one day soon the suns shall both rise, illuminating the darkness – and the new age shall be ushered in; as our dissonance reaches its most violent and bloody, it shall come, and then a glorious light shall engulf these lands, curing all of our collective sorrow."

Luther's eyes watered, and if Ira was not mistaken, he could hear the man weeping as he waddled away.

"Is he going to be okay?" Orla asked, after she was sure Luther was out of earshot. "He seems a little obsessed…"

"Luther was born to a rich tycoon off the mainland. Money is all he's known. He will never love the common people, or they him, for he has never been among them. Though his heart appears to be in the right place." He gave his bride-to-be a wide grin, as he placed his hand upon her belly. "So?" he asked. "A boy or a girl?"

"A girl," Orla responded, after a moment's thought.

"Yes," Ira agreed. "I think you may be right."

Twenty years had gone by. Ira stood in front of Orla's grave, the wind swirled around him as he placed the red roses upon the headstone. As he stared at the burial place, he remembered all the moments they had shared together and all the moments they had missed.

"I wish I'd had a chance to meet her…" said Karina, placing her head upon her father's shoulders.

"The day you were born was the happiest I had ever seen her. I know it hasn't been easy on you, all these years."

"You have been a great father," she told him. "I couldn't have asked for a better role model. Not only for me, but for Syros also."

Syros was holding onto his mother's hand. Ira knelt upon one knee to face the young lad.

"You're going to be a brother soon, Syros. That's a lot of responsibility."

The lad acted shy whenever Ira was present and sheepishly hid behind his mother. "So…" Ira spoke to Karina. "Have you heard any news?"

"They say it's going to be a boy."

"Have you thought of a name?"

"Ednon."

"Ednon…" Ira repeated. "I can't wait to see what kind of man he grows into. You have a long life ahead of you. I'm sure they will both grow up to be kind, gentle and wise. Are you happy, my dear?"

"Yes, Father. Very."

"Good, then that makes me happy also."

Ira was back in his cottage in his home of Jovian. And in the flickering candle fire, he got out one of his many paintings of Orla and caressed the picture. A storm was brewing outside; he could hear the roars of distant thunder yet, despite this, he felt content. Just as he leaned back upon his chair, his mind and body drifting off into the dream world, he suddenly heard loud banging against his door. Wondering who it was that wanted his time, Ira got up from his chair, made his way to the entrance and slowly opened the door.

"Ira, can I come in?" Fergus spoke, the harsh downpour from the torrent drenched the man from head to toe. Ira studied his friend's face – he was now old and grey much like himself. After all these years apart, Ira didn't know how he felt in this moment, but if he could have described it, he would have said he was overcome with joy.

"Yes, Fergus," Ira said, opening the door further. "Please do…"

21

Transcendence

1 Day until the New Year

It was the morning before the night of Sechen's passing. *I must get to Ira's grave soon*, Ednon thought, as he scanned the skies to see black rain-clouds heading over the mountains. He had already bought the flowers earlier that morning from the florist girl he now knew as Dashera. He continued to walk through the packed streets, past the Central Asterleigh School, when a hand grasped his shoulders from behind.

"Good morning, young master," a low familiar voice spoke in his ear.

He turned his head to see it was none other than the exceptionally massive Memphis holding onto him, preventing any movement.

"Memphis!" Ednon stammered in shock. "I thought the military had caught you?"

"They tried, young master." The Elder gave a menacing smirk. "They broke into my home, but only to find a highly shocking surprise… One with a most explosive quality."

"I—" Ednon began. He did not know what to say. He thought all the Elders apart from Luther had already been apprehended. Memphis had always scared him, but never had he been so close. In this moment, Ednon now realised he was utterly terrified of this man.

"Young master, I must ask that you follow me. It is of the greatest importance."

"Why? What is it?"

Memphis's foreboding smile did not diminish. "There is a way we can save Abacus. Now, young master. If you wouldn't mind following me."

"A way to save Abacus? How?"

"All in due time…" Memphis replied. Ednon could tell the man's patience was wearing thin.

"I need to lay these flowers at Ira—" he began, before he suddenly felt something cold and sharp press up against his back. *It was undoubtedly a blade*, Ednon thought, beginning to feel himself sweat.

"I'm afraid I'm not asking, young maverick." Memphis pushed the blade closer. "Come, Ed, I wouldn't want to break those little legs of yours."

He stuttered a response, but, before he could find any words, he heard a loud booming sound. He turned around to see that the school had disappeared into a sea of flames. The Asterlieghians on the streets began to yell – falling into complete pandemonium. Ednon watched in dismay, while Memphis just let out a cold laugh.

"Come now, Ed, we must go before the commotion dies down..." and with that he started to drag Ednon, leading him down a nearby alley. All eyes were upon the fire, so no one noticed as Memphis forced him into the shadows of the alleyway. It seemed like any other, a dead end, with piles of rubbish. Memphis pushed on one exceptionally large barrel. Ednon was startled. There was no way one man alone could move such a thing; it was too filled to the brim with all sorts of junk. Nevertheless, the sheer strength and might of Memphis did manage to move the barrel enough to reveal a hidden passageway, completely darkened, presumably leading to the subterranean network. Without giving Ednon any time to respond, Memphis viciously grabbed his hand, knocking the flowers onto the floor and took him, for the second time in Ednon's life, into the world buried far beneath the surface.

Back within the underground web, Memphis led him from out in front, constantly glancing back to check if Ednon were indeed following. *What kind of man is this?* Ednon thought to himself, watching the back of the tall Elder as they journeyed through the darkness of the corridors. To be able to take life without even a second thought or feeling. This man may even be worse than Luther. *No*, Ednon reassessed, *this man was merely a lap-dog*; he even tried to copy the same fashion sense as his pear-shaped boss. Memphis clearly was not blind, as his movements were free, yet it still appeared that he never took off the shades. *No, this man was not worse than Luther.* The two times he had previously met the short man, self-proclaimed with safeguarding the new age of humanity, he sensed only the darkest of evils. But to save the life of Abacus, which would then in turn make Amelia and Jernett happy, he would have to endure being in their presence. Even if it did make his stomach feel violently ill.

"Who are we going to meet?" Ednon asked, after a few minutes of silent travel.

"Don't talk!"

And with that Ednon returned to silence; the man was clearly not in the mood for idle chatter. In fact, it appeared as if he was doing all he could to prevent himself from attacking Ednon outright. So, he instead decided to focus his mind on other things as they moved through intersection upon intersection. He began to study the ground, trying to find markers in case the time came when he would have to make his escape. He was surprised to see the network so desolate and empty; he had assumed after he and Jung had told Ethna of this place's existence that it would be swarming with military men loyal to the state. Despite this, there did not appear to be anyone. He realised the web went on for miles, so perhaps the military hadn't been to this specific area. Or maybe even they were too scared to venture into this place, so dark and foreboding it seemed like only the vermin of the sewers could ever truly call it their home.

After what felt like hours, they reached a door much like the one he had come to last time he was here with Abacus and Levy by his side, but now he was alone. Feeling so very vulnerable, he watched as Memphis loudly pounded upon the door. There was an unlocking sound from the other side, before it slowly creaked open to reveal a sight that startled him immensely.

"Jung? Fergus?"

The room was small. However, it was big enough to be filled by ten people. Jung was tied to a chair in the centre, while the others stood behind a desk, where Fergus was sitting opposite the beaten and torn old man. Among the ten who stood around the room was Luther, standing much shorter than the other muscled men. He gave a sinister grin as Memphis pushed Ednon inside.

"Fergus, don't!" Jung pleaded. "Ednon is only a child; has your heart really grown so cold in your old age? Don't make him pay for my crimes."

"I feel your darkened mind leads you astray, old friend. Ed is only down here for a chat, nothing more."

"Ed…" Jung spoke desperately. "Run… get as far away as you possibly can!"

At that moment, Memphis, who was still standing directly behind him, placed his hands on Ednon's shoulders, meaning even if he had wanted to run, he couldn't.

"Come, Jung, Ednon has no reason to be afraid of us," Fergus said, standing up from his desk and walking around to stand next to the tied and battered ex-Elder.

"He has every reason in the world to be afraid of you…" Jung responded, his eyes flowing tears of red from newly opened scars. "Fergus, please… he's Ira's grandson."

"Ira's dead," Fergus said softly, placing his hand over Jung's face to quell the stream of blood. "And soon you will be as well… Take him," he demanded to two of the men

269

behind him. "Take him into the next room and make sure his death is a quiet one."

With kicks and loud curses, Jung was taken screaming out of the room by the two large goons. Ednon watched in shock, his mind unable to process what was happening.

"Meet death with some degree of grace, old friend! And rejoice! The moment we have been working towards for so long is soon approaching!" Jung's yells started to become fainter, as Memphis once again pushed Ednon forwards.

"Sit, Ednon," Fergus continued, pointing towards the chair from which Jung had just been dragged.

"Please, don't kill Jung, please…" Ednon begged, as Memphis forcibly placed him onto the chair before tying his arms and legs.

"The man is a traitor. He turned against the very Order that he, myself and your grandfather gave birth to all those years ago. How can I allow this type of parasite to be in my presence for even one more moment?"

"Because he's your friend…" Ednon stared into the eyes of the old man. "Ira wouldn't have wanted this either… "

"I have known Jung for almost fifty years; your grandfather also. However, I feel no regret. A smidgen perhaps…" he re-thought to himself suddenly, "for the way things used to be. But for the future, I feel only happiness. And, to be honest with you, I don't care what Ira thinks, because he's dead, so it really doesn't matter how my dear old comrade feels. My work is for the living, not the dead or indeed their memories."

"What do you want with me? Why did you bring me down here?"

"You have some very valuable information. Our dear young fellow Abacus told us this, before his death."

"A-abacus's... death..."

"The man served his function. Come, Ednon, you act as if the man did not have it coming. However, he was loyal to our Order right to the very end. For this, I give him some credit. Now, Ed," he promptly spoke up, changing the line of conversation. "Tell me who the Supreme Leader—"

"And what makes you think I will ever tell you?"

"Because if you don't, then we will kill the girl," Fergus said in a way that lacked all emotion. "The mother also."

Ednon began to breathe heavily. He gazed around the room at the others who were staring back at him as eagerly as wolves eyeing a carcass. There was no way out of this, Ednon lamented, as his eyes fixed on Luther's smug face. Abacus was dead, but that did not mean Jernett and Amelia had to die as well.

"Her name's Ethna Gibbon. She lives in the Temple of Yashin," he told them, his heart and mind filled with shame.

Fergus gave a slow nod, before gesturing to two of the men behind him. "Dispatch the orders. You two..." he continued, pointing to two more. "Patrol the halls. Make sure no one has followed Memphis down here." In unison, all four of the men agreed, before they made their way out of the room to do the newly given tasks. "Thank you, Ed. We tried to get the information out of Jung, but the man seemed to prefer death. Silly really, how when he tells our secrets he does so with a mouth as wide open as Medzu, but whenever we want access to his knowledge of someone who has ordered the deaths of thousands upon thousands, he remains so very tongue-tied."

"Fergus!" Luther guffawed gleefully, stepping forwards. "The hour is upon us. It is time for the two branches of our Order to unite, so we may lead the masses into the new world." The short man started to smile, but quickly lost it after noticing the abrupt silence that had engulfed the room.

"The two branches?" Fergus uttered, as if what Luther had said insulted him deeply. "There has only ever been our branch. Since the early days, when the teachings of Ira were first implemented, we have always been the true pacifists." He made his way over to Luther, who was visibly shaking, before removing the shades to reveal the beaten and burnt sockets where the short fat man's eyes had once been. "I thought when we did this to you all those years ago, you would have learnt your place and realised your ambition was as blind as your vision, but it seemed only to strengthen it. And for this, I must respect you." Luther's trembling grew, as Fergus slowly outstretched his arms. "Embrace me, friend. For the dream is finally realised."

Luther blindly stepped forwards, attempting to locate the elderly Fergus. As he moved close enough to make contact, Fergus retrieved a knife from his front pocket and quickly jammed it into Luther's neck. Memphis started to yell, but promptly stopped himself, realising the position he was in. The blood from Luther's neck rained through the air as if from a burst pipe, spraying across each of the onlookers' faces. Desperately trying to prevent the rampant flow of blood, Luther fell to the floor, twitching violently, before turning completely still.

"What kind of a man are you? Just what is life to you?" Ednon asked Fergus, who was cleaning off his blade as if it were mere cutlery retaining a small stain.

"You act as if people don't die, Ednon. Are you really going to tell me you will weep tears for this man?"

"Life is precious!" Ednon snapped, trying helplessly to break from his confinement. "To be able to take it so easily is nothing short of demonic. You truly believe this is what being a pacifist is?"

Fergus moved, step by step, closer towards him. "If life is so precious, then why do men kill other men so easily? Why do parents murder their children? Why are wars fought so viciously over such trivial matters? The individual's life is meaningless. All of our lives are nothing but expendable – do not kid yourself into thinking it is anything different."

"Why are you doing this?" Ednon found some hidden courage from somewhere. "You aren't doing this so the Alpelites can reclaim their homeland. What's your true goal?"

"My true goal? Well… I'm doing this for God."

"God?" Ednon returned, taken aback; *which God was the man referring to?*

"I hear the voices calling to me… As I go on my morning strolls through the meadows, as I care for the flowers in my garden, as the trees gently sway in the wind. This world wants our deaths. I have heard it from the soil itself, with as much clarity as anything that has ever before befallen me…"

Ednon looked at the man, startled. *He is insane*, Ednon thought. *He heard Vena talking to him? How is that possible?*

"And then…" Fergus continued, his voice filled with

reverence, "once as I walked through the star-filled night in the meadows near my home in Lowton, I saw him beneath the moonlight. I stared back into the two empty voids of a God and he told me salvation in the stars would be waiting for me, as long as I carried out my mission."

"And what is your mission?" Ednon asked, staring at Fergus, who was now completely lost within his own awe. *The two empty voids? The same he had been seeing constantly over the past couple of months? Was it a coincidence? Or was it all true, what the phantom had said about the world ending on the night of Sechen's passing?*

"Listen carefully, Ed…" Fergus said, closing his eyes and placing a hand against his ear. "The bombs have begun to set off. Any second now, the Venians alongside our Lord and Saviour will enter the city and bring us all our end."

The other men in the room quickly glanced at each other; apparently, they had not been told of this grand scheme until this moment. He attempted once more to break from his confinements, but to no avail. *Amelia*, he thought desperately to himself, *please, I need to find Amelia.* He heard a loud thunderous roar in the distance as the room began to shake. Then a second. Then a third.

"Stop this, Fergus!" he yelled hysterically, the dust of the ceiling falling upon them as the explosions and shaking continued. Fergus moved steadily towards him, blade in hand, pointing it directly towards Ednon's heart.

"I'm sorry, Ed…" Fergus said sadly, moving the blade only an inch or so from him. "When you see Ira, do tell him I'm sorry. Just close your eyes… it's all a bad dream, Ed… it's all just a bad dream…"

He did not even feel the blade as it entered his chest; it was as if he were viewing his death from some place that was not his own self. The blood gushed from his chest onto the floor and he felt his eyelids closing as he began to lose his senses. *My death…* he thought to himself, as his mind started to turn completely blank. *Ira… I will be with you soon.* His thoughts went to Amelia and how he was never going to see her again. *I'm sorry, Am. I'm sorry I couldn't save you…* The moments passed as he desperately tried to cling onto his consciousness. His vision blurred; he witnessed Fergus cleaning off the blade. He was dying… this was it… *Am…* He felt something rustling up against his feet, as two long blue antennae came into his view. It was the creature, curling up beside him.

"Orla…" he spoke faintly, feeling his consciousness slowly dissipating into the unknown.

"What did you s—" Fergus began, before the creature's spiralled forehead started to rotate and everything was engulfed within the ethereal lights.

Ednon found himself once again floating through the blackness; shooting stars and comets were flying past him. Was he dead this time? His body was numb, yet he still felt wild sensations course through him. He was making his way closer to the familiar hole, which had covered all his vision. He stopped for a moment, just as he was about to make contact with the chasm, but like last time it was not sucking him in. His movements were free. He stayed motionless, feeling adrift and at peace, gazing upon the hole as it spiralled more intensely than it ever had previously. As anticipated, the hole disintegrated before him and changed into the kaleidoscopic eye of which he was all too aware. The giant orb of vision parted and he was once again immersed in the astral light.

He opened his eyes. He was back in the room of his death, but something seemed different this time. He could see all matter and energy; he saw the very fabric of the universe coursing throughout the room like sparklers being set off in every corner. Ednon studied his hands; *Why were they illuminating like this?* In fact, it was not just his hands, but his entire being. He felt power surging throughout his body, the power of life itself… He stood up from his chair, breaking through his confinements as if they were nothing but the flimsiest of fabrics.

"God…" Fergus blurted, his eyes filled with astonishment. "Please forgive my blindness, Lord! For I did not know it was you!"

He watched the molecules of the old man as he helplessly tried to get away. *What a silly collection of atoms you are*, he thought to himself and, with a slight wave of his hands, he dispersed them, leaving only a pile of blood and guts where Fergus had once been. He turned to see Memphis and the other men bowing before him. Ednon inspected his hands once more, before he made his way out of the room now drenched from top to bottom in crimson-red blood.

The sound of deafening explosions could still be heard as he weaved through the darkened corridors, now lit only by the glow he himself was creating. The rats came out to watch him as he passed by, beginning to follow the source of the unworldly brightness. His chest was still bleeding. However, with a simple caress, the bleeding ceased and the wound started to heal. *What are these powers?* he queried silently, tensing his hands, watching them pulsating with the purest of energy. He could not slow down to think. The Star of Sechen was soon going to eclipse the moon Vurtus, and after that... who knows?

Ednon continued his travelling, making his way through the web of the underground network as if he had made the journey many times already. He did not need markers to show him the way; it was as if the memory section of his brain had completely awakened. After forty or so minutes of walking through corridors, he eventually reached the surface. The night had come, fire and stars filled the air. He gazed above him to the majesty, the golden Star of Sechen was shooting past – the largest star in the sky by quite a margin was making its annual course towards Vurtus. *Only an hour or so away*, he lamented, watching its glorious journey through the blackness of space. He heard screams and his eyes fell back down to the city of Asterleigh, which was now filled with carnage. Homes and temples were either ablaze or utterly destroyed; many ran through the streets fighting and killing one another. He perceived the rain falling upon him and the ground below his feet as he began to walk on the stone-cobbled pavement. The Asterlieghians watched him as he approached, sharing the same level of astonishment that had been upon Fergus's face. They pointed their fingers at him and lifted their weapons.

"Get out of my way..." Ednon said in a voice so distant

and strange he was sure it could not have come out of his mouth.

Two bloodied men, who were scrapping in the road blocking his path, looked up towards him, their faces scared and stiff. Muttering awestruck babble, they both stood up, allowing Ednon to pass.

All eyes were upon him as he walked through the utter destruction that was Asterleigh. He walked past the Temple of Yashin, whose immaculate green gardens were a sea of red flame. He walked past the Grand Library whose structure had toppled entirely. Eventually, he made his way into the centre of Asterleigh, where many of the people had congregated. Most did not know whether to bow before him or to reach for their weapons. Citizens, ranging from the oldest beggars to the youngest nobles, were staring at him in disbelief and he gazed back with the two black empty voids of his eyes.

"Monster!" He heard one of the voices yell. "He is the one who has brought this destruction upon us!"

Monster? he thought to himself, as he felt a single arrow strike his chest. He removed it and disintegrated it within his hand, as if it was never truly meant for the substantial world.

"He's not human!" Voices continued to shout in pure delirium. "Kill him! Kill him!"

He felt not only arrows but rocks and throwing knives strike him. He did not mind the physical pain because that felt like nothing more than tiny midges biting his skin. What caused him discomfort were the ear-splitting shouts and rapid movements that he saw every particle make. His oversensitive brain was beginning to swell in agony; he felt as if he were about to explode. He let out a deep roar, and with a single wave of his hands the onlookers flew backwards as if the strongest of eastern winds had grown into a violent hurricane, knocking down a few once sturdy buildings. He placed his hands in front of his face and let out another yell as loud as thunder. He slumped to his knees. He felt so scared; he didn't want these powers, he wanted things to go back to the way they once were. The windswept crowd had arisen back to their feet and, losing themselves to the insanity of the blood-soaked night, they charged towards him again.

"Stay back!" Ednon begged, but to no avail.

He saw a figure striding out in front of him, arms outstretched, attempting to block him from the assault of objects being tossed through the air. "No…" he uttered softly, recognising the sweet aroma of Amelia.

"Ed…" she whispered as an arrow struck her through the back. He stared at her helplessly as she collapsed into his embrace. He did not acknowledge the crowd anymore; the only thing that mattered was Amelia dying in his arms. As he felt he was reaching breaking point, the small transparent diamond-eyed creature appeared to him once more, before its spiral rotated, and he knew this was the last time he would ever see this planet. Still clutching Amelia, he gazed one last time at the crowd, only to see his brother staring back at him among the sea of faces. He must have been hallucinating. There was no way that could truly be Syros? But it looked so much like him. It was Syros, there was no doubt about it. Ednon shouted desperately, but it was too late. The small creature's eyes started to beam and he was once again engulfed by the ethereal lights.

22

Sechen's Passing

New Year

An awed silence took hold of the streets. Only the windswept disjointed rubble lay where the disappearance through space and time had taken place. Startled faces turned to each other, completely unsure of what they had witnessed. And in the middle of the crowd stood Syros, panting heavily, his eyes wide with the most dumbfounded of wonderment.

That was Ednon, Syros thought, as he moved away from the mass of his ill-starred fellow species; Ednon, his eyes as vacant and black as the Entity that was leading the Venians. His body too had seemed to be illuminating in the same unworldly manner. But if that was Ednon, then where was his little brother now? Was he within the stars themselves? A fitting life for someone who had spent the better part of his own stargazing. Better to be up there than down here like a doomed rat clinging onto this accursed floating rock. He gazed up towards the Star of Sechen making its annual course through the night sky. It was only an hour or so until the star hit and his species, so long destined to die out, would finally meet its end. *Well*, he re-examined, *most of them anyway.* He still had a way out, and it appeared that Ednon and their young green-eyed neighbour had also survived. Plus, who knows? Perhaps when his kind first left their world of origin, this was not the only planet that they were able to inhabit. For all he knew, there could be millions, maybe even billions, of human beings living out there on the other distant wandering stars.

He gave one last look at the congregated mob, who had again broken into fights and pandemonium. *They're like bacteria*, he mused, watching a young man savagely bash an elderly woman's head in with a newly bloodied rock, *spreading their virus throughout the universe.*

Syros walked back through the burning streets of Asterleigh, moving at a steady pace, his mind on his next move. Was he actually going to do what he was planning? He had run here ahead of Saniya, Bora and the rest of the Alpelites in one last attempt to find Ednon, but never in his wildest dreams could he have imagined finding what it was that he had seen. Ednon was always unequivocally the perfect one, but who knew it was to such an extent? The rain and wind picked up pace as he neared the entrance of the southern Asterleigh gates, where he spotted Saniya running up towards him.

The Alpelite horde had already entered through the city

gates; having sighted their God, they instantly bowed in prayer before the vacant shell. *Fat load of good that's going to do*, Syros thought, as he watched the Alpelites falling to their knees. *If Medzu honestly cared, would it really have allowed things to get this far?*

"Syros, were you able to find Ednon?" Saniya said, embracing him.

"I—" he began, before stopping himself. He gave one more look around the burning city, to the men, women and children and the look of terror in each of their eyes. From out ahead, he saw a few Alpelites running up to engage the humans in a brawl. *It's always the same. Nature is consistent, no matter where in the universe you go.*

Saniya joined him in scanning around the ruins of the golden capital. "Syros, what happened here? Was it the Venians?"

"I don't think so… I heard explosions as I first entered the city." Syros caressed the back of her hair, for he knew, in this moment, it was the last time that he would ever be able to do so.

"What do we do now?" Saniya asked, looking into his eyes.

I'm so sorry, he grieved, as he let go of her embrace for the final time. "I'm sorry, San… but I can never love you… not in the way that you want."

He could not look at the expression on her face as he spoke these words, for it would have broken him entirely. He merely walked away from her.

"Syros?" he heard the voice of Bora calling to him. "Why are you leaving?"

It's her own fault, he reasoned to himself, walking through the burning streets. *To believe in love and all its child-like wonders. She was always destined to break.* Yet, despite his reasoning, he could not get the image of her dying alone out of his head; this, and the vow to her and Torjan that he had broken, he was sure would haunt him continuously until the day that he died. *Oh god, why did I tell her I didn't love her?* He felt worse than a monster, viler than all demons and evil entities. However, in a strange contrast to what was playing through his mind, he felt something monumental change inside of him. For the first time, in what must have been his entire life, he no longer felt depressed.

Amidst the raging devastation, he spotted a young girl crying alone. "Smile," he demanded, walking up and giving her the widest smile that he could. The girl did not smile, but stopped her crying and was now studying him with what seemed like a strange curiosity. They shared mutual stares for a moment, until Syros remembered how little time he had left. *Poor thing*, he thought, giving the girl one last glance. But did he truly care? He wasn't too sure anymore. He once again looked to the sky. *Not long left; best to continue forwards.*

The wind was building strength as the time of the New Year grew ever closer. Even though Sechen had still not passed Vurtus, the night sky was slowly beginning to fill crimson. "About half an hour…" he declared, watching the Star of Sechen above him. Maybe he should go back. That would be the honourable thing to do. He cursed himself for his weakness as he passed through the West Asterleigh gates and onto Yima's Fields, where, as previously instructed, he found the Venians.

There were millions of them, stretching out for miles in an ocean of twinkling life. Their large emerald eyes faced upwards as they watched the star crossing through the blackness, with mouths wide-open, emitting a strange melodic tune, almost as if they were singing. This must be every single one in existence, he imagined, walking through the Venians, who had opened a pathway for him to pass. Every Venian on the planet had come to the surface for this – their final night of salvation.

He assumed the path they were forging would lead him to the glowing Entity. The sparkling life forms took no notice of him as he made his way past; they solely carried on gazing towards the stars, while continuing their sweet melodic humming. It was a surprisingly soothing end, Syros reflected, as he listened to the hypnotic harmony of the plants. An odd way for a planet to meet its destruction, not the type of end-of-the-world stories the old drunks spoke of.

Yet, he suddenly felt guilt flowing through him as he pictured Saniya once more. "Stop…" he grimaced aloud, clutching his head. "Please, stop." It was not only Saniya that was entering his mind, but he was also unwillingly seeing Torjan's cheerful face. "I'm sorry, Torj," he whispered aloud. "But what else would you have me do?" He pictured Bora and the other Alpelites with whom he had travelled so far. He visualised the dead; Captain Raynmaher, his comrades Hurus, Petula, Steph, Freckon, even Mercivous's menacing smile – he was seeing them as plainly as if they were standing just in front of him. *You were wrong*, he pondered, as the image of Mercivous's face dissipated into the nothingness. He was not a born hero after all, he was only human, carrying all the imperfections that came along with that most strenuous task.

It was the next face, however, that saddened him most. He saw Ira appear before him. *What would you have done?* he queried to himself, looking upon the old man who had raised him for almost his entire life. *You have it easy; you're already dead.* Tough choices were for the living, all the dead had to do was sleep. But he knew in this moment, as he watched the face of his grandfather slowly disappearing, that he had always been a failure in his eyes. He was not the pure and perfect Ednon, and there was no one who reminded him of this more than Ira. "All your teachings on hatred were meaningless!" he shouted aloud at the elderly phantasm who had invaded his mind. "They held no value, because the whole time you hated me!" The sad spirit of his grandfather gave him one last mournful stare before it too faded into the fiery ether. "Please don't go, Ira," he sobbed, falling onto the grassy field. "I'm afraid."

His mind was darkening as he walked through the twinkling life forms, as if he was becoming less human with each step. He was forgetting his past self, losing the memory of the faces and cleansing himself of all his misgivings. All fragments of fear, joy, sorrow and love he had ever previously held were slowly evaporating – just as he knew they would.

Although the Venians were softly illuminating the darkness with their bodies, he could make out what he assumed was the unworldly Entity not too far ahead, as his light by far shone the greatest. It must be quite beautiful to gaze out over these fields from one of the high buildings in Asterleigh. That would be a nice last sight to see, better than being one of those on the streets violently attacking one another. He continued across the hills and meadows to the largest source of glow. Eventually, he came close to the light, close enough to touch it. The wind was howling and the rain poured yet, despite this, he heard a low calm voice. "To pass between the black void. To reconfigure the fragments and matter. To separate the spirit from its transient shell. To be reborn in the endless dreams." The Entity was sitting alone upon a rock, eyes closed and body in the meditation stance.

"You have come…"

"You're surprised?" Syros returned, shockingly not feeling unnerved in the slightest, despite the being's overwhelming presence. "I thought you would have already known my decision."

It closed its eyes. "My celestial awakening has given me many different powers, but to be able to see into the future… that is beyond me."

"Then at least tell me why you are doing this?" Syros had so many questions he wanted to get answered. "You said you were human once. If so, then who are you?"

"I am nothing but a server of the Gods… nothing more, nor am I anything less. I'm a servant, given a task that he must abide."

Syros looked towards the city of Asterleigh. It was the perfect view to watch the city burn, as the flames rose to almost the heights of Medzu itself. "My brother has the same powers that you appear to have. I want you to teach me these abilities also."

"You will learn them…" The Entity held still within its trance. "But that will be for another time, on a different planet entirely… and first you will need to die…"

Die? He must have misheard the glowing being, so he decided to ignore this part.

"Why me? Why me out of everyone in the whole world?"

"I will tell you sooner or later," the Entity said, as if it was completely disinterested. "All our actions have been orchestrated for you to meet me here upon this night; you will be needed in the wars soon to be waged… please, human… I need to concentrate all of my energy," it continued, waving him away.

Syros slumped to the bespattered ground beneath him. Was that really all the explanation he was going to get? All of that wondering, to get no answer? However, not wanting to ruin his chances of escape, he sat there quietly in the mud and joined the Venians in their stare towards Sechen. Only two or so minutes until the star passed. The Venians beside him continued their singing, which caused his head to sway gently from side to side. He had no idea how he felt anymore; he was sure the real Syros must have died somewhere along the journey from Ankor, as he could no longer feel any connection to his old self. Maybe an Alpelite killed him in a great battle that he could not remember, or maybe the Venians? Or even a human for his treachery and murder of Mercivous? It could have been the hunger that finally did him in, travelling through the forest in the search for the human borders? Or he might, as he had planned so many times throughout adulthood, have finally found the courage to take his own life. The Venians' sweet song was making him drowsy – *how he wished this was all a dream. All dreams finally end*, he pondered solemnly, and this one appeared to be meeting its close. *Oh god, why did I tell her I didn't love her?*

"All preparations are done…" the Entity opened both of its eyes and stood high upon its rock. "This is your last chance to appear…" It outstretched its hands; it seemed to be talking to Medzu itself. "Awaken, Lord Medzu!" the Entity called in a booming voice. Medzu, as Syros expected, did not appear to have heard, or if it had then it didn't really care, as its shell remained motionless upon its clouds.

Syros considered the mass of congregated Venians; he did not understand how they would all be able to leave this world. There didn't appear to be any kind of ship. Nothing resembling a transporter. Plus, there must have been millions of Venians spread out across these fields.

"How are we travelling? How will we be able to take all of these Venians?"

"Let them die here along with their planet," the being uttered, with no ounce of sympathy in its cold and emotionless voice. "You are the reason I have travelled all this way."

Hearing this, the Venians frantically fell to their knees. "Please, Lord!" they cried, holding their hands up. "You promised us salvation! You promised us peace!"

The Entity widened its arms to them all as if it were giving a sermon. "Do not despair, oh beautiful sentient life. For in the stillness of nothing, you shall find what it is you have been searching for."

The Venians no longer sang their beautiful humming

melodies, and instead let out a loud wail that echoed through the air, sounding not too dissimilar to human weeping.

Syros watched the Venians as they pitifully grovelled on the floor before them. *At least there will be some justice there,* Syros thought, as he watched the pretty flower-like life forms wallowing in despair. Yet, despite all they had done, he could not deny he felt sympathy for them.

"Are you ready?" the Entity asked, indifferent to the Venians' pain. "When the star hits, keep standing here next to me."

Syros gave a slow nod, then, continuing to watch the Venians cry for what would soon be their evanescence, his mind drifted to a question that he had wondered about so relentlessly ever since he was a small child.

"What happens after you die?"

For the first time, he thought he saw an expression cross the Entity's face. It did not answer, however, and solely continued to stare skywards.

Finally, he thought to himself, *time to leave the nightmare and awaken a new person, on a new world entirely, underneath a new sky.* It's what he had always wanted and now, remarkably, he was going to get it. The rain continuing to fall and the gushing wind continuing to flow, the Star of Sechen hit and the sky plunged flame crimson. The Entity beside him started to glow and he could feel himself disappearing.

Then, his eyes spotted something that must have been wrong. Medzu was stirring on its clouds; first, it moved its hand, then its head, before staring towards them. With loud crashes and shakes, Medzu lifted its legs and planted them upon the world's surface. Standing at its highest, it was taller than a mountain, larger than anything Syros had previously ever seen. Completely lost within his wonderment at a sight he had never believed he would witness, Syros did not notice the single Venian rising from the ground behind him, or indeed it burying its sharp piercing arm through his back. Blood flying out of him, he gave an ear-piercing howl, before quickly withdrawing his blade and slicing the creature's head off.

Lost within the light that the Entity beside him was illuminating, he collapsed onto the floor. The pain was unimaginable. His mind feeling light and woozy, he desperately clutched his chest and the arm-sized wound, attempting to stop the blood that was coming out at such a rapid pace he was surprised there was any left inside him.

Losing awareness, he watched as Medzu moved towards them, its massive hand outstretched as if it were about to squash them beneath the weight, in one last attempt to stop the Entity's actions. But it was too late, the ground beneath them collapsed as Vena started to rip apart. Syros gave out one last curse before he felt a tear roll down his face, which seemed to be for Saniya and all his mistakes. *I'm sorry, San. Come meet me in death so I can love you properly.* He pictured her face along with Torjan's as he felt the stiffness overcome him. As the glow of the Entity beside him strengthened to its celestial brightest, he finally let go of his old self. He could sense himself transforming within the endless astral light. He was changing. He was luminous and vibrant. He was eternal. And then... he was nothing.

23

Medzu

Ednon opened his eyes and all he saw was white; *is this nothingness?* No, even whiteness is something. The floor below him was moving gently as if he were standing on the purest of clouds. He turned his head to the side and found Amelia next to him. The small creature was beside her, cheerfully waddling round the vacant space. In this moment, he remembered the events that had just occurred; the arrow hitting Amelia in her chest and the creature appearing in front of them, before they all disappeared into the light. He checked Amelia's body, but there did not appear to be any wound from the stray arrow. He checked his own being; his hands had stopped glowing, his vision along with it, so he must have returned to his normal state. He surveyed his chest for the wound that Fergus had inflicted on him in the underground network only moments before, but that had vanished as well.

"Ed...what is this place?" Amelia said cautiously, as if uncertain whether she was dreaming.

"I'm not sure..." he responded, continuing to scan the surroundings. Were they dead? And if they were, did that make this the afterlife? No, he was sure that he had not died. He still felt, still thought. Everything was the same – inside of him, at least.

He proceeded to survey the location. And what he found directly behind him was a strange being. It had no eyes, indeed no eye features of any kind, but what seemed like an endlessly spinning spiral filling the entirety of its rounded head. There was a thin body, just as a human, made up of strange patterns and textures, with hands and feet both. And even though this place was completely white, he could tell the being was glowing. It was Medzu itself standing before them, but unlike the one hanging above the clouds over Asterleigh, this one was much smaller; in fact, it stood only an inch or so taller than Ednon and Amelia.

He did not know whether to bow before the God or let out a scream; instead, he did neither and stood in awe as he watched the divine being moving upon them.

"You have made it to the in-between, child," it said in a calm voice, aiming its words towards Ednon. "It seems you were able to escape your planet just in time. For this, you must be either exceptionally lucky or have some higher powers working for you." Its voice sounded distant, and even though the being did not appear to be opening or closing its mouth, he could still hear the words as if they were sent directly into his consciousness.

"What do you mean we managed to leave our planet in time? What has happened to Vena?" Ednon asked, deep down already knowing what had happened, for it had all been foretold to him.

"My lad…" Medzu responded, with an air of sympathy in its voice. "I'm afraid Vena has turned to nothing but vacant stardust."

"What happened? Was it something that I did?" Perhaps when he had awoken in his omnipotent state, he might have accidentally done something to contribute. Was it the moment that he had disappeared into the light while Amelia lay dying in his arms?

Medzu gave a shake of the head. "It has nothing to do with you, young one," it informed him, still in a manner that denoted concern for his wellbeing. "The world was under attack by someone whose sole purpose appeared to be to antagonise me. I'm afraid the gods can be just as petty as all other life forms. The man who destroyed your world seemed to have been trained to have such unlimited power, and as soon as I find out who it was that organised these cruel events, I promise I will bring you justice. For Vena, being under my jurisdiction, means that this attack was an attack on me as well as on you."

"Are you saying another god ordered the attack on our world… who?"

"I don't know that yet I'm afraid. I am saddened for these are worrying times… it appears the war of the gods may soon be approaching."

He did not care about the war of the gods; he didn't care about any of that. He wanted to know why his planet had been destroyed and all the life that had populated it had been ruthlessly wiped out. "Why didn't you appear?!" Ednon demanded angrily, forgetting he was shouting at a god. "You could have appeared and prevented everything… if only you had shown yourself to us for one moment. How could you have let us all die? As if we were absolutely nothing!" He felt tears streaming down his face as he fell to the floor, utterly overwhelmed by all that had transpired throughout his short life. "Everyone we ever knew is dead… I never got to say goodbye to Syros… And you act as if you don't care at all."

"You must despise me… mustn't you?"

Ednon looked up, shocked by the emotion he had heard. It sounded so human in the way it had uttered these last words, like a child grieving for its lost loved ones. He gazed towards Medzu; the God did not have eyes, but he was sure if it did, it too would have been weeping.

"No, I just want to know why. I saw you within my dreams every night, and during the day I would look up to you in the sky and wish that you would save us… but now it's too late…"

Medzu moved upon him, before placing its hand upon his head. "My child, you have suffered all too much. It hasn't been easy for you and I know that more than most. The pure-hearted ones always end up with the most hardship. It's a sad fact of the way that life is… you have love in your heart. But you do not know what it is like to watch over millions as I do. To watch day after day as they butcher one another. My love is not unconditional. I did not act because I could not bear to watch, for it broke my heart. And when I did show, I was too late. I am not infallible. None of us are.

You must take the hardships when they come. But also try and hold onto the good, and when it comes, hold onto it for as long as you can."

"Then where do we go now? We have no home to return to."

"Go to another world." Medzu pulled him up by his shoulders. "And be happy."

In this moment, the small transparent creature moved towards them and started cheerfully playing against Ednon's leg. "What creature is that?" Medzu said, contemplating the life form. "I have never seen a species of life quite like it."

"You truly do not know?" Ednon said, wiping away the last of his tears while caressing the small creature's forehead. "I assumed you knew all life within the universe."

"I do," it said, perplexity in its voice. "Perhaps this creature is from another universe entirely."

"Her name is Orla," Amelia said, picking up the little life form and cradling it in her arms.

"Stick close to your shining lodestar, for I feel it will be an imperative light in your hereafter." As Medzu uttered these last words, a void in the whiteness appeared behind the god, a spiralled passageway through space and time itself.

Medzu relinquished its grasp of his shoulders. "It is time for you to leave. Go to your new world and pray that it won't be like your last. But be forewarned, the universe may not be through with you yet."

With that, Ednon, alongside Amelia and the small creature, moved past Medzu and headed towards the rift in the cosmos.

"Farewell, starry wayfarer. I shall be replaying this

moment within my dreams," Medzu called, as the three of them started to move through the portal.

Side by side with Amelia, he placed his hand against the spiralled rift, and in a flash of white light they began their new lives in the stars.

Epilogue

Shores of Xerus

They found themselves standing upon soft silken sand. The suns ahead of them were rising past the white cotton clouds, reflecting off the slow-moving tides. It looked very much like Vena, whatever this place was, only more peaceful and still. They seemed to be the only ones present here upon the shores. The small creature beside them gave out a joyful squeak before immersing itself within the waters. Ednon and Amelia watched the life form as it jumped in and out of the sea, while it looked back towards them as if it was daring the two of them to come and join in its fun. They continued to stare, marvelling at the glorious new suns rising until a voice from behind caught their attention.

"You have arrived…"

Turning around, they saw a figure, its face veiled by white bandages, wearing a long black cloak that trailed past its feet. Two bloodshot eyes stared back, meeting their gaze. It was the phantom he had met in the Grand Library all those months ago. As if the small transparent creature had recognised the figure, it made its way out from the water, trudged its way over towards them and moved to stand beside it, as if seeking approval.

"Well done," the figure said, kneeling down and petting the wide-eyed animal on its forehead. "You have done well."

"You knew you would meet us here all along. How did you know this would happen?"

"I didn't," the figure told him, standing up once again, eclipsing the three of them by a good couple of feet. "There is no planned destiny, Ed; we can only attempt to forge our own futures. However, when you have help like from this little one… then that makes everything a lot easier." He motioned to the creature, which gave out another happy squeak, pleased to get the recognition.

"You sent the creature to help us?" Ednon's mind and heart were racing. "And 'Ed', you know my name. Who are you?"

The phantom stared back silently and for a moment Ednon suspected he would not get his answer. But then, the figure unwrapped its bandaged head to reveal the face of his grandfather. He focused in awe on the face he had imagined he would never see again. Ira surveyed him, his wrinkled face healthier than Ednon could ever remember.

"Are you…" Ednon began, stuttering his words, feeling overwhelmed with emotion, "… truly my grandfather?"

"Would it make you happy if I said that I was?" the face he recognised asked him.

"It would…" he cried, embracing the man. He was half expecting the phantom to disappear into the air once again.

However, as hard as he enfolded the phantom, it stayed whole. "This doesn't seem real... This whole place is like some wondrous dream."

"If it is..." Ira told him, returning his embrace, "then be happy, and enjoy the rest of your life within the endless dreams."

Moments passed. The suns had moved over the clouds, covering the entire morning horizon in pure white light. They watched the creature as it once again played in the tides. The figure had gone, disappearing into the air, much like the first time they had met in the Library. However, searching inside himself, he felt content, for he knew they would meet again someday. He turned to Amelia, who gave him a smile and outstretched her hand, which Ednon in turn took into his own, with no intention of ever letting it go.

Preview

To Bypass the Empty Void
(Book 2 of the Endless Dreams Saga)
By Michael Georgiou

Prologue; Beasts from another World

The strange esoteric allure had firmly embraced the troop as they journeyed through the desolate woods. Death was in the air. It was right under their noses, almost palpable in its strength. Like loose hounds, they followed the scent, looking for their prey. The night was ominously stygian and the woodland shared in this absence of vibrancy. Ento stared skyward, but he could not make out the starry laced veil through the thick mass of pines and oaks. For the first time ever, he was going to miss the passing of Sechen. Ento considered this as he felt a branch entangle itself around his ankle, causing him to sprawl on the ground.

"What's wrong, Ento?" Xavier smirked, turning around to face him. "Lost your nerve?"

"Sorry, Xavier… I must have forgotten myself."

Xavier let out a loud snort before placing his hand upon his halberd. "Rookies…" he grumbled.

"Get up, lad…" the grey-haired Jozef smiled, lifting him to his feet. "This is not the time for you to be making mistakes. Not now. Not tonight."

Ento gave one more glance at the front of the troop, where Xavier was angrily blitzing his way forwards. "He hates me. Ever since my first day at the special ops, he has always hated me."

Jozef shrugged. "I think he hates everyone, to be honest with you. It probably comes with our line of work. The Leper did tell you what our mission is?"

"Aye, the Leper told me."

"And… it doesn't bother you?"

"No," Ento returned without a moment's hesitation, "I hate the Aureuts, even more than Xavier hates me."

Jozef patted him on the shoulder. "We all do, lad. We all do. Come, we mustn't get left behind."

Simultaneously, the two men turned and continued with the rest of their squadron as they followed the captivating scent. Excitement filled Ento's stomach. He was going to see it. He had only heard stories, fiction that seemed so fantastical and inconceivable that they were surely myths conjured by a madman. But now he was going to see it. He clutched his blade cheerfully. He was going to see the ripple within space and time with his very own eyes.

There were eight of them in total, dressed in black, each trained, armed and eager to kill. Ento had spent the last five years of his life with the special ops unit, learning just how to be an effective and useful cog for the Lowesby kingdom. His mentor Shani, whom most of the populace referred to solely as the "Leper," had finally informed him what the special ops' true purpose was in assisting their kingdom. What he had heard that day thrilled Ento. He had always hated the Aureuts and had long hoped the day would come for him to enact his hatred. They were nothing but a nuisance upon his proud Kingdom, their mere existence a direct insult to his heritage. He spat upon the ground as the troop made their way to a clearing drenched in glossy afterglow and gripped his blade once more. The forest was making a strange noise, like a low-key whisper in an exotic foreign language. Remaining covert behind an array of bushes, the fierce, yet soothing, feeling all he could perceive; his mind turned blank and sweat was beginning to manifest. The time was approaching.

"This way, lad…" Jozef motioned to him.

Ento obliged the old man's wishes and stealthily crouched his way over. Jozef gave him a sly smile, before parting the bushes with his hands. "There it is, boy, the phenomenon that defies all reason."

Ento's eyes widened as his gaze fixed upon the clearing. There it was. Shrouded within the trees, almost as if it were a natural part of the forest. A spinning void, almost his height and double his width. He stared in wonderment and in this moment got an inexplicable urge to throw himself forwards to touch it, until a loud grunt from Xavier promptly reminded him of his mission.

"Does anybody know when they're going to appear?"

"Should be on the hour. Just as Sechen passes above us," Nanuk informed them.

Xavier slumped to the floor. "Okay, we have about half an hour. Get comfy, gentlemen, we're in for a wait."

"How many times does it appear?" Ento questioned, turning back round to Jozef, his mind not on anything else apart from the bizarre cosmic occurrence.

"Usually for just over an hour or so… Always here, but I cannot be certain about the other far reaches of this world."

"Does anyone know where it comes from?"

"How the hell should I know, lad? Just because I am old does not mean I hold all the answers. All I know is whatever that thing brings I don't like. So, fuck it. If you ask me, there is no greater threat to our way of life."

Ento studied the ripple further; it looked almost alive, as if it were some type of wondrous eye staring back towards him. Thoughts were beginning to race at such a pace it made his head feel faint. He dropped to the ground and averted his stare. It was all beginning to overwhelm him.

"You alright, lad?" Jozef took a seat beside him. "Don't worry, it had the same effect on me the first time I saw it; not the type of New Year you were expecting, eh?"

"No, not quite." Ento attempted a smile.

He remembered the passing of Sechen the previous year; he had been out with a couple of friends drinking in the capital. After moving on from the bars and taverns, with a rowdy buzz they instead turned their attention to the Aureut population of the city. Usually, the humans and the Aureuts stayed segregated; however, in the chaotic drunkenness of the New Year, the two species often found themselves mixed. And there, in one of the taverns, he saw her. Mohana, an Aureut girl around his age. He had not previously found any of the Aureuts attractive, but Mohana seemed to excite something inside of him. He would have liked to have thought it was just the ale that had taken hold of his reasoning, but deep down he knew it wasn't that. They had spent the night together, but as they did not speak the same language they could not properly converse. Nevertheless, during that evening, as he considered her fierce golden eyes, he could tell what it was that she wanted from him. They lay together that very night, as the Star of Sechen crossed the twinkling sky above; he could not lie and say in the moment he did not find it enjoyable. But, as the suns rose, and the drink wore off, he felt unending guilt. He had done it; a proud member of the human race, none other than a special ops unit trainee, had slept with some common Aureut whore. The shame he had felt was astronomical and after that moment he never saw Mohana again.

However, unwillingly, some nights he would dream of her, before awaking in anguish; he pictured her being with others of her own kind and the thoughts consumed him. He often considered whether he should return to find her, but resisted the urge. She could not have truly loved him, he was very sure of that. Species should stick to their own. That's what they had taught him. *That's what mother and father did.* What if Xavier had found out? Or even Shani? He was already enough of an outcast without them knowing this dark secret about himself. No, best he forget Mohana. She was probably out there tonight, with some other poor human boy who had no idea of the torment he was about to undergo. They were nothing but pure filth. They should have never come to this planet.

Jozef raised his eyebrows. "You alright, lad? You look as if you're about to faint."

"When will they arrive, Jozef? I need to kill..."

"Calm yourself, boy," Jozef gave a worried glance over to Xavier. "This is a stealth mission – quick clean kills and then we can go home. You must keep a level hea—"

Jozef's speech was interrupted by a sound utterly unlike anything Ento had ever heard before. The clearing was engulfed in bright lights and the void was spinning at an increasingly accelerated pace.

"They're here," Xavier announced. "Gentlemen, ready your bows."

Ento's heart pounded. He squinted his eyes to try and focus in on the brightness. There they were, as previously foretold. Aureuts were making their way from out of the rift. Although Shani had already informed him of this, he had not believed him. It all seemed too outlandish for his mind, but now he had the proof. Ento noticed how afraid the Aureuts appeared as they exited the ripple. Males, females and infants of all ages held onto each other as if they were families. It all seemed so very human. He decided to dispel the similarities; for his own sake, he best not dwell on them.

The killing did not take long. Only thirty or so had made it through the void on this trip and none of them held weapons. Killing the children, however, left a sour taste in his mouth.

At this moment, he questioned his own morality and ethics and whether Lord Yashin would look down upon him for his actions this night. He feared his soul might never be able to ascend into the endless dreams and in non-existence he would reside forever dormant. And yet, surprisingly to him, it was Mohana he thought of, as he studied the lifeless gold eyes of a young girl while he buried her corpse. The portal had now vanished and the strange intoxicating feeling along with it. Jozef gave him a smile, as he wiped the blood from his blade.

"Happy New Year, rookie."

"Happy New Year," Ento responded, studying the remnants of blood left from the young girl. It was red, just like his own.

Xavier strolled round the empty clearing. "Good job, gentlemen. Now let's go home and enjoy the rest of th— "

A loud and thunderous roar had interrupted the fierce leader before he could finish. So chaotic and violent, it shook the forest. Each man swivelled their head in a frenzy, looking to uncover just what could emit such a monstrous noise. Then, suddenly, Ento noticed the portal had reappeared five yards or so behind Xavier. Xavier turned and, just as he did so, a beast leapt upon him, ripping him apart effortlessly with its teeth. The creature was enormous, larger than any life form he had ever previously seen. With what looked like twenty eyes, maybe more, a mouth the width of an oak and teeth each the size of table legs, it looked much like a lion concocted in a dark and savage nightmare. The beast rapidly shook its head from side to side, flinging Xavier out from its mouth, leaving his bloodied corpse smashed upon the ground. With panicked yells and insanity driven cries, the men withdrew their weapons and charged towards the demonic horror. But it was no use, the creature was too strong and riddled with too much bloodlust. It tore through the men as if they were nothing more than bothering insects.

"Run, Ento!" Jozef yelled, as the beast's teeth closed around the old man.

Ento gave one last panicked look and turned, before sprinting through the forest. He ran as fast as he could, not daring to look behind. He slipped and fell, but quickly got up upon his feet. The night had darkened; he could no longer see to where it was he was running – but he did not care. He needed to get away, as far as he possibly could. He heard a monstrous roar and he could tell the beast had finished with the others and had now turned its attention to him. *Oh god, why me, why me...* Ento thought, frantically pushing past the branches. *Oh god, what was that thing?* He needed to return to Lowesby to warn them all. To inform them of what he had witnessed. He could hear it approaching. Thud. Thud. It was gaining ground on him. He could hear its thunderous roars ever louder. Completely sapped of all energy, he eventually made it to the edge of the forest. From where he was standing, he could see the fires of the celebration of the New Year rising to the sky. The Star of Sechen was making its annual course through the cosmic dark above them. He fell to his knees, unable to keep going; he was almost there, he was almost home. Thud. Thud. *Mohana...* was the last word that Ento thought, as the beast finally caught him. It was death itself he saw in the depraved voids of its crimson pupils. The beast opened its mouth, and to non-existence Ento subsequently arrived.